Cell-Jacked

Cell-Jacked

PORTIA BLACK VOLUME 2

WALL STREET JOURNAL BESTSELLING AUTHOR

PASCOAL ANTONIO

Published by Best Seller Publishing®, St. Augustine, FL
Best Seller Publishing® is a registered trademark.
Printed in the United States of America.

ISBN:978-1-966395-07-2

For more information, please write:
Best Seller Publishing®
1775 US-1 #1070
St. Augustine, FL 32084
or call 1 (626) 765-9750

Visit us online at: www.BestSellerPublishing.org

Disclaimer:

Dedication

To Christiana, my love

CHAPTER 1

Right before the trunk slammed shut, I thought of how mad my grandmother would be.

I wonder if this what we all feel. Not fear, but guilt. Shouldn't have gone to that bar. Shouldn't have had that drink. Shouldn't have talked to that guy. *Mea culpa.* My fault. He knew it too. Before he pulled the trunkdoor down, he smiled at me. He didn't have to say anything. Guys like this were all thinking the same thing. *Be quiet. Be good. After all, you asked for this.*

I didn't.

Just in case you were wondering, I didn't meet him at a bar either. I met him at a church. Our group met in the basement. There were nine of us, arranged in a semi-circle. We were seated on hard-backed chairs, heads hung low like prisoners awaiting a sentence.

A woman sat across, alone, thumbing rapidly through the big book in her hands. In this small room she was judge, jury, and executioner and she seemed anxious to get it all over with.

"Would anyone else like to share?" She looked around, mustered up a kindly stare, then threw it in my direction like a spotlight. "You're new here, yes? Do you want to say something?"

I didn't. But I stood anyway. "My name is Mary," I said. "I'm an alcoholic. I've been an alcoholic for nine years."

That's when the others looked up, their lips moving soundlessly, counting, calculating. I'm twenty-five but can easily pass for nineteen. "I've been sober for seven…" I paused. "Six days." I sat down immediately and dropped my head.

So far, so good. Perfectly executed. Here comes the disclaimer. My name is not Mary. I'm not an alcoholic. I've done my fair share of street drugs but I'm not an addict. I'm just a working girl. My job is justice, the messy kind. Under the ten-dollar wig, and drugstore makeup, messy doesn't begin to describe it.

My driver's license lists me as Portia Black: five foot three, brunette, brown eyes, organ donor. If the description sounds average, invisible even, then thank you very much. Under the contacts my eyes are wolf-amber, the dark freckles on caramel skin are Pollock paint-splatter, and whatever masquerades as hair grows so coiled and matted it begs to be buzzed to the scalp. Organ donation? Trust me, you don't want anything I have to offer.

"Would you like to say anything else?" the woman asked.

What should I have told them? That I was born in the heroin epidemic of ninety-six? That I didn't have a name till I was six months old? That I found my mother dead in a bathtub, smeared with vomit and excreta?

"No," I said. "That's pretty much it."

The heavyset older woman next to me looked over, raised her hand to her heart, and tapped it. She had a white pearl rosary wrapped tightly around her fingers. When her fist tightened, the silver beads looked like the studs of a knuckleduster. Like she was ready to give someone a mouthful of Jesus. She was the one most likely to offer sponsorship, so I moved on quickly before my gaze was taken as encouragement.

There were two women seated beside her, both red-headed; one black, one white. They could have been sisters. Sisters from another mister. An old man sat next to them, bald and white, ruddy Irish nose pockmarked, starburst veins intersecting like a roadmap. We were twelve miles from the Southside of Boston and the stereotype was cringeworthy.

A family sat beside him, faces screwed up, arms locked, like they had marched here in protest. The boy in the middle of the knot was skinny, late teens, shackled to his bird-like parents. They took turns pecking at him, pruning him. Jesus, I commiserated, I'd have turned to drink too.

"Anyone else?" the woman asked.

At the very end of the semi-circle was an empty chair. Its owner paced the far wall of the room. He was on the bad side of fifty, paunchy, black baseball cap pulled low over his brows. I could already tell he was a thirteenth stepper. There used to be plenty of his type. The seedy kind. Guys who used the anonymity of these meetings to score. Drugs. Sex. A fix. Whatever was easy, quick, and painless.

That was before the internet came along and screwed the game. I mean, why sit through endless recaps of *Trainspotting* to get what you want when there are thousands of needy people online? I mean seriously needy people. People who will set out for love and settle for being bent over a dumpster in a back alley. As the old-timers say, puke on the lips and chlamydia on the hips.

"I guess that would be it then." The woman led the group in a hastily mumbled serenity prayer and shut the book with an air of finality. She draped her coat over one arm and rushed for the door. It swung back behind her before anyone could protest. There was the scrape and clang of chairs as they were pulled across the floor and folded up against the wall.

The older woman and one of the redheads straggled out but the rest mingled at the table where a paltry spread of dry donuts and a bag of crushed chips cozied up to a chintzy coffee pot. A large portrait stood above it, encased in an oversized gilt frame. The engraved script on the border said *Judas*.

"Ironic, don't you think?" The man with the baseball cap stood beside me. There was an unmistakable bulge in his pants. Small and hard. A Ruger LC9. Or a Beretta compact. A purse-gun.

Loser, I thought, but I indulged him. "What's ironic?"

"That they'd hang a portrait of Judas in a church. After hanging him."

"Judas Thaddeus," I said. "Not Iscariot."

"Ah," he said. "You're a *Christian*." He spat the word out like a sin.

"No. I just have a thing for Jude." Dark hair and beard, almost Jesus-like, Judas Thaddeus is the patron saint of lost causes. J.T. and I go way back.

"Judas over Jesus. I like it." He pressed a cup into my hands. The heat bled through my thin cotton gloves. "How come I haven't seen you here before?"

"Haven't been here before." I stared at the pool of murky liquid and counted the number of illicit substances that could be swimming inside. Alprazolam. Brotizolam. Clonazepam. Diazepam. Estazolam. Flunitra-

"Don't worry," he said, interrupting my meditation. "It's not Irish." He removed his baseball cap and placed it ceremoniously over his chest. "Unless you want it to be."

There was a dark patch on the front where the embroidery had been painstakingly removed, thread by thread. I wondered if he was good with a razor. Guys like him were always good with blades.

"Are you offering me a drink at an AA meeting?"

"No." He popped the cap back onto his head. "Of course not." His smile was lopsided, I could see where his fillings had tarnished and discolored. Yellow suns and silver moons. "I was just making-"

The other red-head squeezed between us and poured out a cup of coffee. She double fisted a pair of doughnuts and balanced the cup between her chin and two jellies.

"Need some help with that, Audra?"

"Fuck off, Will."

Wow, I mouthed. "You're popular here, aren't you?"

"Nah," he said. "I sponsored her once. I might have been too rough on her."

"So, if you sponsor me, will you promise to be rough on me too?"

"I never said I was going to sponsor you."

There was a curse from across the room as a jellyroll hit the floor. Audra stuffed a lump of fried dough into her mouth and made her way back.

"Come on, Will. You come over here, make the lamest attempt at conversation. Try to pick me up with *free* coffee and doughnuts. God, I had a better time at my grandma's funeral last week and no one else turned up but me."

Will's shoulders hunched and he looked like he was almost ready to cry. I wondered if I'd pushed too far.

"Look, I'm just not good at this." He moved aside as Audra barreled through. "I'm not much of a talker, okay?"

"Then what can you do?"

"I can make you feel good for half an hour."

I smiled. "That's the smartest thing you've said all day."

"Cool." There was the hint of a sniffle. "Let me get my stuff." He returned with a large black duffel, the kind meat-heads live out of. Wrist straps, Valeo belts, ammonia pellets, and gallon jugs of water. Very unusual. Especially for a guy that pudgy. The bag clinked as he came over.

"What you got in there, a couple of forty-fives?"

"More like forties." He grinned and flexed. "Milk is for babies. *Ah-nold* drinks *bee-yah*." The front double-biceps was pathetic and he knew it. The laughter turned into a sheepish smile. "I'm just starting. Trading addictions, you know."

He opened the door, making space for me to pass through. I was taken aback. I'm not the kind who expects doors to open or chairs to pull out and I'm jealous of girls who do, the ones who accept it without awkwardness. I stepped out, trying not to touch him.

The night air was muggy and I breathed it in. A faint odor of trash sifted past, like a garbage truck had just rolled by. In the distance a car horn blared, a drunk couple stumbled along, arguing entirely too loudly about where they had parked.

Will lingered on the stoop. I assumed he was waiting for approbation, but he wasn't. He was busy rummaging through the duffel.

"Let me guess. You're going to pretend you lost your keys, because you're embarrassed your license got taken away."

"You got me, *pardner*," he said. "That's the whole game, isn't it? All I need is a little *hoodsie* with her own set of keys, else I'm riding the bus home."

He zipped up his bag and came over. There was something in his hand. Soft. Balled-up like a sock. There was a familiar smell too. Sweet and sour. Nail polish remover. Wood stripper.

"So, do you? Or don't you?"

"Oh, I do have a license. And a car too. It's not a Cadillac, but it'll get you where you need to go."

I watched him jingle a set of keys held together with a belt clip, custodian style.

"Come on, I'll show you." He sauntered off down the road, the bag clinking as it bounced of his hip. We took a turn down a blind alley. The darkness sucked us in with a single breath. Fifteen, thirty, forty paces.

And there it was.

A late-model Sonata, navy-blue, with Massachusetts temp plates. It was parked behind a large green roll-off, pushed up against the brick wall.

I turned slowly.

Car. Dumpster. Fifty feet of blackness. *Well played*, sir. The dumpster shuddered. There were footsteps within, too heavy to be an animal.

"It's him or me, baby," Will said. He was smiling, his eyes glistening and cat-like. He popped open the trunk. As I tried to run, I noticed his hand had recently been gloved.

Chapter 2

The trunk space of a 2014 Hyundai Sonata is a class leading sixteen and half cubic feet. Almost three average-sized humans if packed just right. Alone, it felt positively roomy. I pushed my bound hands out, the zip-ties cutting into my skin. There was a hacksaw and club-sized rolls of duct-tape strewn across the floor. Bags of different sizes, plastic and burlap, a coil of rope and a jug of generic bleach.

I couldn't see any of these things in the darkness, but I knew they were there because I saw them before the trunk slammed shut. I kicked up and down with my legs, scraping the trash-laden floor with my boots. I couldn't feel the hacksaw. Maybe he took it out before he left. I knew he had straightened up the bleach and tucked it into the corner. I had an auburn wig, and he might not want a blonde tonight.

These are the crazy, irrational things you think of when the numbness of a kidnapping wears off. You think of everything and nothing at all. You start to think of all you left behind; not much really, not in my case at least. You start to prepare yourself for what might come. Rape. Death. Or worse still, years and years of darkness. Of nothingness.

You start to think of grandma. About the day she sat you down and gave you the talk. Not *that* talk. The other one. Stranger danger. Creepers. Peepers. Pervs. You start to think of the cop who came to your class in junior high and talked to you about abduction prevention. You think of the rules.

Rule one. Don't talk to strangers. I broke that rule at nine thirty.

Rule two. Don't go home with anyone you don't know. Broken at nine fifty-one.

Rule three. Don't let him change locations. Broken at nine fifty-nine.

Three basic rules. Three broken. The handsome cop should have added another one. Don't go out looking for trouble. But I've been breaking that one my whole life and-

The car stopped suddenly. There was a breathing hole drilled through the sheet metal, probably the size of a 3/8 bit. Through it I could see the cracked surface of pavement. It was wet. It hadn't been raining in Southie. Then I heard it. Not rain. This was ocean spray. Fresh. Sharp. I could almost taste the salt.

The engine cranked up and the car peeled left. My eyes adjusted and the hole became my window on the world. The streetlamps flickered like moths as they disappeared. Pavement changed to gravel, then dirt. No lighting now. Midnight blue turned into black.

I could finally feel the edge of something sharp, the claws of a carpenter's hammer. Not a saw, but it would have to do. As I began to scrape it against my ties, the car started to slow. Bad timing. It's a chronic condition with me. If you asked my mother, the crack-head who delivered me in the depths of a nose-bleed high, she would've agreed.

I heard the parking brake pop and the sound of work boots circled the car. The nylon hadn't even begun to splinter. The trunk opened and a sweaty pair of hands ripped me out. The flashlight bit into my eyes, blinding me. I saw him inspect me like a piece of meat.

"You're not as pretty as I thought."

"Go to hell."

"I'm sure I will." The light splayed across my body, toward my legs.

"Well," he said, "beggars can't be choosers."

This really pissed me off. I'm no pageant girl, but I'm not butcher scraps either. Will pulled me up and over his shoulder. I was bounced up a series of steps and squeezed through a bowed porch door. A cabin, not a house.

"Mother, I'm home." Will laughed hysterically, like this was the funniest joke ever. He carried me through an unkempt country kitchen, dirty floral wallpaper peeling down the back of the washboard. There was one dish and one glass in the dishrack, no pictures on the ancient refrigerator door.

A knob clicked and we took a turn downstairs into a musty smelling basement. A black satin curtain hung across the back wall, two spotlights aimed in a studio set-up. A rack of plastic-wrapped women's clothes had been pushed to the side and an old dentist's chair was bolted in the center.

This was where I ended up, my zip-tied wrists wedged over the back of the chair, the occipital rests digging into my neck. My cut-off shirt and jeans were pulled off, folded neatly, and placed on an antique dresser.

He turned on the umbrella lights and looked at me. He pulled at my hair. The wig, held in by spray and bobby pins, hung off the side of my head like a dead animal.

"Damn you," he said. "You know that's why you girls are such shit. All promise on the outside, but inside? Lies. Just damn lies." He was an ugly beast. Under the black baseball cap, his face was all nose, red and pockmarked, blackheads and whiteheads competing for prime real estate. And he smelled.

What was I thinking? If he had been handsome, a Patrick Bateman type, would this be any better?

"I like to dress my girls up first, you know, take some pictures, but…" He pulled the strap of my cami to the side, exposing a sunburst of scars, and made a face. "What a waste." He made a throw up sound in his throat. "Pitiful. At least you wore clean underwear."

He rolled out a mechanics' chest and popped the accordion top open. "This used to be a dentist's fishing cabin, you know. Used to store a lot of his old junk here. Those guys know how to have fun." He laid instruments on the table, picks and explorers, scalers and curettes. A hand driven drill for root canals.

"What do you do, huh? Root a canal? Or canal a root? What about extractions? Picks or pliers? No, the correct term is *forceps*. Wouldn't want to use a Home Depot needle-nose on you, would we?"

I gave him no reaction. Monsters like this feed on tears. He wasn't getting any of mine.

Will's shoulders slumped, like he was disappointed, but he pushed ahead. "Guess how I kept their mouths shut?"

He picked up a curved needle locked in a hemostat. The silk thread that dangled from the needle was stiff, crusty with dried blood.

"I mean it's not like anyone else can hear, but the constant crying, the bitching, the moaning? Man, oh man! It gets to you, know what I mean?"

Jesus, didn't I know it? I mean, this guy just wouldn't shut up. *Just get on with it.*

"Now, I know my instruments are rusty, but don't worry. It's not the infection that'll kill you."

He picked up a Bard-Parker and laid the blade against the skin of my knee. It went pale and blanched as it compressed. Dull blades? Not just a loser, I thought. Grade A, premium loser. The scalpel finally penetrated in a thin red stripe.

"This ligament holds the bone above and below your knee together, see? Holds your kneecap in place like a band-aid. It's the anterior cruciate. I call it the ex-cruciate. Get it? That's only how it will *feel*. The good thing is it doesn't really bleed much, so we'll have plenty of time to examine other parts. I've spent a lot of time reading, watching. Learning how to make this last. I like to last long. *Law-ong*."

I'd finally had enough. "I thought you held your girls."

"What?" The scalpel hovered. The cut on the knee filled and bubbled like a teardrop. For the first time he looked uncertain. Till now it had been a well-rehearsed play and he had gone through the motions with the confidence of one who possessed the only script. He pulled back. Slowly. The brim of his hat still covered his eyes. I wanted to see him desperately, look right into his eyes.

"I thought you held your girls. Didn't cut them up. You know? A slave in the pantry is better than meat in the freezer."

He finally looked at me, his eyebrows knit together like a bird setting for flight. *That's* it. *That's* the look I wanted. *Good boy!*

"What the fuck are you talking about?"

"Linsey White? Twenty-eight. Pretty. Skinny. Green eyes. You probably liked her, didn't you? Wore a yellow dress when she was last seen." I bobbed my head. "That one. On the end of the rack. And Jessica. What was her last name? Oh yeah, Fitzgerald. She was only sixteen. You probably didn't care for her, though. She had a tramp stamp above her butt-"

"Stop." He was on his feet now, his head clamped between his hands. Gone was the swagger he had shown when he shoved me into the trunk. Now he was just a fat, balding man with a knife.

"Want to see something interesting, creep? Take a look in my shirt pocket."

He grabbed the shirt off the dresser, ripped the pocket open so quickly it sounded as if it might tear in two but he wasn't that strong. Not anymore. He stared at the photo, *his* photo, a bubble of spit growing at the corner of his mouth. He flipped it over, looking at the name scrawled on the other side.

"Portia Black?" His breath was hot, a plume of fear. "What the hell is this? Who the hell are you?"

"Doesn't matter," I said. "By the way, if you think I'm not pretty you should buy a mirror." I paused for effect. *"Bob."* I waited another beat. "Robert Benson Pullman."

"I said, *stop!"* He screamed, lunged forward, the scalpel handle clenched in his fist like a dagger. For a moment I thought I had overplayed my hand. Or mistimed it at the very least. He came to a stop, inches away, suspended in midair. His breathing turned shallow. He was trying to push words out where only gasps would fit. A dribble of blood appeared at the corner of his mouth, splitting his lips.

"Oh hell," I screamed. "No, no! *Hell!"* I pushed him into a seated position on the chest and pressed him back, lifting his legs above his chest. The venous return would keep him going for a few minutes at least. The knife I had taped to my back, the one that had sliced through my ties, the one that had then sliced into his chest, was barely visible in the blood seeping through his clothes.

I pulled it out and dug through a pulsing well of meat and gore to find the artery. It wasn't as easy as it sounded, not on a beast that fat. Next time, I reminded myself, leave the goddamn knife in.

"You stabbed me." His voice was a hoarse whisper.

"I'm sorry. I didn't mean to get you so hard. That was just to immobilize you. God, I never do this. I'm better than this." I *am* better than this. I'm very good. Ask my references. I'm the best.

"Here." I rolled up his cap and staunched the puncture. I folded his hands over the wound and pressed down. "For God's sake, don't you die on me. Please!" I took the rickety steps two at a time, my heart slamming. It's weird, I know. But I needed to keep him alive, even if he would have thought nothing of disposing me.

There was a wall-mounted phone hanging by the fridge. Please be working. I pulled the handle to me. A dial-tone. Finally, luck was on my side. Then, behind me, I heard the click of a hammer. I knew this sound, heavier than a pistol, clunkier than a rifle. I felt the cold nose of a shotgun in my back. Twenty-two, maybe twenty-four gauge.

"What did you do to my boy?"

I turned, slowly. An old woman faced me. Her clothes were soiled, her grey-white hair kitchen scissors-cut with a heavy hand.

"Seriously? He has a mother?"

"Everyone has a mother, child."

"Not me."

She smiled, her mouth pink and toothless. The skin around her lips was cracked and peeling. "Not you, huh?"

"I just meant, it's weird that he does all this with you around."

"He does it *for* me, child."

"Oh," I said. "I get it. You pick the keepers."

"Did you hurt my boy?"

"A little." *A little?* I hoped he wasn't braindead yet. I hate lying but I'm sure Judas would be okay with me in this instance. "You have a choice here, Mrs. Pullman. Kill me. Or save him. You can't do both." I turned slowly to the basement door.

"No. You don't move. I'll blow your brains out, honey. And I don't want your crap all over my nice kitchen floor."

As if following up on the threat, the shotgun traveled in a straight line up to my forehead. Bad move. The old woman's arms were short and the angle was weak. I pressed forward like a soccer player at the goal line. The headbutt pushed the rifle up into my hairline. By the time the blast went off it caught just hair and singed my scalp. The stock went backward, and I followed through, plowing it into her throat. She fell to the floor, knocking her head on the linoleum.

I felt for her jugular. Faint, but still there. Two for one, I thought. But I had to get Pullman stabilized first. I went back to the phone. *Please, please, please* be there.

A male voice answered. Old and tired. "Yes?"

"Mr. Fitzgerald?"

"Yes?"

"It's done. But you have to come fast."

"Where? You're still at the meeting?"

"Dammit," I said. In the rush, I had forgotten that Pullman had ripped my jacket off in the parking lot. My GPS tracker was in the pocket. The cabin was… *think, damn it!* Where was the cabin? I looked around. There were papers on the table.

"Mr. F., keep the line open, put your coat on, and get your keys."

I rummaged through the mess. Notes, clippings, recipes. I tore through the drawers, throwing handfuls of scrap onto the floor. A bill peeked through. Overdue electric to one Mrs. Geraldine Pullman.

"Mr. F., you there?"

"Yes. Of course."

"Six nine oh eight. It's about a quarter click off Wilderness Road."

"Oh my God."

"I know," I said. It was less than fifteen minutes from the Fitzgerald home. I tried not to cringe. All business now. I had a killer to save. "Quickly, Mr. F. And bring the medical bag. I'm going to need it."

CHAPTER 3

The truck pulled up in eleven minutes. James Fitzgerald was only fifty-four, but he looked ninety. That's what losing a daughter does to you. It stops your heart but your body keeps going, trying to outrun the pain.

"You hurt?" he asked.

"Just a scrape. Needed a haircut anyway. Come on." I grabbed the bag and took it into the kitchen. The old woman hadn't moved. I dropped to a knee next to her and felt for a pulse. *Hell*, I thought. Too late.

"Who is she?"

"The mother."

"Fuck," he said. He was a polite man, and the word seemed bitter on his lips.

I shook my head at him. Then I relented. Whatever. I guess it's called for sometimes. I loaded a couple of hypodermics and took the stairs. I half expected Pullman to be waiting for us with an axe or a chainsaw, but that stuff just happens in the movies. When a person bleeds to death, the body goes into hypovolemic shock and it conserves just enough to flush the brain and vitals.

"He's on the bench, Mr. F." That was stupid of me. Anyone could see the three hundred-pound whale beached on the Craftsman tool cart. But I guess Mr. Fitzgerald hadn't seen him. He was staring into the distance.

His legs bandied, and he reached out for the handrail like the room had suddenly gone dark.

"Oh damn," I said. "Oh hell." The clothes rack. I moved quickly, trying to block the second dress, the pink flowery one behind Linsey White's yellow frock. It was the kind of outfit I'd never consider wearing. If I were a dress wearing kind of girl, that is. *God*, if I was a boy I'd probably wear a dress once or twice. But never as a girl.

I grabbed it and clutched the hideous thing to me, trying to hide it, but I saw Mr. Fitzgerald's face and it was obvious that this whole thing was about to go to pot.

"Give me the dress."

"No. Mr. F, you have to focus."

"Give me my daughter's goddamn dress."

I relented and passed it over. He hugged it. He sniffed it. Under the must and dirt smell of the basement, he had found something he could relate to. There were tears in there, somewhere deep inside of him. I don't believe you can ever be cried out. But if he started, this would all be over.

"Okay," Mr. Fitzgerald said. His eyes were red and rheumy. "Okay, let's do this."

I injected Pullman with the painkillers, a pop of epinephrine, and slapped him till he responded. "Bob. BOB! I need you to answer me."

"Wha..." His voice was bubbly, filling with blood. I could've kicked myself.

"Bob. Wake up."

"Yeah?"

"This is James Fitzgerald."

"Mother?"

"No, Bob, follow me. This is not your mother. This is James Fitzgerald. Father of..." Shoot, with all that was going on, I had forgotten her name.

Fitzgerald pushed me aside and shoved the dress in front of his face. "This is my daughter's dress. Jessica Fitzgerald. I want the rest of her."

"She's in the... she's in the woods. Near the old oak."

"The one with the lightning strike?" I had seen it on my way in the door. A large unwieldy tree with half of its branches severed and strewn around the barn.

"They all are."

"All?"

"Yeah. All." He coughed. A stream of dark blood sprayed upwards, then landed back on his face and chest in a fine red rain. The knife had pressed too deep, under the xiphoid, near the middle lobe of his right lung. God, I wish I could have that back. I've worked in hospitals before and seen what just the nick of a blade or a bullet can do to a lung. The last thing I wanted was for his larynx to fill. I knew he was going to want to talk and I needed his throat to be clear.

"How many, Bob?"

"Eleven, twelve." He smiled dreamily. "I have their photos in a book up-"

Mr. Fitzgerald slapped him so hard the huge body almost slid off the cart. "Are you bragging, asshole?" He turned, grabbed a curette, and stuck him with it. It quivered between his ribs like a dart.

"Easy, Mr. F. You want to take your time." I needed to control Fitzgerald. And fast. If murder was a dance, this would be a minuet.

"I could give you amateurs some pointers," Pullman said. "I have... I have pictures. Figures. Diagrams."

"Goddamn you!" Fitzgerald launched at him.

"Mr. F., no!" I pulled him back. Gently.

"No, I won't let him. He's mocking us. He's mocking my girl."

"I know," I said. "I'll handle this." I turned to the beast. "Bob, how about we keep you alive?"

"What?" Mr. Fitzgerald protested. "No! I can't live through a trial. Not with him like this. He likes it. This is what he wants."

I raised my hand sharply. It cut off all protest. "Only for a minute. I've got someone you might want to see." I went upstairs and dragged the old lady into the basement. I tried to do it gracefully, but the stairs were old, the woman was limp, and I had to give up halfway. Her dumpy body slid down to a comical seated position at the bottom of the stairs, limp like a marionette. There was no blood, but the large purple bruise on her neck had welted so badly it looked like a scarf.

"No." The word was almost imperceptible, but I could tell Pullman had seen her.

"She wasn't supposed to be home, was she?" I asked. "But she's just as much at fault as you are, so maybe we start with her while you watch." I hoped he hadn't realized she was already dead. Mr. Fitzgerald grabbed a kitchen knife, sliced off thick chunks of her hair, and threw it at him. Limp white strands stuck to the saliva and blood dribbling down his cheek.

The triumphant look had gone from Pullman's face. He was staring at the old woman. The no came again, mumbled, fragmented, swallowed between a trail of sputum and blood. "Ma!" He was crying. Sobbing. My work here was done. I leaned over to the beast, my lips almost touching his ear. "Not that it really matters, bud, but when you get down to that big black hole down there, tell the boss man that Portia Black sent you."

I may not believe in heaven, but I do hope there's a hell. I picked up the scalpel, wiped it on his face and tucked it into my pocket. No sense in leaving any DNA. In my line of work, you can't afford to leave anything behind.

"He's all yours, Mr. F. Enjoy."

I climbed the steps and leaned over the sink. Everything finally hurt but there was no time for that now. I was good at plenty of things, but not arson. I had to be extra careful. I piled together every flammable thing I could find. Gasoline, K-1 Kerosene, linseed oil. At least six cans of hairspray from the basement.

There was no way this wouldn't look suspicious. Having bodies together in the basement during a fire never looks good but I was too tired to stage them. I hoped Mr. Fitzgerald remembered to keep them in one piece. What the hell, let the man have his fun.

Fitzgerald finally pulled himself into the kitchen. He was still standing, but his body had crumpled, his movements slowed to a crawl. There were pieces of flesh and trails of blood all over his shirt and skin.

"Well?" I asked.

"Burn them," he said. "Burn the motherfuckers."

We stood outside the cabin and watched the flames lick up the curtains. The dress was folded up under his arm. "This part of my life is over," he said. "I hope I never see you again."

"You won't."

"Promise?"

"I can't promise anything, Mr. F. Every time you tie another knot, it only gets tighter. Your car tracks are all over the ground, you've got pieces of them on you. They've got you on them. It's messy." I paused. It was more than messy. It was a pile of manure, and I hoped no one would sniff too closely. The smoke was beginning to seep out of the window. Time to go. "I found the book."

"What book?"

"Pullman's book."

He looked at me, aghast.

"Not for you. You don't want to see it, trust me. But I put the photos in Pullman's glove compartment. When they find the bodies, the cops aren't going to be looking at anything else. At who chopped up his body. At who set the fire. But…"

"But what?" he asked.

"Those knots? They're always going to be there. I can just promise that if they find me, I won't know you. And I hope you won't know me." I turned my fingers like a key over my mouth.

"You're acting like we're criminals. This shouldn't be criminal. This is justice."

"Sometimes what this country calls justice is criminal." It's a cheesy line, but I truly believe it. "Mr. F?"

"Yes?"

"Time to go."

He looked at me, his eyes dead. "Don't you need a ride somewhere?"

"I've got a job in California." I pulled a washcloth from the backpack and handed it over. "Besides, if you get pulled over for a taillight, I sure as hell don't want to be next to you."

James Fitzgerald opened the back door of his car and a large black creature flopped out. There aren't too many things that can make a day like this better, but that animal sure does try. She came to a heap at my feet. Dog was old, and her eyesight was failing, but she could still smell. She retreated, whimpering.

"It's okay, Dog, it's done. He's gone." She prowled around, sniffing at the blood stains. She watched the flames lick out of the windows and growled. "Fine. Like you've never seen anything like this before? Let's go."

Dog's whine grew louder. There's a little Husky in her and she's convinced she can talk. But her ears were pricked. It wasn't the smoke or the blood. It was the sound. I could hear it too, from way beyond. Sirens.

As Mr. Fitzgerald's car rumbled off, I walked in the opposite direction.

The beach was dark and sweet smelling. I thought of Jessica Fitzgerald. Linsey White. Of the twelve other nameless girls. I thought of how easily I could have been number thirteen. An envelope lay crumpled at the bottom of my bag. There was a Polaroid in it, a young woman tied up on a bed, hands and feet trussed together in a slaughter pose.

"Work's a killer," I said.

Dog whined at the water's edge.

"Okay, girl. Just five minutes."

I stripped off my clothes, bundled them tightly, and doused them with lighter fluid. I had a sealed pack with the same outfit in the bag, two more in my van. Black sleeved shirt, standard blue jeans, fingerless gloves. No more underwear. On the road underwear and socks were an extravagance.

I ran into the freezing surf. I had a long cross-country drive coming up. And the ocean was cleaner that a Flying J bathroom. Dog bounded in beside me, paddling around in circles. The cut on my knee, the bruise on my neck, the gouge on my forehead, the assorted rope burns all cried out instantaneously. I ignored them. In minutes, the salt would heal all the wounds.

California was a long way off, four, maybe five days drive. I would probably have to call in a few favors along the way. A bed. A meal. A few bucks to tide me over. I knew a couple of people I could call on in Tennessee. That would break the trip up nicely. I pushed the thoughts to the back of my mind. I'd worry about it in the morning.

I bobbed in the current, watching the black smoke spread out into the clear moonlit night. And as a strobe of red light cut across a distant road I dove down as deep and as far into the surf as I could and disappeared into the inky black.

CHAPTER 4

The package arrived at Dr. Arthur Zahn's lab at 8:00 a.m. The specimens had been picked up from a garbage can in East Memphis the day before and overnighted to L.A. in a FedEx mailer.

In the plastic packing was a foot of dental floss and two used Kleenexes. There was a half-inch bloodstain on the nylon and a thick clump of materia alba on the end of the fiber. Oral samples were usually a gold-mine of exfoliated gingival cells, but the bubble mailer was ripped in two places and the inner bag was a grocery-quality plastic liner.

Sloppy, Zahn thought. Guys who were that sloppy tended not to use sterile gloves and if the gloves weren't sterile, if there was even a trace of someone else's DNA on the sample, then-

The phone rang suddenly, Verdi's *Libiamo* lighting up the dull room.

"How's my favorite doctor doing today?" Hunter asked. Zahn winced. Every time Hunter said the word *doctor*, he made it sound like an insult.

"Did you get the specs? How are they?"

"Not good," Zahn said. *Not good?* Working with specimens like this nowadays was like street racing a Yugo. Zahn hadn't seen such shitty samples since Bush had been president. And he meant *H.W.*

"What's the problem?"

"First, I'm not even sure if the items are hers. Second, the chance of nailing down a decent sample from this?" He paused, searching for a better word and failing miserably. "This garbage? The chances are slim to none. And third, even if we can get a hit, all the samples have to be amplified."

"So?" Hunter sounded bored.

"Have you read Fujimoto's paper in 'Forensic Science'?"

"Of course not. Isn't that your job?"

"There's a new test for DNA methylation. It's cheap. Simple. Amplified DNA is non-methylated," Zahn said. "If the forensic labs test for it then we're screwed."

"Didn't we do the Francke girl with amplified DNA? That was just last year. And the Kreiner kid? Her parents paid up real quick."

"You're not listening, Hunter. Times have changed. People expect more. We can't just sneak in a couple of drops of blood or saliva, a pube, or some skin cells anymore. Parents aren't ponying up a twenty-five mil ransom without real proof. If they even suspect that the DNA is fudged, it's over."

Zahn's first attempts at DNA transfer were rudimentary. He had taken genetic fragments from a skin sample, amplified it, and transferred it onto a host red blood cell. It was cheap backyard science, but it worked. All it took was a few drops to contaminate a crime scene beyond repair. Or arm twist a reluctant parent into co-operation. Unfortunately, like most scientific breakthroughs, last month's wonders were little more than afterthoughts today.

"What do you need?" Hunter asked.

Zahn looked at the wall-sized incubator, rows of petri-dishes bathed in infrared light. There were five trays with slabs of flesh, slivers of bone. Fragments of tooth. This was way more than traces of blood. These were slam-dunk, *pay up or your daughter comes back in pieces* cases.

It was knock-out evidence. Proof of life and proof of imminent death all wrapped up in one. But creating evidence was messy. It was expensive. Zahn needed money and time. He knew Hunter was usually only good for one at a time. "What do I want? Or what do I need?"

"Let's start with what you need," Hunter said.

"What I need is a real sample. If you want this done right, I need live cells. Not shit you picked out of the trash."

"If I can get you some facetime, how long will it take to get some tissue? I mean the *real* stuff."

"Like skin? Anything more is going to cost extra."

"This isn't about money, Zahn. Do you know what this girl is doing to our business? She's public enemy number one. I want her off the streets permanently. I want a chop-shop. Bits and pieces. Blood and guts. Toes and teeth. I want puke-tacular. I want to lock her in a hole and throw away the hole. How long will it take?"

Zahn took a deep breath in. There was a long list of things that Hunter lacked. Patience was at the very top. He steeled himself. "Three months. Maybe four."

There was silence on the other end of the phone. Silence from Hunter was never good.

"Then you need to find a way to keep her in town for a few months," he said finally.

"How?"

"Use something you've got. One of your test cases."

Zahn looked at the nitrogen freezer. He had bits and pieces they weren't using. Experiments. He had most of a foot, but he hadn't been able to grow the toe-nails right. He had an ear, but it was built on a titanium frame. His eyes settled on a small object the size of a shortened pencil. It was a finger, the bone severed at the metacarpal, the nail bed pink and bloody. "I might have something that would work."

"Excellent," Hunter said. "I'll set it up for this weekend."

"This weekend?" Zahn paused, looking at the Memphis return address on the mailer. "You mean she's already here? In L.A.?"

"Not only is she in L.A., doc, I happen to know exactly where she's staying for the next couple of days."

There was a chime as a message popped up on his computer.

It was a screenshot from a surveillance camera, a convenience store or gas station, grey and grainy. Zahn zoomed in to the girl at the counter.

Five three, black hair, brown eyes. The kind of girl who brushes by you in the bank, on the bus. The kind you'd forget in five minutes. If you noticed her at all.

"Who is she?" Zahn asked, intrigued.

"Her name, at least the one she's been using of late, is Portia Black."

Chapter 5

"Well?" I asked.

"Well what?" Stephanie was at her mirror, peering at her eyes.

"Does this look okay?"

Steph looked up briefly, too briefly. "A little makeup wouldn't kill you, honey." She went back to the mirror, turning up the back lights to their fullest power. I could swear she did her lashes one by one.

"I didn't put any makeup on, Steph."

"Exactly, honey. That's why a little wouldn't kill you."

"But a lot will? How much?" Getting Steph's attention was like prodding an alligator. Slow steady pokes or it would bite your arm clean off.

Steph's shoulders dropped, but she didn't turn. "God, why are you always so difficult?"

"I'm not being difficult. I just asked what you thought about the dress and-"

"Oh my God, P!" She turned and jumped around, squeaking and screaming all at once. I hate it when Steph calls me that, for obvious reasons. "Why didn't you tell me you were wearing a dress?"

"I didn't tell you because I was already wearing the dress."

Steph wasn't listening. She was still running circles around me like a puppy. I like to think of Steph as incandescent. She's bright, she's plugged in all the time, and she burns through money like no one else. I tried to change the topic.

"Reminds me, I have to get Dog some dinner."

"God, that animal eats like…"

I followed Steph's stare and folded my arms over my ribcage, embarrassed.

"Like you don't. I'll call Simon. He can do it. That's what he's here for."

"No, he's not…"

But she wasn't listening. She circled, poking and prodding me like a mannequin. Steph was rich and pretty. In her world no one really questioned her. She's the kind of girl I was talking about, the one who always has doors opened for her. And Steph never notices. In fact, had I not rescued her from a situation involving duct tape and a roto-zip, I'm sure she wouldn't notice me either.

"Omigod, Shay." She had finally finished the inspection. "The dress. I'm perfectly shook." Steph was in a permanent limbo of shook and lit. She had a litany of other words that I couldn't understand. Bussin. Drip. Rizz. "You listening? I'm a stan. No cap. That dress is so you."

I knew that wasn't true. I looked at the endless drape of lavender and noticed how skinny my body was. "This dress is not me. There is no dress that's me."

"It's a Givenchy, doll." She pronounced it *Jay-Van-Chay*. "It's everybody."

It was all I could do to not stick her with my knife. But Steph was being nice enough and putting me up for the weekend so I let it go. "Thanks, Steph. Really. I mean it."

"Twelve Gs," she said.

"Grenades?"

"Grenadas. As in thousands. That's a lot of cheese. Cheddar. Gouda." Steph had a lot of names for money too. Most were variants of dairy products. Some days they were all leafy greens. I looked at the dress again, finely stitched, no doubt, but not something Grams couldn't have put together with three yards of discount satin and a box of leftover buttons. At current Jo-Ann's rates, probably under ten bucks.

"Come on, Portia, don't look at me like that. You're wearing Mr. Givenchy himself."

"I don't think Mrs. Givenchy would care for that. It's very Ed Gein."

"Who's Ed Gein? Does he have the new store on Rodeo?"

"No, he's a serial killer. Used to dress himself in his victim's skin."

"Jesus, I wonder who's sicker. Him? Or you for knowing him? Can I trust you to be normal for just one night?"

"I promise I won't mention death and dismemberment."

"Or skinning?"

"The word is flaying."

"Don't say that again either and we're square." She pushed me to the mirror. "But the hair, girlfriend, has got to go. We're not slumming at *The Whiskey*." My hair is usually buzzed enough to see scalp. Like early eighties Sinead O'Connor. After three months on the road without electricity, it was in desperate need of a good set of clippers. She plastered the messy locks down with gel.

"I usually use spit."

"Shut up. Close your eyes."

I did. I felt pins going through my hair. For someone who didn't trust anybody, I trusted Steph way too much.

"Don't you dare open your eyes until I say so." I heard alternating humming and cursing. "Okay, now." The weave was big and ginger, but it looked real.

"Well?"

"I'm thinking B-52's."

Steph put her face next to mine. Her hair was bigger and blonder. All natural. Mostly. "Oh, my God, you're right, Shay. It's so nineteen eighty-nine. Perfect for a B-52's party."

My heart sank low enough to knock at my knees. "It's a B-52's party?"

She patted me on the cheek. "It will be when we get there."

I could see it in her face. She totally believed it. It almost made me puke. Steph was bouncing around again. "Now let's get you some real shoes and slap some face on you."

"You sure this is a good idea?"

"What is, honey?"

I extracted the picture from the envelope. The bound girl looked up plaintively, the duct tape reflecting in the camera flash. "You sent this to me, remember? You said you needed help?"

"Yes, it's terrible, isn't it? But isn't that exactly why you're here, Portia?"

"I'm here to make sure you don't get into any trouble either. I definitely don't think clubbing is the best way to do that."

"You want me to hide?" She knocked on my wig. "Jeez, Portia, is it still you in there?"

"Steph, this is the third girl in your circle to go missing in, what, two years? I think it's time to-"

"I'm not scared. Especially now that I have you."

"I'm not a bodyguard, Steph. That's not what I do."

Steph came over, put two hands on my shoulder. "Believe me, Portia. I know what you do. Everyone knows what you do. Now, come on, let's get to work." She swiveled and bounced out of the room.

"That's not comforting," I said. It wasn't comforting at all. Being in the shadows was crucial to my success. And the last thing I needed was someone finding out I was in town on a job.

CHAPTER 6

Fifteen minutes later, we were rolling down the driveway. Simon was in the front seat, big and bald, his square face hidden behind oversized sunglasses. At night. I think Simon fancied himself as a secret serviceman. In truth his real name was Shimon and he might have been one back in Tel Aviv. He certainly looked the part. Broad-shouldered, thick-jawed, squinty-eyed. A creasing of thin lips that sometimes passed for a smile.

Steph's driveway was gated and took most of ten minutes to traverse. An hour if you were on foot. It was the kind of layout that needed a park just to keep the house in perspective. Steph's parents owned a quarter of the Hollywood Hills and she was one of those golden kids who once dreamed of getting famous for doing nothing, then pretending that she never wanted it at all. But she's changed a lot since I met her. I think that's why she keeps me around. I remind her of what could've been.

The car rolled down Mulholland to Outpost, winding out of the quiet hills into the raucous setup of Highland and Franklin.

There were uber-rich kids everywhere, preening, posing, hanging out of expensive cars, wearing one of a kind couture that would probably end up in a back closet after a single wear.

"Sick," I said.

"What?"

"All of this. You know there are kids out there who don't get to eat. Makes me want to puke."

I saw Shimon smile in the rearview mirror. He likes me, I think. We have this little-people bond.

"Not on the dress, honey. And FWIW, most of these kids don't eat either."

Steph pulled her hair up and pursed her lips. The flash was blinding in the dark cabin.

"Jesus, Steph," I said. "Some warning."

Steph flipped her hair the other way. "You really need to get yourself one of these, Portia. Make your life a whole lot easier."

"Probably make my life a whole lot more dangerous."

"Oh, that's right, cloak and dagger and all that. It's a pity. You'd blow up on Instagram tonight. A million followers in less than twenty-four hours. I could make that happen. Guaranteed. Right, Simon?"

"Yes ma'am," Shimon replied.

"Does it matter?" I asked.

"Does what matter?"

"How many followers you have?"

"Jesus, Portia. How old are you? No, I mean, not literally, but how old are you? This isn't the sixties. You only have so much time. Don't you want to be remembered?"

"Actually, no."

"Wow," "Well that's really the whole point of life isn't it? The only point. That someone misses you when you're gone? What I wouldn't do to just be missed." She jumped, squealing, face plastered to the window. "Here, Simon. *Here.*"

Shimon spun the Maybach around like it was a Supra. The back tires drifted and bumped the curb, the door opened, and we were engulfed.

The street sign said Argyle. We were at a large industrial looking building attached to the Hollywood self-storage. Two years ago, this was probably a coke-motel. Now it was a way overpriced nightspot.

A weathered mural covered the brick, a host of dead Hollywood stars staring down disdainfully at the kids waiting patiently in line. And the line was endless, wrapping around the corner, two, sometimes three deep.

"What are you doing, twinnie?" Steph pulled me toward the entrance. Steph liked to call us twins. The Winter twins. She thought it was funny because we looked nothing alike. Except for the skin tones. She spent way too much time trapped in a tanning bed, and I spent way too much time trapped in someone's basement.

"Come on, sister, lines are for losers."

A young woman sucking on a hand-rolled cigarette and wearing a Michael Jackson-red jacket pulled out of her group. She puffed out a billow of mist that smelled sweet against the muggy acid air. Her eyes were sunken in, drugged out.

The bouncer elbowed her back, making way for us. Steph turned and winked at me. Know your place, she always said. You don't have to like it, but you had to know it.

The warehouse doors ahead of us were covered in faux graffiti. Hugs and air-kisses abounded all the way to the entry. Aluminum sliders opened up to a brutal dubstep beat, knee-deep foam, and an array of electric blue lasers. The light cut through the cavernous dancefloor like a lightsaber.

I stalled at the entryway, already nauseous. I was used to clubs that looked and smelled like back alleys and the sensory overload was toxic. Words cut in and out in the pounding bass line as Steph was surrounded.

"Does it --- to be this ---?" I screamed. I could see she hadn't heard. "Does it have to be this --- bright?"

"Look at you talking," she yelled into my ear. "--- punk rock. Like --- didn't have strobe-lights back --- nineties."

"No --- didn't. And --- the seventies."

"What?"

"Punk was seventies ---"

"--- you kidding me? You --- even born then. You coming ---not?"

I stared at the kids on the dancefloor. They were moving like animals in a cage, fighting and clawing their way to the stage or bar. Arms waving ritualistically, they pushed themselves slowly back into the throng.

Others hung about, half-empty glasses in hand, disaffected, waiting for something interesting to happen. Nothing ever did. Yet they came back night after night. They all looked uniformly rich. Even those trying to look poor. I felt the nausea worsen.

"Not." I stood my ground, knowing that it wouldn't do any good.

"Suit your ---" Steph threw her hands into the air. I suddenly realized how alone I felt without her. People stared at me like a bug that had strayed into a room.

I looked back at the steel doors as they slid open again. The Mercedes had gone. Another large yacht had pulled up and was disgorging another group of inebriated kids. I looked at the Blahniks that cut into my ankles. I wasn't getting far in these deathtraps, and I didn't want to spend the rest of the night on the curb either.

The bouncer noticed me standing there and gave me the once over. "You in? You out?" His voice was baritone deep and limited to well-practiced single syllables. He pulled a device from his pocket and scrolled through the list.

I turned and looked around for Steph, but she was long gone. The girl with the red jacket was going to love this.

"Hey, Cindy!" A young man pushed his way through the crowd, two drinks in his hand. "She's with me."

He tipped one of the drinks at the man. It was unlikely that the bouncer had heard but he left me alone and returned to the door. The boy motioned me over to a break in the black industrial curtain. It was twenty feet away, but it took almost a full minute to squeeze through the crowd. I was wet by the time I got there, champagne, sweat, and other indeterminate body fluids lashed across my clothes.

In the next room, the bass still thumped but it was quieter and the lights were dim. A small bar stood up against the partition and the glasses rattled and blinked in the low-lights. Kids were perched on ottomans and sprawled on thick rugs.

The girls were Gia Carangi clones, dressed in satin and skin, sunken eyes and bombed-out faces. It was called heroin chic and it hadn't been this popular since the nineties. Packets of powder and pills scattered like dice. The red velvet draperies completed the opium-den ambience.

He was standing there with the glasses in hand. I was amazed that he hadn't spilled a drop.

"I'm not Cindy," I said.

"Course you're not Cindy!" He had brown hair cut in a traditional crew, his clothes were JC Penney rack sale, and there wasn't a hint of makeup or surgical intervention on his face. He didn't look like any of the other kids. "I mean you could be a Cindy, but you aren't, obviously, *Cindy*. And I'm not Bas. Look at me, I'm blabbering. Here, this one's for you, *not*-Cindy."

"Thanks," I said. The word was dry and distasteful on my tongue. "But I don't drink." I began my silent recitation. Alprazolam, Brotizolam, Clonazepam-

"I'm sure you don't." The drink was still proffered. "But it's organically grown cactus. Ecologically sourced. Farmer supported. All that bullshit." He stopped and frowned. "Oh, you mean you won't drink because I'm a stranger. Good choice."

He switched the glasses and proffered the one he had held close to him. "Still no? Okay, I'll double down." He lifted the glass over his open lips and poured half down his open mouth. "See? Safe."

I took the glass and looked at the half-inch of amber sloshing around at the bottom. Steph wouldn't allow me to wear gloves with her dress, and I knew I was leaving prints all over. The last thing I needed to do was to add saliva to the evidence. Stalling seemed appropriate.

"Do you make it a habit of offering people half a drink? Or are you just too poor for this club?" I asked.

He laughed. "No, actually *you're* too poor for this club."

I was shocked for a moment. I *was* too poor for this club, but I wasn't expecting to be called on it. Mr. Givenchy was supposed to be a suit of armor protecting me from these kinds of questions. The drink wavered in my hand. I wasn't sure whether to suck it down or dunk it onto the little shit's head.

"Don't worry, I'm too poor for this club too. See? We have something in common." He tossed his drink down. "I work the lighting," he said. "I set up, then I'm free to-"

"Hit on the patrons?"

"Yes." He bowed. He was not bad looking. In a kind of strap on your tool belt and fix the plumbing kind of way. I nodded appreciatively. He did look poor. Not food stamp poor. Ramen and Chef Boyardee poor. Without thinking, I sucked my drink down.

"Here." He took it. "I know the bartender. He'll get you a refill at half-off." He pushed away to the bar. "And it'll only cost me two weeks' pay."

I felt like an idiot standing there alone. The bathroom seemed like a safe option. It was open door and unisex, the stalls separated by thin, transparent panels of frosted plexiglass. Two were occupied by couples in copulating poses. There was a girl at one of the urinals, cutting powder on its rim and sucking it up with a paper straw. A boy in a lemon-yellow pantsuit stuck his tongue out at me. It was forked down the middle, twin-tips pulsing and purple. He flicked a double rope of saliva at me. I retreated back into the den. Conversation floated around like a purple haze. A kid next to me was talking about cutting Ketamine with MDMA.

"You do realize that's a horse drug?"

"So, what? A racehorse horse is worth way more than you."

"Five mil, then?"

"You know you're only worth that dead."

Fantastic, I thought. I moved on to another group of girls slicing open a plastic packet with a scalpel. They eyed me suspiciously as I passed.

"God damn it, Lexi," one said. "This had better last longer than the crap your boyfriend got us last time. I was only high for an hour, then I fell asleep. When I woke up I had shat myself green. And not Kale green. Lucky Charms green."

"Told you not to use it as an enema."

"What's a girl supposed to do? I hate needles."

If I only had a dime for every shooter who started off hating needles.

"What the fuck do you want?" It was the girl with the green excrement. She was staring me down like she was prepping for a fight. "You got something to sell?"

"Nope. But if you hate needles you might want to try grating." I wish I hadn't said anything. Most of what passed for conversation in my life was with guys duct-taped to chairs. They tended to be avid listeners which made me an avid talker. So much so I rarely knew when to stop.

"What the hell are you talking about, bitch?"

"You scrape the underneath of your tongue until it gets raw and tuck a fentanyl patch in there. It's a sublingual overload."

The girl looked at me carefully. "I don't give a shit about your life-hacks. You selling something, or not?"

I shook my head.

"Relax," the other one said. She pointed the tube at me. "She's one of Steph's girls. She's in the game. You in the game, honey?"

"I have no idea what you're talking about."

"God! She doesn't even know. Where are you from? Nebraska? I asked you. Are you in the game? A Bella Donna?"

Her face was close enough to smell her breath. Licorice and acid. Her pupils were so dilated, there was only a hint of brown iris. I wasn't looking for a fight here and I decided to go with the safe route. "No," I said.

She dropped back into the cushions. "God, she really is from Nebraska." The others giggled, translucent skin rubbing up and down their bony ribcages like silk on a washboard.

I felt a hand guiding me away from the table.

"I wouldn't get involved," Bas said. "Used to be kids would fight about who drove the best car. Who lived in the swankiest neighborhood, wore the best clothes. Now it's all about who has the best drugs, the best dealers on speed-dial. Who's got the best game. Like I said, you can't compete."

"You're not exactly endearing me to you."

"Seriously, you want to be one of them? I might have misjudged you."

"I guess you have me all figured out then."

"You don't look all that mysterious to me." He raised the glass.

I laughed. "You'd be surprised."

Bas looked at me carefully, handed me the drink, toasted, and sucked his down. "So, would you?"

We ended up on the terrace above the club looking down at a line that had grown impossibly larger. The warehouse roof was little more than cinderblock and air vents, but the breeze was cool and the noise was limited to the rumble of the 101 freeway behind us.

Bas balanced on the edge of the roof, straddling the ledge. One leg dangled off into space.

"You're wondering what would happen if you pushed me, aren't you?"

"No." I paused. He had me there.

He laughed. "I know that look. You like to peek over the edge of buildings, wonder how far it is till you hit ground. What it'll feel like when you finally hit."

I looked at the crowd below. "Probably feel like a lot of silicone and Restylane. I might bounce."

"You know there's a myth that being God-smacked-me gorgeous would always get you into a club in L.A.. That was then. Now everyone's beautiful. Everyone's platinum blonde and pretzel skinny. Even the guys. And everyone's rich too. Know why they come? It ain't for the crappy music."

"Ah, it's one of *those* clubs."

"Every other club is one of *those* clubs. This is *the* club. And I don't mean street-shit like heroin. Meth. Molly. I mean good stuff, stuff nobody knows about. Think they're lining up for some shitty 'ludes? They're looking for the new drug. The next drug."

"And what's new? I mean, in case I was interested. Which I'm not."

"Betty Grables, Rita Hayworths, Jane Russells. Beautiful ladies."

"Aren't they all dead?"

"Yeah. I don't know if these suckers get it, though. Or maybe they do." He looked at me, his eyes shiny. "I'm not sure which is worse."

I glanced at the crowd again. The kids were shifty and aimless, Romero-esque. The girl in the Jackson jacket was still around, the zipper all the way down, a lacy brassiere pushed up in the face of one of the bouncers. No one was interested.

"Look at the big guy up front with the pointed beard. They call him Lucifer. Guy's a goddamn Rockstar. He's been known to take a chick or two into the back room and get some head just to let them in. Seriously, you think they'd do that for Skrillex and a shitty bottle of Cliquot?"

I laughed, my contempt evenly distributed for the sluts and the storyteller. "You're such a damn liar."

"Cross my heart." He made a cutting motion across his chest. "What would you do? If you had to get in."

"I wouldn't be caught dead." I stopped, realizing how stupid it sounded.

"No, you wouldn't. And yet here you are. Let me guess, best friend, lots of money, needs a lot of attention?"

I reached out for the drink in front of me, then pulled back. He knew I was warming up, and I hated him for it.

"You seem to know a lot about me."

"Maybe I do. Let's see. The accent's Mid-western but there's an East Coast edge. Like you moved there when you were a teen. New York City area but not anywhere terribly cool. Staten Island? No, New Jersey. Hoboken or Weehawken. Someplace where you can see the lights at night without having to remind yourself that there's a big old river between you and everyone else."

I shrugged.

"You listen to something edgy, not commercial," he continued. "Garage punk. You take pride that it's local, but it annoys you that they try so hard to be the Stripes. You auditioned once but they wanted you to play bass and you don't-"

"Okay," I interjected, "this is getting excruciating."

"That far off?" He laughed.

"Yes." I paused. "Well, except for the band part. It was old school punk. Ramones. The Dolls."

He leaned forward. "Show me your tats."

"That's a little forward."

"Okay, I'll go first." He pulled up his sleeve. A single flower drooped amidst a bed of thorns. I'd seen my share of tattoos and I could tell it was not a rose. Or a lily. Or any kind of flower usually featured in body art.

"What is it?"

"Atropa Belladonna. Deadly nightshade. Your turn."

"I don't have any." I'm not against body mod, but my line of work calls for discretion. No ink. No piercing. I don't even wear jewelry.

"Punk rocker with no ink. Now that is rebellious." He pointed at my chest. "What's that?"

"I'm guessing you missed fourth grade health."

"No, that." He pointed closer, at the neckline of the dress. A slender pink spider peeked out from under Mr. Givenchy. I pulled the strap back further and more legs appeared. A starburst of a scar trailed over my breast and deep into my heart.

"Let me guess. 2:00 a.m. Lower East Side. Double Down? No. Mars Bar. Stared down some asshole with a broken beer bottle."

"Close enough." I was nine. The boy was eleven. It was my second month in foster, first in the Wilson home. He had tried ripping my shirt open with a Bowie knife. I pulled the dress back, covering the scar with a thousand dollars of silk. "Let's just say this isn't the crowd I usually hang with. And I think I'd take *crazy-eyes* Mike with a broken bottle of Labatt over some of these idiots."

"I get it. Given a choice, you'd be anywhere but here. But then you'd never have met me. So fuck 'em." He stood, took a deep swallow, and forced up a wad of phlegm. He pointed at the crowd. "Pick one."

"Lucifer."

"Why? Because he could break me with his pinkies?"

"No, it's because I'm giving you an advantage. He's bald and his head is bigger than Barry Bonds."

"Okie-dokie. Bombs away." He leaned over, his chest balancing on the railing as his feet lifted off the ground.

"No!" I grabbed him and pulled him back.

He burst out laughing. His teeth were white as Tic-Tacs and perfectly shaped. The t-shirt had lifted halfway up his abdomen and I saw a hint of muscle underneath. Not rock hard and chiseled like he lived for it. But just enough to keep me looking. The lights from below were shining on his face. It suddenly struck me how handsome he was.

He pulled out an e-cig and flicked it on. "You chickened out. What happened to the punk rock baby? Rock and fucking roll and hell with the rest."

"Spitting on people isn't my idea of fun. I already had my share of that tonight."

"Okay, then it's your turn. You do something stupid you're going to regret tomorrow."

"I will," I said. I went up to kiss him. And, boy, did I regret it.

CHAPTER 7

There's a romantic notion that suggests that if you wake up alone in a strange bed, the guy you slept with will be up early, puttering around, cooking breakfast.

It was something that only occurred to me as I passed the empty kitchen, dress half-on, shoes in one hand, the other trying to erase the millstone of a hangover that weighed on my shoulders.

I paused at the door, my hand on the knob, a nibble of curiosity setting in. I didn't really expect bacon and eggs but I expected *something*. The drawers were empty, so was the refrigerator. Not a pizza box or beer can in the trash. There was, in fact, little evidence anyone lived here. I walked back through the apartment, small but luxurious, barely furnished. The floors were shiny travertine, arranged with animal furs that felt only too real. The vacuum lines in the carpet were undisturbed.

The bedroom I had just woken up in was under-furnished, white walls, splatters of paint meant to be art. A single blue silk rug meandered its way lazily from bed to wall. I ran my hands over the bed. The satin bedsheets were messed only on one side and still tucked hotel-room tight on the other.

The roiling in my stomach that had dragged me out of the bed was simmering down now. My mouth was dry and my jaw hurt. I ran a finger down my cheek to where the bone of mandible curved up to the joint. There was a ragged bump, sore to the touch. A wisp of something silken wiggled above the skin.

But that was it. Maybe nothing had happened. I slipped a hand below my dress, below the waistband of my underwear. Still nothing.

I looked down on a breathtaking view of the sprawling city below. The wrap-around balcony leaned over others exactly like it. The acid crept back up my throat. I couldn't remember the drive up the Hills. I couldn't remember an elevator. I couldn't remember stairs. After the club, I couldn't remember much of anything. Behind me, I heard the door open.

"Listen, I know I stayed, but that doesn't mean anything. So if you went to the trouble of getting breakfast, I'm sorry but-"

"Ma'am?"

I turned slowly and faced the muzzle of an LAPD-issue Glock 22. The officer was young, barely into his twenties. His posture screamed rookie. Both hands were wrapped tightly around the pistol grip and he circled the room warily.

Two more officers took up crossing positions at the door, keeping me in their sights.

I stepped up, raised my hands, and tried to defuse the situation. "Seriously, guys. He told me he was eighteen, I swear."

Humor rarely works with the LAPD. I saw the rookie jump and I regretted it immediately. My face slammed against the edge of the bed and I heard the click of cuffs as they bit into my wrists. It was a little excessive, even for breaking and entering.

The ride down the elevator was slow, silent, four uniforms flanking me, hands at their waists. As we hit the lobby I saw flashing lights and noticed the number of squad cars.

It was only then that I realized it. I wasn't being hit with trespassing. Someone was probably dead.

The ride to the station was a blur. In the hour that elapsed between being Mirandized and booked, there was nothing more than the occasional nod and grunt on my part. For Hollywood jail, it looked and smelled very East Coast.

There was a major drug problem on the strip, and most of the women lounging in the intake were still sweating stuff out of their systems. Like the population, the drugs were varied. Khat from Africa, Kratom from Thailand, God knows what from trailer-labs in the prairie.

There was one woman rocking on the floor, scraping her tongue with the tip of her shoe. A puddle of spit and blood collected in a ring around her neck. She was sitting across from another woman, barely out of child-hood, picking at her raw skin and arranging the shims on the floor like a bloody snowflake.

The one thing being an alumnus of the U.S. foster system had taught me was to set a tone right away. I eyed the biggest woman in the room, a two hundred and fifty-pound white girl with cornrows so tight her eye-brows were pulled back into her hairline. Tattoos that specified gang affili-ations were etched along her neckline.

I knew she would come in handy if I was dropped in the clink for an extended amount of time. She also didn't look strung out. That was a big no-no. You never took on a druggie. They fought with the strength of ten women. And they would use everything, and I mean everything, they could.

I walked up to the woman and stared her down. I bet she'd never been attacked by a girl in a Givenchy gown.

"What the f-" she began to drawl. That's when I popped her. When you're a hundred and none pounds and unarmed, that's the only way to do it. The old handshake to the face.

The woman looked more offended than hurt. She swung but I was way too quick. Duck. Punch right. Wait for the swing to complete and left finger jab to the neck. The next blow connected under her right eye, com-pressing the infraorbital nerve as it exited the foramen.

The result was like an electric shock to the face. I once worked jani-torial at a cadaver lab in Fargo. There was a lot you could learn from an anatomy text and a freshly dissected human. My fingers felt for the thyroid notch near the border of the sternomastoid as she reeled.

The internal carotid artery splits here, the primary supply to the brain. My fingers found her pulse and squeezed. It was quick and vicious, just my kind of fight.

She was on her way down as the guards blew in and pulled us apart. Most of the druggies were on my side of the room now and they had to peel through a dozen inmates to get to me. I got in a couple of extra licks before they had me immobilized.

"You! Out!" The officer pushed me out, past the large woman who was now sitting on her haunches. Her eyes were glazed and red, her neck a scarf of bright pink. She pointed at me with one finger, but her throat was too bruised to make any sound.

I was pushed into an empty cell. "Five minutes and you're already creating trouble."

"Should see what I can do in ten."

"Shut up. The chief wants you in one piece or else I'd throw you back to the wolves there. And Myra? Bad choice. You might have gotten away with it once. But if that was a ploy to get attention? Prove yourself? Bad, *bad* choice. Myra will break you like a little girl."

The metal doors slammed, and the locks clicked. No keys, no cards. As old and decrepit as the jail was, the security has been upgraded recently. I could be lost here forever, and no one would care. Myra or no Myra, I knew I was a lot safer in the hold.

The sergeant came back an hour later and looked at me like a bug on a napkin. It was a look of half-pity, half-fear I've been subject to on occasion. Squish? No squish? Depends on how nice the napkin is.

"Chief's in. He'll see you now."

"Chief?" I felt a soreness in my mouth, the taste of blood from chewed up tongue. I wondered how Myra was. Not very forgiving, I'd bet.

"Yeah. You screwed up big time. Better have a good story because he's in a foul mood."

"I don't have any kind of story at all."

The sergeant looked at me. "Then I suggest you make one up."

"Isn't that against the rules?"

The sergeant shook his head. "I'm a cop, chickie, not a lawyer. I get to bend the rules, so when I say good story, I meant it. Now, come on."

I glared at him, then relented. I've known plenty of lawyers. Judges too. Everyone bends the rules. Even the good ones. Live long enough and you won't have a choice.

He prodded me into a small white room with a single bench and two chairs. A large brown man with an almost-bald head and a handlebar mustache sat on one of the chairs, although he could have easily used both.

Once there might have been an imposing frame on him, wide shoulders and hips, a powerlifter or wrestler. Now there was just a weathered mass of softening muscle and overlaid flab.

"Sit," he said, without looking up.

The door shut behind me and the room suddenly seemed whiter and smaller. I know interrogation rooms are painted white to make them seem more open but the room made me feel smaller than I ever anticipated. I had never been in one before, and it felt like a vacuum had been pulled, sucking the air right out of my throat.

"So," I finally managed to speak. "You interview everyone who comes in here or-"

"Shut up." He still hadn't looked up. His stylus kept scribbling on the tablet before him. Another minute passed, and I realized he was working hard to make me feel inconsequential.

"Candy crush?" I ventured.

He finally looked up, his eyes cold and black.

"You're facing some pretty serious charges. I wouldn't be flippant."

"Okay, are you going to tell me what-"

He raised his hand sharply, like a knife ready for slicing. "My precinct. My job. I do the questions. You just answer. When I'm done, I get to go home. When you're done, you get to go back to your cell. See the difference?"

I waited. He returned to the pad. A minute, maybe two. Finally, he looked up. "Looks like you have a question."

I shook my head.

"Good. I have a question, then. Why did you kill Nathan Hunter?"

I was right. L.A. was crawling with squatters. They wouldn't have made all this fuss about just breaking and entering.

"Who's Nathan Hunter?"

He looked at the folder, a photocopy of my driver license. "You're MacKenzie Bricker, aren't you?"

"Yes." For today, at least.

"Well, Mackenzie, whose apartment did you think you woke up in this morning?"

I shrugged.

"What, your Tinder app doesn't have names anymore? Is it name-free hookup now? I'm surprised you don't just do it at the street corners like the pros and save some time."

"I met him at a club."

"So, you do know Mr. Hunter."

I held up my hand like a truant child. "I don't know who I met."

"You never asked for his name?"

"I don't usually do names. It's safer that way."

The man stared at me, his eyes cold. He wouldn't say it, but I knew what he was thinking. I went home with a guy I was too afraid to exchange names with.

I relented. "He said his name was Bas."

"Bass? Like the fish?"

"One S? Two S's? I don't know. I didn't ask for ID."

"So, this Bas. He looks like this?" He pushed over a black and white photo.

I nodded. The captain pulled the photo back. "It's Hunter. You just met him at the club? No previous encounters? Internet chats, snapchats, whatever you kids do nowadays?"

"No," I repeated. "I met him at the club. He said he worked the sound and lighting."

"Sound and light?"

"Yes, you know, the setup for the DJ." "Nathan Hunter sets up the sound and lights for the DJ?"

"Yes, he-"

Again, the hand cut through. He leaned in close, his eyes narrow. "Nathan Hunter sets up sound and light for the DJ. The DJ he pays. In the club he owns."

"He owns?" The last wisps of air sucked out of the room.

"Nathan Hunter owns three of the most popular clubs in L.A.. A restaurant in Malibu. A high-end jazz club on the strip. You getting the picture?"

"Got it. He's rich. It wasn't him."

"Because he told you he did sound and light." The chief passed over another picture. In color. "Nathan Hunter. That him?"

I nodded silently.

He passed over a couple of pictures of the apartment.

"Hunter's apartment."

"I don't know."

"How do you not know?"

"I was drugged."

"Ah." He pulled back. "How convenient."

"For him."

"Him? He's the one missing."

"Missing." There was a sense of relief here, like a cloud had blocked out the burning sun. It was temporary, I knew, but still. "You said he was dead."

"Missing. Kidnapped. Dead. I don't know. I wasn't there. You were. Let's go back to last night. You go to the club. Alone?"

"With a friend."

"Name?"

"Stephanie Winter."

The man looked up at the mention of the name. He had to know, but he gave nothing away.

"Where is she?"

I shrugged.

"So, you meet this guy, he tells you he works sound and light."

"Yes."

"And you believe he drugged you. Why?"

"Because I woke up in his apartment this morning. And I don't know how I got there."

"Pretty nice apartment for a lighting tech, don't you think?"

"Like I said, I woke up. I had no idea where I was. I tried to leave. That's when your guys got me."

He kept his eyes on me like he was waiting for more.

"Your guys can fill you in with the rest."

"That's it?" He swiped the tablet off and put the stylus into his pocket.

"Maybe he just went out," I said.

"For coffee. A smoke. Couple of morning-afters?"

I shrugged.

"Okay, then." He brushed past. "Tell Myra I said hello."

I wasn't worried about the Hunter kid. There was no blood. No sign of a struggle. But something the chief had said was eating at me. It wasn't the accusation of homicide. That was bullshit without a body.

He had said kidnapping. If there was some truth to that, then it cut close to home. Really close.

Everyone has secrets hidden deep in their own back yard. And if they started turning over the dirt in mine, that hole was going to be pretty damn deep.

CHAPTER 8

"What the hell were you thinking?"

I looked up at Steph as the car peeled out of the lot. She had given me the silent treatment all the way out of the jail, through the parking lot, and to the waiting red Tesla where she insisted on holding the door open herself, like she wasn't giving me the slightest option to run.

"Well?" A scarf was wound around her head, a pair of oversized sunglasses covering most of her face.

"I'll pay you back," I said.

"First, you can't." She pointed to a well-dressed woman entering a white Cadillac. As her perfectly sculpted calves disappeared, I saw the red tongues of her Louboutins, still showroom shiny. "That's your attorney, sister. You can't afford her. And second, it's not about the money."

The car screeched around the divider, crossing four lanes of traffic and bumping the opposite curb. If she was trying not to attract attention, she was doing a terrible job of it.

"And Nathan Hunter. I mean, seriously? What were you thinking?"

"I wasn't."

"Damn right you weren't. I mean, what about the rules? Like, isn't this what you *do*?" She pulled to a hard stop at a yellow at Franklin. Cars screeched and honked behind us. "What do you mean, *I wasn't.*"

"I think I was drugged. I don't remember a thing after I left until I woke up the next morning."

Even under the sunglasses, I saw her eyes roll. "Great. That's just eff-ing great."

"I didn't ask for this. God, Steph, I'm the victim here."

"Victim? Look, if you were any other dumb broad in Hollywood, I'd feel sorry for you. But you know better. Fuck, even I know better. Because I learned from the best. You. You're the one who's supposed to be keeping these motherfuckers straight. Never put anything in your mouth you don't know. And I'm not just talking about drinks either."

"He drank it too."

The light turned green again and a medley of horns blared. Steph raised a single flippant finger and let it fly over the canopy of the roadster. She gave it a minute to let it settle in and then roared across the boulevard. "Suck and switch."

"What?"

"He drinks but doesn't swallow. Pretends to chase it with beer and spits it into the bottle."

"He drank half. I drank half. No chaser."

"And you didn't drink anything else?"

"One. At the bar." As soon as I said it, Steph shot me a look of disgust. Now that it was out in the open, it sounded terrible. Steph was right. It was okay for an ordinary girl. One without my history. This was my job, I shouldn't have been so careless.

"Oooh, just one. At the bar. That he owns. Poured by a bartender he pays." She curled her lips and slurred her words. It was hard for someone like Steph to look ugly, but she could come pretty damn close. "It's okay, Steph." Her voice drawled. "It's no big deal, Steph. It was just one drink, Steph. *God!*"

"Stop. I made a mistake, okay? I didn't know who he was."

"Let me guess. He said he was the valet. He gets to sneak in for free."

"Pretty much."

"And he dropped you a dumb line. Like, oh my gawd, your tats are so amaze. You're nothing like the dumb society girls who come in here all the time. You're just my type. Let's go home and get this on."

Despite the seriousness of the situation, or perhaps because of it, I burst out laughing. "I don't have tats, Steph."

"Oh, that's right. You're supposed to be untraceable. Well fat lot of good that did. Stop laughing. It's not funny. How about I get my bond money refunded and send you back in." The car yawed widely across the boulevard, narrowly missing an old Chinese couple who had stepped too close to the curb to take a photograph.

"You should." I'd probably be safer in the clink anyway. "When was the last time you drove yourself?"

"None of your business." She turned away but through the sheer pull of the scarf I could see she was finally smiling.

There were three cars in the semi-circle in front of the house, all black Suburbans with reflective windows. Full tint is illegal in California, and it's just the gang bangers and dealers who risk the fines.

"Steph, what the hell did you do?"

"Nothing. Just a little backup."

"Looks like an NSA convention."

"It's your attorney, honey."

I winced. "I thought you said the model in the Caddy was my attorney."

"She got you out. These ones will keep you out."

"These?"

"Did OJ have just one attorney?" Steph wouldn't look at me but it didn't matter. I didn't know a single lawyer in the Hills who drove a Suburban, let alone a fleet.

Steph pulled in, one wheel on the driveway, the other straddling the bottom step. Shimon was already running down the steps and retrieving the keys. I shot him a look of compassion.

Strange, I thought. I had just got out of jail and I was sorry for him. I saw it in his eyes. He was sorry for himself too.

Dog was waiting for me at the steps, her mottled tail wagging furiously. "Sorry, girl," I said. "I don't think Aunt Steph is going to let us play now."

"You're damn right, I'm not." Steph dragged me through the carved oak double doors, through the grand entryway. "Playtime's over, Portia," Stephanie said. It sounded like a line from a movie and Steph delivered it like one.

"You," she commanded. "In there." She pointed to a door headlined by a family portrait, the only evidence that Steph had a mother and a father. I've met both of the Winter parental units and they both were as distant in real life as they appeared in their portrait.

By reputation, Father Winter, a small-time real estate salesman done right, divided his time between his Century City office and the golf course. Mother Winter, a former interior designer turned artist, ran a children's foundation and a studio in Taos.

I knew better. Mr. Winter spent most of the year with his mistress in Napa while Mrs. Winter visited with a certain Mrs. Ford on a regular basis. I often wondered if Steph's childhood was any better with parents than mine was without.

"I'm waiting." Steph stood at the door, her foot tapping.

Two men and one woman sat around a large walnut table in the study. The room was off the foyer, lined by built-in mahogany bookcases and a matching Queen Anne desk so large and heavy, there was barely enough room to fit the table and people at the same time.

A hand stuck out in front of my face. "Medina, Jacqueline. That's Carlson and Guerrero." They all wore dark, department- store suits without any embellishments. Including the woman. No ties. No pocket squares. Just black t-shirts. *Definitely* not attorneys.

"So, let's get this straight before there are any misunderstandings. You got in two days ago. Texas Eagle from Chicago? Used the name Reagan Simon."

I shook my head.

"We have another reservation you made. Routed through Salt Lake," Carlson jumped in. "California Zephyr. Name on the res was Tania Jeffrey. Another one on the City of New Orleans from Kansas City."

"Kansas City, Kansas? Or Kansas City, Missouri?" If this was a game, I was going to play to stay.

"Does it matter?" Medina asked.

"I don't know. Does it?"

Medina blinked. She looked over at Carlson.

"Kansas," he said.

"Nope," I said. "That one I did not take."

"Okay," Carlson said, "which train did you take?"

"I drove."

"From Chicago?"

"Boston."

"And the multiple reservations?"

"Nervous habit."

"You have that much cash on you?"

"I have enough."

"There's a red van in the garage. Belongs to you?"

"Yeah. Piece of garbage Dodge Caravan. Blew up on me in Death Valley. Head gasket popped and almost took the entire hood off. Want to make me an offer? I know it's not your color but-"

"Okay." Medina shut the folder in front of her and crossed her arms. "We can go around in circles all day. That what you want?"

I crossed my arms to match. "I don't care. Obviously. I don't need you guys."

"That would be a little presumptuous. You booked three train tickets with three different names and skipped on them to drive cross country. You got booked under another alias. Mackenzie Bricker. Idaho driver license. Birth certificate in Pocatello checks out. But Mackenzie Bricker died three years ago. Fentanyl overdose."

She paused, waiting for me to answer. I didn't.

"I'm going to assume you're hiding something," she continued. "In fact, I'll wager it's something big." She waved her hand over the folder. "Bigger than this mess. So, if you don't want the cops to stick their nose in your dirty laundry, you might want to make sure it's washed and put away first."

The woman had a point there.

"No cops. No attorneys," she said. "Everything is completely confidential. And outside the system. You can get up and leave, handle this on your own. But the clock is ticking, it's not the best time to bet on yourself."

"Okay."

"Okay." She opened the folder again. "You came here because you have a prior connection with Miss Winter."

"We're friends," Steph jumped in.

I looked at her carefully. The first time I met Steph she was tied to a chair in a dingy basement with electrical wire. "Acquaintances," I said.

"And no one besides her knows you're here?"

"Just Shimon. And Frida."

"The housekeeper?"

"Yes."

She turned to Steph. "Your parents?"

"They haven't seen her since…" She paused. "Since, you know." She didn't have to finish. I guess everyone knows how Steph and I met.

"How long have you been here?"

"Forty-eight hours. Give or take."

"Since you got here you haven't left the house, haven't made any calls. Completely out of communication."

"Not till we went out that night."

"And your cellphone?"

"Don't have one."

"You're twenty-six?" Carlson asked.

"Twenty-five."

Again, that look. He was suspicious, but who wouldn't be?

"Internet communication. Chat rooms. Twitter. Snapchat. Instagram. Nothing?"

"Not a thing."

"How did you tell Miss Winter you were coming?"

"United States Postal Service."

Carlson started on me angrily. "Okay, you're going to have to cut with the attitude, missy. I'm not the one facing serious jail time."

Medina raised her hand. "Mike, let it go. You're here for a few hours, maybe a day, then you go out with Miss Winter and you meet Mr. Hunter at a bar. The first time you've ever met him."

"He said his name was Bas."

"Like Bassanio? And your name is Portia? Interesting."

Crap, I thought. It annoyed me that Carlson had made that connection first. A printer whirred on the table. He dropped a sheet of paper onto the desk.

"This you?" Medina pushed the photograph along. The picture was a freeze-frame from a security camera. The lighting was dim, but there was no denying it.

"Yes."

"That him next to you?"

"Yes, that's Bas." I paused. "The guy who called himself Bas."

"It's Hunter. Any drinking involved? Drugs?"

"Two drinks. Shared."

"Then?"

"We went up to the rooftop."

"Door was open?"

"He had a scan card."

"Odd for someone who only works temp."

"I didn't think of it then, but-" I realized there were a lot of things I hadn't been thinking about.

"Twenty minutes later he drives you to his apartment. What kind of car?"

"I don't remember."

"You don't remember anything after the roof." Medina placed a print-out on the table. Grainy. An expensive silver sports car. Two occupants with blurry faces. "That's his car. Remember?"

"No."

"This was from a camera at his apartment building's parking garage. That's you."

"That doesn't look like me."

"No. Not that one." Medina pointed again. "Other side. Driver's seat."

I could see myself in the window. Even through a plate of solid glass I could see I was out. "I couldn't have driven, I was-"

"Under the influence. I know. Plenty of people do it."

"That's ridiculous. I wasn't drunk. Or doped up a little. I was out. Roofied. Besides, what kind of guy lets a girl he's just met drive his car?"

Again, the unsaid accusation. What kind of girl lets a guy she's just met drive her home?

"Did you kiss him?" Carlson asked.

I got up. "Get the hell out of my way."

"Did you?"

I raised a fist. "I've taken guys bigger than you down."

Steph came over and put an arm around me protectively. "They're on our side, babe."

I pushed her off roughly. "There's no *ours*. You're not on my side either." My head was pounding again, but now there was another ache, rising from my neck to my ear, stabbing across my face like a knife. I tried to storm out of the room, but Medina was at the door, a photograph in her hand.

"Before you go. I got this from the DA's office. Don't ask me how, just look at it." It was grainy print from a camera phone. A picture of a picture.

"What the hell is this?"

"It's a finger. It was found in a jar in the refrigerator. In Nathan Hunter's apartment." She pulled open the door and extended her arm. "But you have places to go."

CHAPTER 9

I spent the afternoon outside, trying to clear my head. My ears were ringing. My nose was clogged. My jaw throbbed like I'd been punched. I was in the middle of nowhere, on a snake-like street, surrounded by million-dollar homes that would probably sell for a buck and a quarter in Memphis. A car horn blared loudly as I stepped off the curb. A bunch of girls swerved around in a drop-top Cayman. One of the girls turned around in her seat and flipped me off. A cloud of smoke billowed from a pen-like device.

I refrained from returning the favor. I wasn't afraid of East LA Cholos in their Chevys, Compton gangbangers in their Cadillacs. I definitely wasn't scared of four girls from the Hills who probably just paid a thousand bucks for manis and new dresses. Chicks like that don't like their nails broken or blood on their clothes. I wasn't scared, just sorry. They were wasted, or high, choosing to burn up the best part of their lives. Then it came to me. Burn. The cigarette. There was smoke. But no fire. Before I could stop myself, I was running back up the pavement to Steph's house.

"Is it his?" I asked.

Medina was sitting in her truck, playing with the radio. The rims of her aviators were as dark as the lenses. They straddled her crooked nose like a bird. "The lab's still running tests." She took off her sunglasses and pursed her lips. Behind the nose she was an attractive woman, dark eyes and skin, large sculpted teeth, very white beneath red lips. "You know, once a body part is involved, even a minor one like a finger, the chances of this turning into a murder just skyrockets." She stopped. "This morning he could've been sleeping on a beach in Cabo, but without a finger? It changes everything."

"I didn't kiss him."

"What?"

"You asked me if I did. I didn't. He was smoking. I don't kiss guys who smoke."

"But he wasn't really smoking, was he? Did you see the vapor coming out of his mouth?"

"No."

"Electronic cigarettes have a heating element in the barrel. Vaporizes the nicotine liquid so you suck it in. What you see coming out of the mouth is vapor. But you didn't get hit with an e-cig. You got hit with a propellant cartridge. You don't inhale."

"You blow." I began to tremble. I was cold. It was like being attacked all over again.

"Yeah, but it's not blow, if you know what I mean. It isn't any of the usual street narcs that get you high and tip you back the next morning. If it was, we wouldn't be here. How did you feel when you woke up? Woozy? Cold? Dry eyes and mouth?"

"Yes." I was beginning to get nervous that Medina remembered all this better than I did.

"You probably got hit with an anti-muscarinic. Interferes with the acetylcholine neurotransmitters. Depresses cognition but motor function is spared."

"A zombie drug?"

"I'm going to have to ask you to co-operate a bit more and get a blood test and serum analysis."

"It's been over twenty-four hours. Besides, the cops already did one."

"The cops did the usual battery. Weed, heroin, coke, PCPs. They didn't test you for Scopolamine."

"Burundanga?"

"Not the Colombian stuff. Natural Brugmansia gets a bad rap, but it's remarkably ineffective. Powder it, blow it into someone's face, maybe it knocks them out for a couple of hours. But this isn't a street drug; it's a Frankenstein, structurally potentiated. A chemist we consulted called it Scope. Get it? One swish and it cleans your mind out. But you're lucid, open to suggestions. Of any kind. It's the perfect date-rape drug. Especially because no one knows what it is. Or where you get it. We don't even have a name."

"Betty Grables."

"What?"

"Betty Grables, Rita Hayworths, Jane Russells."

"I'm not sure where you're going with-"

"Hunter said people came to his clubs for the newest drugs on the street. Beautiful ladies. *Bella donnas.* Isn't scopolamine a belladonna alkaloid?"

Medina turned to Guerrero. He scrolled through his phone. "Kissing cousins," he said. "Atropine from Belladonna, Scopolamine from Brugmansia."

"What's the half-life?"

"Nine and a half hours."

"If you got a significant dose we should still be able to run an alkaloid panel. If not, we're going to have to try urine analysis, maybe liquid chromatography and a mass spectrometer on a hair sample. It won't hold up in court, but it's a start."

Medina put her hand out of the window and the second truck pulled up. Carlson slid in, pulled open a wrapped medi-bag and laid a series of vials and needles on the tray between the seats.

"Right here?"

"Sooner the better. Do I have your permission?"

I nodded blankly. Before I knew it, my arm was being ligated and scrubbed with alcohol.

"Portia?" Medina asked.

"What?"

"We're professionals. This is what we do. Let us handle it."

"And what about me?"

"Just don't do anything stupid."

I didn't even feel the needle. I was already thinking of my next move. The only ideas that jumped out at me were pretty damned stupid.

But I didn't care. There was one thing I knew about guys like Hunter. They never stopped at one.

CHAPTER 10

Hunter had tracked the girl for much of the morning and well into the afternoon. A couple of times he had gotten close, leaning in on an escalator, brushing against her in the midday crowd. Close enough to smell her hair.

It was strawberry blonde but without a hint of straw-berries. Instead, there was the heady scent of oil. Something woody; eucalyptus, camphor perhaps. It was a smell that would drive him crazy, and he made a mental note to buy shampoo. He wouldn't risk what happened last time. This time, everything would be perfect.

He stopped, waited for her to gain some distance, and he began trailing again. It was this part of the game, the stalk, that he enjoyed most. He was a wealthy man and could easily pay someone to do the dirty work, but the hours spent preparing, dressing, waiting, yes, especially the waiting, were soul-cleansing for him.

Even in the middle of the Las Vegas strip, surrounded by thousands of tourists, there was a certain solitude, a single-minded purpose that made the stalk an almost spiritual purpose. Tracking a human, Hunter mused, was much like tracking an animal. Except you didn't have to stand in line and buy a permit.

The girl finally stopped at a swanky nail salon, perched herself on one of the throne-like chairs as her feet soaked. Epsom salt and spearmint? he wondered. Or sea-salt and lavender? If so, he would have to add peroxide and a jug of distilled water to the list.

He dropped into a massaging recliner across the concourse and waited. This was her fifth stop of the day. It was approaching evening time and he was sure she'd be tired. The girl had broken up with her boyfriend that morning and she had responded, stereotypically, he thought, with a shopping spree. She had already been to Balenciaga to pick up a metallic envelope clutch, a stop at Mac for a laundry basket-sized haul of cosmetics, the Cristophe salon at the MGM for the aforementioned oil treatment. Now, after a working stop at Pinkberry and a quick pause at Frederick's, she seemed almost done. Hunter decided to make the first call.

"That room I had pre-booked?" he said. "I'd like to confirm."

The woman on the other end sounded like she'd been waiting for the call. "Yes, Mr. Hunter. Anything else for you?"

"I'd like the limo pick-up, something nice. Maybe the Escalade stretch?"

"How many passengers?"

"Just one."

"And will it be you, Mr. Hunter?"

"No," he said. He thought for a moment. He looked at her relaxing on her throne, eyes closed, lips moving to a song he couldn't hear. "The pick-up will be for Mrs. Hunter."

"I didn't know there was a Mrs. Hunter."

"Neither does she."

The woman on the other end laughed. "You're a devil, Mr. Hunter, you know that." She confirmed the pick-up and he snapped the phone closed.

The girl was finally done. The sun had begun to set, and she headed off to the lounge at the Mandarin Oriental. Hunter followed her and perched himself at the bar across from the banquette where she sat alone, surrounded by her day's purchases.

He ordered two drinks, a *Jacques Selosse* for her and a virgin nojito for him. The bottle was a Grand Cru but not the precious ninety-nine vintage. He wanted her to feel special, but not *that* special. He wanted her to know that he could splurge on a bottle that she might never drink but he wanted her to know that he could upgrade her too. He watched as the white-gloved server presented and poured the champagne. She stared at it, then at him. He could tell she was less than pleased.

"You were expecting Bradley Cooper, perhaps?" Hunter muttered to himself. He turned on his electronic vaporizer, fiddled with it as she came over, bottle and glass in hand.

"I don't accept drinks from strangers," she said. She dropped the bottle and the glass on the marbled bar top. The champagne wobbled in the glass, millions of bubbles exploding to the surface.

"I hardly think Monsieur Anselme Selosse spiked his grand cru specifically for you."

A silent, colorless puff curled out from the vaporizer, caressing her neck.

"I didn't say it was spiked. I said I wasn't interested." Her eyes had already taken on a glazed look, ebony black pupils, ivory white sclera.

"Then I must apologize. Maybe you have a friend who enjoys five thousand-dollar champagne and equally valuable company?"

She grimaced and swiveled on one pointed heel. Hunter enjoyed teasing his girls. They all acted so haughty and cat-like in the beginning. As she turned and left, she stumbled into a coffee table. Hunter winced. He didn't want any marks on her. Not tonight. He picked up his phone and dialed.

A familiar voice answered. Good old doctor Zahn, Hunter thought. Always reliable. Like an old dog.

"Any news about Miss Black?"

"They're doing a DNA profile on the finger. But it's just a finger. Without a body, it's not homicide. And without any real proof of her involvement, there's not enough evidence to keep her locked up."

"Involvement? The girl woke up in the apartment of a missing millionaire. I've seen choir girls convicted on less."

"Obviously," Zahn said, "you haven't visited any of our county jails recently. Unless the girl had had a knife in her hand and a liver in her purse, they're not going to keep her locked up."

"Throws a little wrench in the works doesn't it?" Hunter watched the girl stumble out into the concourse. "Especially since I'm already working on stage two of our plan while you're still piddling around with number one."

"We could throw another bone, pardon the pun, out there," Zahn said. "Make it worth their time?"

"No," Hunter replied. "Let's leave her out there for the time being. Let her scurry around a bit. How much time till her tissues are ready?"

"I told you. Three months. At least. What if she skips town?"

"I think I have a way to keep her interested." He watched the young woman stumble against a slot machine. "In fact, I have the one thing she won't ever say no to."

Hunter ended the call and got to his feet. He turned to the young bartender. "What do you think, Jimmy? Perfect girl or what? Feisty. I mean, I'd prefer her with some red in her hair. It would show up real well in the pictures."

"She's an awfully attractive young woman, Mr. Hunter," the man said. "But you know me. One fish slips through your fingers, there's always another one swimming down the stream."

"Not like this one."

"She's your type, huh?"

"You know me, Jimmy." Hunter laughed. "I'm a sucker for good genes." He dropped a crisp hundred on the bar and followed her out into the night.

CHAPTER 11

I found her in the ladies' room of Mastro's, the exclusive ocean club restaurant perched on Malibu's Pacific Coast Highway. She was halfway through the signature seafood tower when she had excused herself, rightly, I guessed, to regurgitate the gluten-encrusted lobster tail into the first commode she could find.

I stood behind the door, waiting for her to finish retching. As the panel unlocked, I slammed it back, dropping her onto the seat.

"What the hell are you doing, bitch?" she said. "Get out. Get-" She stopped, her eyes widening. "Shit! You were the freak at the club last night."

"Nebraska," I said. "Or was it Kansas? Either way, honored you remembered."

"What the hell do you want?"

"Your name is Alexandra Cooper. Twenty-two. Green eyes, blonde hair. Well, at least it used to be blonde-"

"I told you to get the hell out."

I slid the lock closed and snapped open the knife. She looked like she was going to throw up again, this time without the digital manipulation.

"You grew up in Covington, nice little two-bedroom, nothing fancy. Now you live in university housing at Northridge. Cal-State, am I right?"

"Why the hell does it matter?"

"Oh, it matters. You're not one of them, one of the rich kids. But you hang with them. They accept you. Which can only mean one thing."

"That not all rich girls are shallow?"

"This yours?" I flashed a brown clutch at her.

"Where did you get that?"

"You left it at the table. Jesus, it's small enough, you could have brought it with you to the john. Especially if you have stash in it." I opened the purse. It was a Luis Vuitton and from the looks of the lining, quite authentic. Entirely too expensive for a girl of her modest finances.

"The boy you were with was poking around in it, probably trying to get a head start on whatever was in here." I swiveled my fingers into the recesses, like I was stirring a drink. "You should thank me. I might've saved you a dine and ditch if he'd found this first." I dropped four or five small ampoules on the floor. The glass clinked and rolled on the marble. "So how many of these little guys buys a dinner at Mastro's? Five, six? What about club admission? That should be at least baker's dozen, right? No wonder you broke that glass ceiling."

"Shut up!"

"Oh, I'm not judging, honey. God knows, I've had to make questionable choices too. Once I stayed in a foster where I was fed only if I came to the table in underwear and-"

"What the hell do you want?"

"Belladonnas. Betty Grables. Rita Hayworths."

"What the hell are you talking about?"

"Drugs. Scope. Deadheads. Zombies. I don't care what you call them. I want to know where you get them."

"I don't sell that shit," she said.

"But you do know where it's sold," I insisted. I flipped out my knife and tested it on my finger. It drew a thin red stripe to the surface.

"I swear, I don't know." Alex's face blanched. "You might want to ask Jamal."

Cutting is the best negotiating tactic in the world. If you were willing to do that to yourself, who knows what you would do to next. "Who's Jamal?"

The girl shifted on the seat. Her skin had gone from pink to paper white. "He's the guy who supplies my guy. Shit, he's the guy who supplies everyone's guy."

"Where can I find him?"

"Jamal? I don't know. No one does."

"No, I mean your guy."

"He usually hangs out by the Chevron in Inglewood. Near the ramp. Ask for Bumps."

"Seriously?"

"Shit, I didn't name him." Alex put her hand out and I passed the bag over. As she bent over to pick up the glass on the floor I noticed the little flower that crawled up her shoulder. Atropa Belladonna. I unlatched the door and stepped out.

"How the hell did you find me here anyway?" she asked.

I waved a glittery pink iPhone at her. "You just updated your insta an hour ago. And your friend, Jillian, was it? She was kind enough to give me her phone." I snapped the knife closed and slid it back into my boot. "Didn't even complain. Much." I sucked my finger feeling the tingle of blood on my tongue. "In fact, she showed me how it was done. Which kind of helps because I don't have a clue how these damned things work anyway." I paused. "You do realize that every time you update your socials, you let everyone know where you are?"

"That's the whole point, isn't it?" the girl said.

"Jesus," I said. "You're a goddamn drug dealer, Alex."

"I'm not a dealer. I'm a-"

"I know what you think you are. But you're not. Think Jillian took more than two seconds to give you up? You're not a friend. You're not one of them. You're a service. Get used to it. I did." I dropped the device and kicked it across the shiny floor. "Grow up and get yourself a damn burner."

CHAPTER 12

There was a dead body under the 405. The owner was probably fifteen, but wasted away to the weight of an elementary schooler. Awkward angles, mostly shoulders and knees, pressing out from the rags that served as a blanket. A crusty brown patch of vomit encircled the head like dried oatmeal. A stink that oozed and slapped onlookers in the face.

The ambulance that weaved through the onlookers took its time, its sirens on silent, the red eyes burning lazily through the muggy greyness of another spit-poor L.A. evening.

I watched them pull out of the van, staggering under their burden. I get it. I mean, why rush, right? The medics pushed through the small crowd, bags of charcoal in hand. If you've never seen a drug resuscitation, consider yourself lucky. O.D.'s are a paramedics worst nightmare. Worse than choke-blue babies, four hundred-pound myocardial infarcts. Even worse than jumpers. Jumpers don't fight back. Narcs do. Street drugs are a chop-shop of narcotics, psychotics, and stims. Fent. PCP. Dust. Pop. This was a tour of duty, and these were the IEDs. It wasn't uncommon for one medic to hold back with a switchblade handy while the other shoved a pocketful of charcoal emetic down the vic's throat.

"Stand back," someone in the crowd said. "She's going to blow like a blue whale."

"Ain't nobody blowing," someone else replied. "She's been dead since this afternoon. She pissed herself and shat herself already. She's good and dry now."

Other voices drifted over, low voices, a thick lace of disgust and excitement. "Is that little Mischa Jackson? She's been back from juvie just three days."

"That ain't Mischa. That junkie is a white girl."

"Not white, she's just a pale black girl."

Truth to be told, it was hard to say. The medics had her rolled over already. Her features were bloated, her skin grape-purple.

One of the medics gloved up and went through the motions of pulse location. The other packed his Narcan kit away. It was like disaster-zone triage. Naloxone was in short supply and most medics only picked the ones with a real shot.

I slid over to a short man with earnest black glasses and a stubble that ran down his cheeks and disappeared around his mouth.

"Bumps?"

He looked at me, his eyes puffy. "What?"

"You selling something?"

The man looked at me with disgust. "Little girl dead, shat her bag up and died. What's the matter with you? You want to climb up in that shit-bag with her?" I moved on to the next guy. "Anyone know where Bumps is?" I asked.

He didn't turn. Neither would the next two. I gave up and took the van over to the gas station at the intersection. The Chevron sign flickered, struggling to stay alive.

As the crowd began to dissipate, the man with the stubble approached. He was staring at my hands, then at the dash.

"I don't have a gun," I said.

"Man, I'd be way less suspicious if you did. Sorry I got hard on you there, but you don't want nobody else listening. You know how they get, all bent out of shape because a junkie's dead. You be fine with what I got. A rock or two. You look like a couple of rocks would do you good. I got some new shit, cut with PCP."

I peered at him carefully. *Bumpy.* I was right the first time. The stubble was laced with hills and craters that boiled up in little pustules that threatened to grow and blow. It was a sure sign of an addict who sold drugs on the side, not a dealer who occasionally dabbled.

"You got any Scopolamine?"

"What's that?"

"Belladonna. Betty Grables. Rita Hayworths. Comes in a propellant cartridge. Blow it into someone's face, knocks them out, but they're still awake-"

"Like roofies?" He was still checking the van out. Most dealers are the nervous sort, especially with new customers. They had to be ready for anything. A Glock strapped to the headrest, a jumper in the hold.

"There's nothing back there." Mostly true. The back seat had been trashed a few years ago, it now held a box with a hot plate and a generator. A sleeping bag was rolled up in the other corner. The rest of the hold was taken up by a treasure trove of books from public libraries across the country. When you skip town at thirteen, there's only one way to make up for a seventh-grade education.

"Okay, but I don't know you. And you're a girl. Asking for weird-as-hell shit."

"I don't want to buy it. I want to know who's selling it." I pulled a twenty out of my pocket and folded it into a rectangle. Street is so cheap nowadays you can get a hit for less than a six pack of Coors. Sometimes it's cheaper than a school lunch. "You tell me where I might find a seller and I might consider buying some product."

The man's eyes glazed over. I could see him doing the math. He was going to sell me five bucks of product for twenty and buy another fifteen from a real deal. Then he'd cut it with chalk and weed killer, sell half to another fool, and use the remainder. Home-boy Ec 101. You know the old saying. Drugs don't kill people. *Cheap* drugs kill people. Death rates have gone through the roof because idiots like this are out on the streets selling product they know nothing about. The real dealers are smart enough to keep their customers alive.

"Well? You still selling?"

"There's only one guy who knows every game in town. If anyone knows where to get it, he does."

"Jamal?"

"Yeah." He looked around warily. "Jamal. He's the one who owns Mary Jane." "The marijuana dispensaries?"

"Dispensaries?" he scoffed. "More like Wally World. Especially that big one in Compton. Damn near bankrupted us street dealers. Like Home Depot came to town and all the mom and pop stores closed up. Now you have to walk through two miles of power tools and washers just to get a bolt."

"Sounds like he took your lunch."

"Sure, if you're into baby food." He opened his hand half-way. A crystalline pile of rocks rolled around in his palm. "If you really want to get bombed, though?"

I turned the key in the ignition.

"Wait, you won't find him that easy, honey. His stores might be legit, but he still rides like a dealer. No number, no address. You don't call Jamal. Jamal calls you."

"He's got a hit on him?"

"A couple, twenty, who knows? Nice girl like you? I wouldn't get involved."

I wanted to tell him I had more than my share of money on my head, but I let it go. "Compton?" I asked again.

"Comp-town, yeah. But I told you. You'll never find him."

"Oh, I don't know, I got friends in Compton." This was a blatant lie. I knew people in Compton but they sure weren't friends.

"Hey, wait. I thought you were buying."

I dropped the van in gear and begin rolling off, the guy following, rapping on the window.

"Hey, you don't know what you're missing. It's real good stuff." I stepped on the gas. They always turned belligerent when they realized it wasn't a bargaining tactic.

"Get the fuck out of here, junkie. Don't you come back." He picked up something, a bottle, a rock, and flung it at the van. It missed by a mile. It wouldn't matter either way. My van's been hit with worse. "You're going to get your ass killed, bitch," he screamed.

As I took the exit to the freeway, I could see the medics zip up the body bag and load it onto the stretcher. The pusher was right about one thing. The odds on getting myself killed were pretty high.

CHAPTER 13

I took the Rosencrans exit off the 110, rolling into Compton from the West. A collection of dilapidated buildings and gas stations lined the ramp, plastered with advertising for tobacco, alcohol and weed.

The stereotype of nineties Compton, the one perpetuated by countless hip-hop videos, had a dealer on every block and a banger in every car. Things had changed in the old hood. Apart from the occasional gang sign on a shutter there was little sign of violence. If you looked hard enough, there was even the subtle whiff of gentrification.

Still, I was two blocks north of Alondra, dangerously close to Southside Crips territory. In a red van. I took a left, towards Lynwood. It was all Piru Bloods and Varrio Seventies up here. If I got shot at, at least I had given them a good reason for it.

I found my man playing street craps at the Qwik 'n EZ storage facility in Imperial Courts. His name was Quentin and he squatted by the rolled-down grates of number 43. He wore a white t-shirt and Adidas track pants with matching single strap sandals. There were tattoos on his arm that were new, but not much else had changed.

Quentin flicked his cigarette, dusting his hands on his pants before he approached. Halfway there he paused, shielding his eyes against the glare of the sun.

He took a long look at the road, then down the row of concrete sheds. He fished around in his pocket, pulled out another cigarette and lit it, taking in the smoke in great raspy breaths. It all came out at once, a plume that obscured his face.

Most dealers I knew were creatures of habit, used to their regulars and wary of all others. The drawn-out dance gave him a few extra seconds to see if I might be a cop, a gangbanger, or worse.

"Hey, Q, what's up?" My tone was cool, friendly even. I couldn't sell it though. I hated the bastard to hell and back.

"What's your name, girl?" He approached the van, grinningly goofily, all white teeth and pink and black gums. When he saw me; the smile disappeared. He turned and ran.

"Wait!" I shouted. "I'm not going to hurt you." I struggled with the door latch, unsuccessfully. It was stuck, courtesy of a nine-pound tire iron meant for my face. I cursed myself for not having had that fixed sooner, but when you're on the run, food and weapons come first.

By the time I dropped out of the passenger window, Quentin was already halfway down the row of locked storage compartments. The three men shooting dice with him stood with their hands in their pockets, watching him as he jumped a shutter and scrambled up the metal ribs. One of them had the distinct bulge of a 9mm in his pocket.

"Stay out of this," I yelled. "I'm not here to hurt him." It was a stupid thing to say. The man's hand was wrapped around the duct-taped grip. If anyone was getting hurt it would be me. Even at this distance, chances were my brains would end up spattered all across the farthest shutter.

I kept running, expecting the click of a safety, but they just stood there, waiting, watching.

Quentin had his hands on the concrete roof, and his sandals, half-on, half-off, squeaked against the galvanized steel of the door.

"C'mon, Q, I won't hurt you. I promise."

"Like hell you won't." He kicked downwards as I grabbed at his ankles. "I got a gun, you know."

"So does that guy. But no one's going to shoot an unarmed girl in the middle of the day. It's bad for business."

"Uh-uh," he said. "First of all, you're a not a girl. A dog is what you're more like. Real grade-A bitch. Second, no one knows you're here. I can just stuff your little ass in a can. Like a pickle."

"Jamal knows I'm here."

"What?" His feet clambered up another bracket, just out of my reach.

"Your boss. He sent me here."

Quentin looked down. His eyes were wide, frightened. "I don't work for no Jamal, bitch. I work for me."

"Doing what? You aren't making any sales in this garbage dump. Come on, Q, I just want to talk."

"We're talking." He swung for the rooftop and missed. His voice was raspy, struggling for air. His arms, exhausted, dropped a little and I seized my chance. I grabbed at one of the metal struts on the side of the door and swung myself up and across the shutters.

If I missed, I'd be on the ground, splitting my head open on the cement. But I didn't. My hands latched onto an ankle as I dropped, and I felt his weight come crashing down on me. A shoulder jammed, a sharp pain cut into my ankle. I rolled over and straddled his back, pinning his arms under my knees. I patted him down, finding the gun, an unloaded Ruger.

"Jesus, Quentin, where did you get this from? Toys R Us?"

"I got it from Shawna."

"What?"

"Nothing." He gritted his teeth like he was chewing on pebbles.

My jaw pounded in response. "You said something." I twisted his arms harder.

"God, woman, you'll break it right off."

"I sure will. What's rule number one?"

Quentin groaned. "Never mention her name."

"Right. It's like the *only* rule. But you're too stupid to remember, right?"

"Yeah." He was grunting now, spit trickling out of his mouth. It was laced with crimson.

"You going to remember now? Whose name do we not use?"

"Sh-" He stopped.

"Good." But nothing about it was good. Shawna Cole. Petite. Caramel skin. Cocoa eyes. Everything about that girl seemed sweet, but then Quentin got her hooked on dro. Then crack. And when she couldn't pay, he locked her up in his basement. They only found bits and pieces of her. Bone. Gristle. Fingernails.

"I didn't kill her," Quentin said. "I swear, I didn't."

"Her DNA was all over your car. Your house. But that still isn't proof. Not *real* proof. Which is the only reason you're still out. The only reason you're still in one piece."

Not true. Shawna's grandmother had beaten Quentin to an inch of his death, but couldn't bring herself to finish it. She was shot outside the neighborhood five and dime a week later.

"I also know you had her grandma shot. What I should've done is called the cops about that. But I don't do cops. And you'd just have been out a couple of years later and we'd be doing this all over again. So, as far as I'm concerned, I have no beef with you." I was lying. And lying made me angry.

"What do you want then?"

"I need to find Jamal."

"You said Jamal sent you here." I felt his arm loosen. I pulled it back in and kneed it into the dirt.

"Why would he do something stupid like that? You're the one who does stupid stuff. That's why you're going to take me to him."

"I don't mess with Jamal, man. You going to have to shoot me."

I cocked the trigger and pressed it against his head.

"It's not loaded, you fool," he said.

"I know that. I wasn't planning on shooting you with it." I stuck the barrel into his right eye and twisted it. As he started screaming, I felt a searing pain cut into my side. For a moment, it felt as if a knife had wedged its way between my ribs. My side went numb.

Before I knew it, everything was black.

CHAPTER 14

I woke up in total darkness, my breath echoing back at me from the rough cloth bag that covered my head. Beyond, I could hear voices, two, maybe three. The only one I recognized was Quentin's, and he was begging to have me killed.

I tried to speak, but the words that came out were muffled. Heavy footsteps plodded their way toward me and the bag ripped off, plunging me into the fluorescent brightness of a stockroom. The walls were lined with cheap aluminum rack shelving. Cardboard boxes of indeterminate origin interspersed with old hardware, bits and pieces of junk more expensive to dispose of than store.

A man sat on one of these items, an air-conditioner that had its faceplate missing in an evil, toothy grin. He was bald and white, long scraggly beard, no mustache. His over-sized frame took up half the room, overweight, yes, but in a rounded Mack truck way that made him look more menacing than if he had muscle.

"You're Jamal?" I was tied up in a basement. I had a dope dealer begging to have me shot. And I was trying to suppress laughter. This was not how I anticipated my day would be going.

"Jamal is Arabic for beauty." His accent was Middle Eastern, heavy on the A's. "You don't think I'm beautiful?"

"No, you're a beauty alright. I just didn't expect my drug dealer to be Lebanese."

"I'm not a dealer." He raised his hands, offended. "And I'm from Palestine."

"Which governate?"

"Rafah." His thick eyebrows knotted together like a rope.

"The refugee camp or the town?"

"You've been to Gaza?"

"Couple of times." I had a half-read copy of *Mornings in Jenin* from the Sioux City public library tucked under my seat. I knew it was set in the West Bank, but I was feeling lucky.

"Pleasure, *tifla*?"

"There's pleasure in Gaza?"

"Business then." Jamal smiled and pulled up a chair. "You're well-travelled."

"I get around."

"Jesus, Jamal," Quentin protested. "This isn't a reunion. Give me the damn gun. I'll blow her away."

Jamal raised his hand and waved him off without looking. Quentin sidled over to the back of the room and sulked.

"What's a nice *tifla* like you doing in my basement? Stole some rocks from Quentin? Didn't pay your bill? What?"

"I thought you weren't a drug dealer."

"Dealer, no." He jabbed a finger at Quentin. "He's the dealer. I'm a businessman. You know it's legal now in this great state of California."

"Not all drugs."

"Ah, it's all the same. You open the door to one rat, all the others come scurrying in. Quentin, come here."

Quentin came over, his fists bunched, arms crossed tightly.

"Why is this girl here?" Jamal asked. "Does she owe me money?"

"No."

"Has she stolen any of my property?"

"No."

"I'm not going to keep asking questions, why is she-" He paused, looked at me, then up at Quentin. "Are you scared of her, Quentin? Why are you acting so weird?" He took a small breath. "Wait, now I know. Shawna? This is the girl?"

He turned to me, his black eyes shiny, like beetle skin. "You're not very terrifying."

"Believe me," Quentin said. "She is. If you don't want to shoot her, let me do it." His trigger finger ran around the cuff of the gun.

It wouldn't take much for him to drop me. A slammed door, a car backfiring. I've seen it happen, deals gone wrong because someone got an itchy finger. All it took was the unexpected rumble of a passing train and someone's brains ended up smeared on a windscreen like bird shit.

"Shoot her? You caused me a lot of trouble, *tifla*. But I understand you're in a bit of trouble yourself, yes?"

I shrugged, aiming for nonchalance. It came across as indifference, which is what street kids like me pull off better. "I can take care of myself."

"So I've heard. But not this time." He turned and whispered to Quentin.

"What?" Quentin protested. "You're crazy. This bitch is crazy."

Jamal silenced him with the swipe of a hand. "I have a job for some-one with your kind of skills. You interested?"

"I'm not here for a job interview."

"Then why are you here?"

"I want to know what Belladonna is. And where I can get it."

Jamal burst out laughing.

"What?" I asked.

"It's funny, *bint*, don't you see? You just walked in with a *nankh* full of it. Come on. You want a job, you come see what I do."

The storefront upstairs was brightly lit, with large plate-glass windows and laminated posters of herbs that made the place look like a health food store.

The logo was everywhere, in neon, on paper, laminated onto the win-dows. A pretty girl with an oversized blunt sandwiched between the words Mary and Jane. The address below was Oceanside Avenue. San Diego. My skin crawled. "How the hell did I?"

But Jamal was already onto the next aisle, pattering on. "See? Like a Seven-Eleven. Know why Seven-Eleven's are such great businesses? Good lighting. That's all it is. Makes people feel safe. Why don't people like to shop at bodegas or mini marts? Because they're small. Crowded. Dark. Look like places you're going to get jumped in. Put some good lighting in and all of a sudden it just looks safe. Ever been to a porn shop?"

"Occasionally."

"You know the old seedy shops? Smelled of sweat and bleach and worse. Felt like you were going to get groped. Old men with trench coats and nothing but a shriveled *how do you do* underneath. Now they sell Orange Crush and have pretty girls behind the counters. It's clean. It's neat. Its normal. Most of their business is couples. It's opened up the market like crazy."

"What does this have to do with drugs?"

"Well, we're doing the same with weed. High quality. Great service. Enough stock to satisfy the discerning buyer. Easy to navigate for the first timer. This is like the Whole Foods of weed. Better than Whole Foods. It's the Wegmans of weed."

He was right. The floor was shiny maple, the displays were rich walnut and stainless. The rows were neatly stocked, the glass vials attractive. So were the baristas. Or maybe they were called *bud*-istas here.

I sauntered up to the tasting bar at the counter. Snowstorm. Alaska. Sour Patch. Trainwreck. Diesel. There were two women at a side counter tying boxes of laced gourmet brownies with silver ribbon. It was more like a Starbucks than a weed store.

"Looks like it's working."

"Nah, it's a loss leader. Government takes ninety cents on the dollar. It's ruined the business. Come on I'll show you the rain-maker."

I followed him through the back tables where more employees were busy measuring and packaging product. He pushed me out of a back door. In the back was a wide gravel lot and a raised loading ramp. "Ready to open your eyes, *bint?*"

A white panel van sat in the bay, back doors open. He helped me in and the doors closed, sealing in the blackness. The van rumbled off, taking lefts and rights before the tires began humming on the smooth concrete of the freeway. It felt like hours before it finally slowed.

Jamal had talked the whole time, in the dark, his voice like a rock in the tin-can hold. "Anytime the government gets involved, *tifla*, it screws up the system. You know why? Because they only see what they want to see. Hear what they want to hear."

He popped the doors open as the van stopped. After the darkness of the hold, the sunlight was blinding. "Sometimes they only see what is in front of their faces. And sometimes what they see is not what is actually there. So, tell me, *bint*, what do you see?"

We were in the middle of a gravel-covered square, about twenty by twenty. Large cinderblock buildings rose up on either side; old factories, warehouses perhaps, iron-mesh grilles with long-broken windowpanes.

I could hear the rumble of traffic behind us, but it was two or three hundred feet away, maybe more. There was a service road ahead, crumbly asphalt, tufts of green peeking up in the cracks. In the adjoining lot was a small, church-like building, half-built, dark brick and porcelain tiling emblazoned across its face in the shape of a cross. The structure was still held together by a patchwork of scaffolding and the lawn in front was burnt out from the dry summer heat.

"Bad grass," I said.

"You won't find bad grass in one of my stores. No Bobby Brown, no shway, no popcorn. It's all fire, *bint*. Dank. Primo."

"Not that kind of grass. Real grass. Fescue. Bluegrass. Bermuda."

"Bermuda?"

"Yeah. Or Zoysia. Juneau is a good sub-varietal. Grows well in dry weather. Or Palisades."

Jamal pulled at his beard again. "We still talking about-"

"Lawn grass, yes. For your bunker." I stomped on the gravel, watching the dust rise, listening to the hollow sound beneath.

"I'd put some binder here too. Maybe blacktop. Cut down on the echo. But that's a dead giveaway." I pointed at the building. "You need something hardy. Grass is hard to grow over a concrete slab. I'd recommend El Toro. It's like a mushroom. That shit grows on mulch. By the way the church is a nice touch."

"It's a chapel."

"Whatever. Something Catholic. So that no one's suspicious when nobody really goes in and out. Why do you have a basement, Jamal?"

I didn't need to ask. I had already made a mental measurement from the far end of the church to the end of the alley. I came up with four, maybe five thousand square feet of subterranean working space.

"You're asking the wrong question, *bint*. This is California. Everyone wants a basement. But no one can afford one. So, if I have one, the question would be what could be so valuable for me to build one?"

"I don't care. A heroin mill. PCP. Fent. Designers. Does it matter? The important question is, why are you telling me?"

"Because I told you, I want you to work for me."

"I already have a job."

"Chasing sickos around the country? I don't think it pays well."

"The pay is shit. It's not about money."

Jamal stretched and turned. "It's always about money, *bint*." His arms were small and the gesture awkward.

"Look, I'll do what you want. I just need to-"

"You just need to find Nathan Hunter, don't you?"

I felt like yesterday's news, big enough to be remembered, not fresh enough to still be interesting. "So, you know too."

"Oh, everybody knows. L.A. is a small town. Big city. But a small, small town. And if I didn't, I could have put one and one together. I mean, you're not some stupid druggie. You're asking questions you shouldn't. Looking for shit like Belladonna." He pulled closer. "It's like walking into Pyongyang and asking for the bomb. Now, *tifla*. Want to know how this works and what it's got to do with Mr. Hunter?"

The small back door of the building was open, and it led into the nave, where twelve rows of oak double pews faced the raised altar. Behind the cupola, a hallway led into the sacristy, stacked high with old magazines and paperbacks.

Jamal finger-scanned a glass panel and a door unlocked audibly. Behind it a short flight of stairs ended in a wide, well-ventilated room. I'd seen the set up before. Cruder and smellier, yes, but a dungeon all the same. If Quentin was down there with a hammer and a hard-on, I wouldn't be surprised. But it wasn't Q.

A small, heavily built woman was waiting for us, her face etched in a perma-scowl. She was dressed in an unadorned black t-shirt and shorts. A pair of ill-fitting army boots clunked around under her stubby legs. Slung under her arm was a snub-nosed Heckler and Koch. She placed the weapon on the metal table and pulled a tray out from the stainless locker behind the desk.

"Don't get any ideas, *bint*. She doesn't need the gun, she could probably throw a bullet right through you."

She pushed the tray over. If she'd heard him, she didn't show it.

"Here." Jamal pressed a pair of blue surgical booties into my hands and strapped a NIOSH mask onto my head. The woman pressed a button on her desk and the double-plated aluminum doors slid open noiselessly.

"This necessary?" My voice was distant and muffled under the hood. A single row of suspended fluorescent lights ran the entire length of the promenade, a series of glass-lined compartments on either side, bleached and sterile in the white light.

"I don't want you O.D.-ing, and I definitely don't want you tracking any dirt in and mucking up my purity levels. This is just to walk up and down the catwalk. If you were working a room here, you'd have to have a full decon shower, in and out."

I peeked into the corridor. The first two rooms were empty, save for the large refrigerator-sized machines running at the back ends. Large LCD displays ran a microbial count on the product that processed into a series of small metal canisters.

"Is that a Rensonator?"

"Thirty-five grand a machine, and I need five. It's a fucking scam." His hand waved me on. "Humidity, airflow, temperature, all computer controlled. You know what it does?"

"Ferments genetically altered yeast to produce morphine."

"That's the junior high version. I didn't spend six million dollars for a grade school science project. Just the sequencing costs are in the thousands. Then there's enzyme production, glucose reduction, reticuline synthesis."

"You put sugar, genetically modified yeast, and some enzymes into a fermenter. It's like making dough."

Jamal pulled forward, his eyes angry. His breath through the mask smelled like licorice. Or was that the purified air? "It's like making whiskey. Real good whiskey. Real *expensive* whiskey. But whiskey doesn't sell for a hundred grand a liter."

He continued down the corridor, dark and futuristic, like a theme-park ride. "Scalable roll compaction, hot flow extrusion, precision re-granulation." He paused, proudly, clicked the machine off and on. "We've come a long way from a bathtub of lye, a crushed bag of pseudoephedrine and some red phosphorus."

"Pfizer would be impressed."

"Pfizer would be jealous. Come on, this is the cooking area." The corridor curved around a large, glass-encased room. The walls were lined with beakers, rows of pipettes, and computerized scales. There were ten, maybe twelve, women working around a surgical steel table. A large ventilation hood dropped down above them like a Hibachi. Every occupant was stark naked but for the masks strapped to their faces.

"Before you ask, I've had a few stick a couple of grams up their, uh, crevices. One stuck it so far up, the packaging blew. She died on the table. Can you imagine how difficult it is to find a place to bury bodies under twenty feet of concrete?"

An older woman walked by, her breasts drooping over the beakers in her tray. She arranged the equipment under a vacuum hood, popped her hands into the attached gloves, and peered into the built-in scope.

Her fleshy bottom splayed out over the edges of the stool like an undercooked soufflé.

"I don't pick them for their pretty faces, that's for sure. What do you think?"

I shrugged. It looked like the setup for a reality show. Naked science, or something equally disastrous. There were men and women of all colors. Some were young, their bodies supple and full, others overweight, wrinkly thighs and bulging bellies. An older man walked around with an LED headlamp, inspecting the product being sorted onto the stainless circular table in the center.

"Wouldn't catch me dead."

"*Bint*, you're so skinny, no one would even notice. Besides, I'm not hiring a talented young woman like you to cook or cut. I already have the best cooks. And yes, it matters. You add an extra grain of fentanyl to the mix and you can kill someone. And I'm taking about a grain like a grain of salt. One grain and you go from high to dead in less than a minute. I don't want that on my hands. Everyone wants to push the limits, but a dead customer is a not a repeat customer."

"Then what do you want?"

"Isn't it obvious? It so happens that your problem is my problem. I make good product. Great product. Safe product. Product people can enjoy on a Saturday night, then wake up on Sunday. At home. Not in a hospital. Belladonna? That kind of shit is ruining my business."

He pulled out a plastic packet from his pocket, about the size of a fentanyl patch. "I don't know what this shit is. And I don't know how to make it. The last thing I need is to have it knock off my customers."

"Or cut into your profits."

"Profits, *tifla?* You're crazy. You try to smoke it, inject it? This is the worst high you'll ever have. This is not a recreational drug. This is donkey shit, and the only reason to use it is, well, you know already."

The clamoring in my head, the pounding in my jaw demanded attention again. "So, what do you want me for?"

"Find Nathan Hunter. Take him out."

"Why Hunter?"

"Isn't it obvious?"

No, I thought. "I'm not an assassin."

Jamal laughed, his eyes small and twinkly. "Okay, whatever you call what you do is fine."

"Why don't you just take him out? Isn't that part of your business?"

"No. Of course not. It is a business. I can't just go around putting the hurt on people. I hire that out to independents. How about this. You find him. Then we'll worry about the next step."

"You do realize that the entire LAPD is looking for him."

"Exactly. Which is why I need to find him first. Why you need to find him first. Once we find out where he's making the product, how he's selling it, maybe we can give him a good reason not to, well, distribute."

"Distribute? Hunter's the dealer?" I thought of the girls

in the club, the packets of dope lying around the tables. *Do you think they come here for some shitty ludes?* I could've kicked myself.

"Dealer? God, no. Do I look like a dealer?"

Yes, I thought. "Okay, not a dealer. A producer."

"Yes, of course. He produces it. And he sells it. I mean, he doesn't *sell it* sell it. Like, Pfizer and Novartis sell dope, but they get the MDs to pimp it for them, you know? Lortabs, Percocets, Demerol, good stuff, all legal dope. Real money."

"What about the nightclubs-"

"There's no money in that, *bint.* You make money so you can waste it on that shit. Use it as your showroom. Your dealership. How does anyone make *real* money in this fucking city? We're businessmen. We make product. Nathan Hunter made his money in pharmaceuticals. He doesn't own any of them anymore, not on paper, of course. That would be a big red arrow pointing in his direction, wouldn't it? But yes, he has the means *and* the motivation."

"Listen, Jamal, I'm not sure if you know this, but-"

Jamal patted me on the cheek. The gesture was fatherly, intoxicating. The feeling spread through me like a hit. "I know about the finger, *bint.* Do you know which finger it was?"

"Middle."

"Middle finger." He laughed. "Makes it seem like it had a touch of pre-meditation. Which makes it even more imperative that you find him first. The only way you get out of this whole deal is by finding Mr. Hunter. Alive. You shouldn't need any more motivation. If he's dead, you're dead. So, you want the job?"

I stared at the men and women scurrying around the table, envying the repetitiveness, the mindless simplicity of their jobs. Cut, mix, pack. Cut, mix, pack. I almost wished he had wanted me to cook. Even the nakedness seemed less appalling now.

I turned away from him, only too aware that the more he called me *bint*, the more I wanted to please him. I could hear the breathing sharpen within my mask and felt the urgency build. I was way too close to doing something stupid. Really stupid.

"You realize that I came looking for something and you're turning me around and hiring me to look for the same thing? Why can't you send one of your guys? Don't they know every dealer and spot in the city?"

"Yes, *bint*, but they have no motivation, remember? You do. And you're, how should I say this? More resourceful than the fools who work for me? Look, this isn't a street drug. If it was, I'd have it in check by now." He handed me an object. It was small and red, half the size of a thumb drive. "There's only one way to get an invitation to this party."

I turned the disk around in my hand. It looked like a chiclet with a USB plug. Small enough to be swallowed and retrieved. "How did you get the invitation?"

"Lucked into it. One of our regulars traded it in on a shipment of black tar. Rip off deal, I think, but you know druggies when they're desperate. Girl shot herself up and never made it through the night. Now we have a key and no address."

"And that's my job?"

"Like I said, you're resourceful. And you're desperate. It's a good combination." He paused. "Also, you just happen to know Vincent Kryzinski."

Vincent. My heart sunk. Whenever things got really shitty, I knew I could count on Vincent being involved.

"Deal?"

"Deal," I said.

"Good. You'll need some backup. You take Quentin with you."

The room was suddenly colder. "I don't want Q."

"*Tifla,* you might not realize this, but Quentin is like an asshole. Nobody wants one, but everybody needs one. Well? *Bint?*"

Against my best instincts I nodded and tucked the key into my pocket.

CHAPTER 15

"Where the hell have you been?" Steph stormed down the driveway like an angry pitbull, face scrunched up and hair tousled. "We've been waiting for an hour. You weren't supposed to leave. What, you think this is funny?"

"I don't, Steph. Seriously." Steph's wet bikini bled through her t-shirt, and there was a puddle of water forming around her flip-flops. "But, FYI, the scared-me-to-death routine works better if you haven't been lapping the pool. And Medina didn't say I couldn't leave, she just said I couldn't leave town."

"Screw you, Portia. We're just trying to help, and you're acting like this is a prison sentence." She grabbed me by the arm and dragged me along. Her hands were small and wet, but her grip was a vise.

"Steph, you're hurting me."

"Hurting you?" She stopped but wouldn't let go. If anything, her grip was tighter. The skin around it blanched, a halo of red bleeding through. "Hurting you? You know how much Medina charges? Five hundred. Dollars. An hour. Do that math. Four thousand a day. Twelve thousand a month. One hundred and fifty-"

"One twenty."

"What?"

"One hundred and twenty thousand a month. One point four mill a year. It won't get to that. This thing will be done in a week."

"How do you know?"

"Because there's no ransom demand, no body, no forced entry. Just a spoiled rich kid who date-raped a girl and decided to go off and start all over again. He's probably in Santa Barbara right now scoping some other stupid broad."

"Then how do you explain the fact that you were the one who woke up in his apartment? And he's the one missing a finger?"

I pulled my arm away from her sharply. "Steph, I'm going to let you take that back for a moment. Because it almost sounds like you're accusing me."

She turned and stomped her way back to the house. Through the front window I could see Medina shut the curtains. By the time I reached the dining room, I'd smudged two windows and knocked an ornate earpiece off its handle. Someone was behind me immediately with a cloth and a sprayer of Windex.

"You leave spots behind, missy," the woman said. "Someone else has to clean them up."

I turned on her, fists clenched, teeth bared. Kids at the home I grew up in called it my feral cat look. Fight or flight. Except they soon learned that I never ran. Even if I should have.

"And the phone," she continued calmly, "is decorative. Doesn't work. No one sees it but me. But I have to fix it." She put the piece back on the cradle. "And I had nothing to do with it."

My fists loosened slowly. Truth is, I didn't really fight that much either. Not anymore. You got older and realized that the less you fought the better you got at it. It might be an emotional thing, but if you only punched someone every other month, you made it count.

"What, kid? You're going to knock my block off?"

I walked up to her and picked her up in a bear hug.

Frida is just like Grams, just small enough to scoop, just big enough for it to be fun.

"Good choice." She pointed a long, curved fingernail at me. "You know, I'd have cut you, right?"

"You know, if it wasn't for you and Shimon, I wouldn't last a day in this mad house." I grabbed the cloth and Windex from her and made a valiant effort at the window.

"No, stop," she protested. "You're making it worse. My God, child, how're you ever going to get a husband?"

"I don't intend to." I looked at the window smudge, wider and murkier than before. She was right, though. If I ever did, I'd have to find one who could clean and cook. "Maybe I'll get a wife instead."

"Shush!" she said.

"What? It's a new millennium."

"And I'm from the old one. But you do what makes you happy. Just don't tell me about it."

"Portia!" Steph was at the door to the library, her foot tapping impatiently. She was still wearing the flip flops. The rubber slapping on the travertine floor sounded like wet towels in a dryer.

I winked at Frida. She winked back, and I laughed at her wrinkled little face. Gram's face, except whiter and smaller. "Remember," she said, "that girl owes everything to you. Don't let her push you around."

"Too late," I said.

I dropped myself into the end chair, looking around like I was waiting for a wine list. There were three small bottles of Evian on the table. I took one and unscrewed it with my teeth. Medina and her associates had arranged themselves in the same order as the day before. I noticed they were wearing the same clothes too.

"Do you guys pre-arrange this," I asked, "or do you just never take them off?"

Guerrero was busy connecting cables from a computer to a projector. Medina and Carlson were poring over a stack of eight by tens.

"I mean it works, right? Take a shower and wash your clothes once. Saves time and water. Leaves you with plenty of free time to, oh, I don't know?" I pointed at Guerrero. "He probably scrapbooks." My finger moved over to Carlson. "Crochet? Tatting? What about you, Medina? Pet rocks? Minecraft?"

Medina picked up the photographs and tapped them into a neat pile, like a deck of cards. "Let's not waste any time, shall we?" She slid out a photograph and pushed it across the table.

"What the hell is this?"

"A vaporizer. It's from the evidence bag. It had traces of alkaloid in it. Possibly scopolamine."

"I was drugged. I know. Now can you get off my back?"

"It was in your pocket, Portia."

"Wait a second," Steph interjected. "You're not trying to say-"

"I'm not saying anything. That's what the cops are trying to say. And the DA. They'll show the jury this. Nathan Hunter is missing. And the drug used was yours."

"There are fifty different ways that could have ended up in my pocket."

"Absolutely. But we have to be ready for it. If you think of every case as a fabric, this is a small hole. By itself?" She shrugged. "No big deal. But small holes become tears, then the tears become a rip."

I turned to Steph, but she was no help. She stared at me like a cornered fly. They all did, swatters ready, anticipating my next move.

"Rips, like this," Carlson said. He flipped over the screen board. It was covered in photographs and newspaper clippings.

I suppressed a smile. In a dimly lit room it would look like a serial killer's shrine. I must admit, I always knew I had quite the career, but when you put it all together like this, it was a bit overwhelming.

"Care to explain?"

"I don't know who these guys are," I said.

"I'm sure you don't. You knew them for what, ten, twenty minutes, an hour, tops?"

The elation morphed into rage in a matter of seconds. "This isn't a hobby. It isn't a round of golf on a Sunday afternoon."

"I know it isn't," Medina said. "That's why it's a problem. One missing person is bad enough. But twenty? It's going to come up. So, you might as well come clean to us first."

"You know I write stories," I said.

Medina sighed. "Fiction or non-fiction?"

"Fiction."

"Okay, I'll play." Medina leaned back and crossed her fingers patiently, the pen interlaced between the tips. "Tell me a story."

"The main character's a classic, a damsel in distress; you know, the kind Hollywood loves. Like her." I stabbed a finger in Steph's direction. "Pretty. Popular. But clueless."

I could see Steph color, but she remained silent.

"You know the type. The one who's going to get chatted up by Ted Bundy because, gosh, every handsome man is a prince. The one who's naïve enough to walk down a dark alley because she hears a puppy whine. The one who runs through the woods, being chased by a guy with a chainsaw, but doesn't have a drop of sweat on her face. A twig in her princess hair? Or snot smearing her rhinoplasty?"

"Can we cut to the chase?" Carlson asked.

"What if you took the makeup off that girl? Took the hair, the pretty clothes, the bright-eyed bunny naivete. What if you were left with this? The girl no one wants. A pain in the ass with issues. A chick who keeps a boxcutter in her sock at all times. An ampoule of strychnine in her collar. A girl who makes a life out of taking down the perverts and sickos that live on every corner, but you guys never seem to find."

I stopped, making sure they were as uncomfortable as they could be. "You think that girl would risk her career by getting buzzed and jumping into someone's car after fifteen minutes, going to their little home, their dungeon, and expecting to come out alive?"

"That's exactly what I said." Steph jumped. "It's not like you. But what if you had a bad day? An off day-"

"I don't take any goddamn days off."

"Look, I'm sure she didn't mean that," Medina said.

"She didn't mean to what? Come on. You're being paid, what did you say, Steph? Five hundred an hour? And the best you can do is a corkboard with Polaroids? Why not sidewalk chalk on the driveway? Next get a set of stupid pushpins and a string so you can show me how all this ties in to me.

String it up like a web and put me in the middle so I realize how I'm the mama spider in all of this."

I brushed past Carlson and flipped the board over. I took the Sharpie from the table and drew faces on the back. They were all different but varied on the same theme.

Stick figures with bloated faces and spiky heads. Monsters from a child's imagination. Slit eyes that sloped into a dotted nose. Straight line upper lip that dripped with fangs. Some had hair. Others didn't. Some were fat, others skinny. One had pockmarks. Another had a bull-ring in his nose.

"That's what they are to me. No names. No faces. I know every single one. What they like, what they eat. I know the music they listen to after they've ripped a girl up, sucked on their viscera. I know the ones who like sharps. Knives and picks. The ones who like blunts. Hammers and bars. I know the ones who like to leave a little blood under their fingernails, a little to taste for later. I know them all because I made them up. Because no one ever found a body. It's just a fantasy, isn't it? An overactive imagination. A little chica like me couldn't possibly have done this by herself."

Medina's hand was up, her eyes closed. "We get it."

"No, you don't. To everyone else they're just stories. But they're my stories. Don't you dare say I don't know these characters. I spend months prepping them, I know what they eat, I know how they sleep, I know if they sit or stand when they pee. I go to bed dreaming of them. I wake up in the morning and my mouth tastes like their blood."

I stopped, my mouth dry. I had to hold myself to stop from shaking.

"I live with them every damn day of my lives. I know them. I take offense to the fact that you think all it takes is fifteen minutes and a knife. If I was going to kill Hunter I wouldn't have left a finger in his fridge. And I damn sure wouldn't have woken up in his bed the next morning."

Medina looked at the others. "Okay, I won't bring it up again."

I got up and pushed my way back past Carlson. His chair was out and I almost tripped, steadying myself against his shoulders. "Are we done here?"

"No," he said. He still sounded unconvinced. "Not by a long shot. You said he drugged you. You said you can't remember getting off the rooftop. Or anything until you woke up the next morning?"

"So?"

"Then how did you drive?"

"Excuse me?"

"He asked you how you drove to his apartment," Medina said.

"We've been through this. Belladonna, remember? I wasn't tipsy. I wasn't buzzed. I was out. I sure as hell didn't drive."

Carlson wasn't listening. He had already turned on the video player, a shaky handheld *MOV* file from an outdated cellphone. It wasn't focused on me. There was a visibly drunk young man dancing in the street, cheered on by the crowd as he cozied up to a drainage gate.

"Got moves like *Jae*-ger," the crowd chanted while the phone yawed widely, panning the crowd. The screen paused. In the corner a couple was getting into a silver sports car.

"Recognize the car?"

"No."

Carlson blew up the photo. "Recognize yourself? Driver's side."

"The car isn't moving. You can't prove that-"

"We're not attorneys, remember?" Medina said. "And this is not a court room. Blow it up again."

The image was grainy, but it was impossible to argue. It was my face. And I was on the left.

"That's you, right?" Carlson scrolled through the film until the car disappeared.

"So, let's assume I'm driving. Isn't that what Belladonna does? Keeps you lucid-"

"Lucid," Medina said. "Responsive to suggestion. But if you two walked out and you got into his car and drove off? I mean, at that point, who would a jury think is doing the suggesting?"

"What if we can we prove the Belladonna was in Portia's system?" Steph asked.

"About that," Medina said. "We have a preliminary tox screen back."

Carlson was patting his jacket like he was missing something. "Where's the drive?" He rummaged through his pockets, then his briefcase.

"What's it like?" I asked. "Like a USB drive?"

"Yeah, a thumb drive. Black."

"Black. About the size of a vaporizer? Like the one they found in my clothes?" I pulled the small black object out of my pocket and spun it across the surface of the table. "Jeez, not sure how that ended up on me. Don't worry, I don't need it. I know the results. Inconclusive, right?"

Carlson fixed me with a hardened look. He put the disk back into his jacket pocket.

"But shit happens, right? I know, in your business it probably happens all the time. Like when you forgot to mention that Hunter started his career off in pharmaceuticals. But instead of investigating him, you're wasting your time on me."

I saw Medina turn and look at Carlson. "Oh, wait, it's worse. You didn't *fail* to mention it; you didn't even know, did you? Oh, and by the way, the car you're so worried about? Any idea what make it is?"

Carlson turned the player back on, ran the frames backwards.

"That's not a great picture. Can't even see the hood ornament."

"Does it matter?" Steph asked.

"Of course it does." I stared Medina down and she finally relented. She turned and pulled out her phone.

"What the hell are you trying to prove, Portia?" Steph asked.

I kept my eyes straight ahead, ignoring her.

Medina finally tucked the phone away. She swiveled back, her lips pursed. "Silver Jaguar e-tron. Vin number 1-H-G-B-H-4-1-J-X-M-N-1-0-9-1-8-6. Matches the car in the picture."

I whistled. "All electric, four hundred horses, A Model X killer."

"Where are we going with this?"

"It's not on sale in the US for what, another six months? This must've been a special order. An import."

"Okay," Medina said impatiently, "keep going."

"Nice Brit car. Owned by an Indian company now, right?"

"Tata Motors," Carlson said.

"Okay. If I'm not mistaken, both countries drive on the left side of the road. Which means, well, you get it, don't you?"

"I don't-" Steph protested.

"The steering wheel is on the other side," Medina said.

"Yeah." I got up. "Opposite sides. That's appropriate, isn't it? In other words, I'm back to where I go out and find out who's selling the Belladonna while you guys stay here and do whatever five hundred-dollars an hour buys you. Talk about your shitty tox screen. Maybe paint your nails. Take a bubble bath."

I stomped out of the door. Steph made a half-hearted effort to stop me. "Don't go, Portia, you need to trust us on this."

I pushed her. Hard.

"Right now, Steph, the only person I can trust in this house is my dog."

CHAPTER 16

Dr. Zahn popped in the quick connectors to the compressor and turned up the dials on the mixer head. Nitrous wasn't his preferred anesthetic, that would be isoflurane with a propofol induction, but it was safe, quick, portable. A favorite of hotel room anesthesiologists.

He popped the nasal hood on her and checked her pulse oximeter. All good. The girl was laid out in a rather chaste position, her ankles tucked together, hands folded over the pit of her stomach, a green surgi-drape wrapped carefully around her neck and abdomen. The foldable surgical table was equipped with arm-boards for an I.V. drip, and a self-contained suction unit hummed beneath.

Hunter sat in an easy chair with a panoramic view of the strip, the shimmering gold of the Delano, the obsidian black of the Luxor, the red and blue spires of the Excalibur.

"Do you need help?" he asked.

Zahn looked at him quizzically. His beard was folded and pressed under his tie-back mask, his head covered with a blue scalp cap. Between the two was a set of wide-spaced eyes permanently set on twinkle.

"You did your job," he said. "I'll do mine."

Hunter frowned and looked away. He was sure he could do an adequate job. After all anyone who had butchered an animal was skilled with a knife, and anesthesia was something they were letting nurses do nowadays.

"You know, in Soviet Russia, they would teach monkeys how to do this stuff. Cut and sew. Cut and sew."

"Yeah, but can they golf?" Zahn laid his instruments on the Mayo stand, a standard oral surgical set up. Ronguers, files, forceps, Bard-Parker handles, and a slew of blades.

On the side was a specimen case in a cryopreservation kit. He prided himself on his surgical skills so much that he often set a stopwatch to time a personal best. His killer time was two minutes, thirty-one seconds but that was in a fully equipped O.R., not a hotel room.

Zahn inserted the mouth gag, picked a number 15, and incised carefully into the soft fleshy tissue of the retromolar pad. The incision design was a standard envelope, beveled through the periosteum. He lifted the flap and aimed his headlight on the thick knurl of bone.

The angry whine of a high-torque electric handpiece began to roar as he cut through the cortex, the white puffs of milled bone clumping in the irrigation. He removed the cap with a flat elevator and stared at the surgical field, a single ivory wisdom tooth set in a bed of oozing blood. It was a veritable treasure trove of stem cells.

The procedure took less than six minutes, he had the incisions sutured and the specimen secured in another five. "Done," he said as he tied up the red bag of waste.

"Wait, where are you going?" Hunter asked.

"To the lab. Have to get the dissection started-"

"No, what about her?"

Zahn grimaced. "That's your job, isn't it?"

"You don't want to stick around for the fun part?"

"Look, I don't know what's going on here. I thought we were just going to take some cells. The usual."

"The usual? No, Zahn, this is anything but usual. This is a gift for our old friend Portia Black."

"What do you mean by gift?"

"Well, not so much a gift. More like bait. You need real bait to set a real trap."

"Bait." Zahn tried not to shudder. He knew where Hunter's bait usually ended up. "Can you…" He paused. "Can you go easy on her?"

Hunter looked at Zahn, then at the girl. She lay motionless on the table, the hiss of oxygen still pumping into her nose. She was pretty, barely any trace of surgical intervention. Her hair, flame-red, was tied up in a knot and bundled into a surgical cap. Wisps had let loose around her neck. Not natural red, Zahn thought, but it suited her.

"Little late for that, isn't it?" He grabbed Zahn by the arm. "You're not backing out on me, are you? Having second thoughts?"

"No," he said.

"Good. You know she asked for this, don't you? They all asked for this. Rich kids, pretty faces, got the whole world ahead of them. And what do they want? They want to feel something. Don't we all just want to feel something? Isn't that what we need?"

"I just need to get paid," Zahn said.

Hunter laughed and patted him on the cheek. "And you will, Zahn. Just keep your mouth shut and do your job."

The phone began to ring. "Excellent," he said. "They're here." He pulled out a car battery and connected jumper cables to the hookups. "Time to get this show on the road."

CHAPTER 17

I picked Quentin up on the corner of Inglewood and El Segundo. He slid into the passenger seat without looking at me.

"Rough night, bruh?" I asked.

"Shut up," he said. His side-shielded Sean John sunglasses were covered with enough chrome to cover an Escalade, and his breath smelled of alcohol.

"Seriously? I didn't ask for you to be here."

"Hey, you weren't my first choice either. So, let's get this over with. What the hell is this?" He shifted, pulled a worn copy of Kierkegaard's *Discourses* from between his seat and the console.

"Don't touch my stuff." I grabbed the book from his hands and tossed it into the pile in the back.

"It's not your stuff. It says it belongs to the Helena City Library. That's Montana?"

"I'm returning it."

"Yeah, right." Quentin unsnapped his seatbelt and popped it back in. He searched for the seat adjustment, then, disappointed, grabbed at the release bar under the seat.

"Afraid that airbag's going to bust those pretty chiclets?" I laughed, but deep down I was jealous. My teeth were fine but I'd kill for his. I would've had them straightened but I'd never lived in one place long enough to get the records. Quentin's teeth were natural, perfectly even and sculpted, painfully white against his dark lips. Like Jamal's other guys, he didn't smoke or do drugs and he made up for it with copious quantities of cheap brandy.

"Bitch. I don't know how you drive. You probably one of those bitches who drives like a bat out of hell."

"More like a bat on its way in." I dropped the van into gear, lurched forward a few feet, and slammed on the brakes. Quentin didn't know it, but I hadn't had the seatbelt fixed either. The waist tightened, but the cross strap gave way when pulled. The effect was instantaneous. Quentin's chest lurched forward almost a foot and a half, his head narrowly missing the dash. In a quick motion I pulled at the shoulder strap from over his head and caught him on the back swing. The strap looped around his neck and cinched tight under my fist.

"Are we good now, Q?"

I could see his eyes bulge, and there was an almost instantaneous redness that bled into his cheeks. I pulled harder. The glasses were cockeyed, and his hands were flapping at his chest. His dark lips swelled up, first beet red, then purple. I let the strap go and he dropped back into the seat. He was breathing heavily like he'd run a marathon.

"Now you know how I drive." I gathered the folds of loose belt and patted it on his chest. "So you might want to hold on."

It took twenty minutes to get to the El Capitan Theatre with two breaks for Quentin to lean over and dry heave on the pavement. He sunk back into the seat smelling like battery acid and grain alcohol. The smell didn't get better as we hit the boulevard. The usual suspects were hanging around. Hawkers, buskers, and cranks. The few tourists who had turned up hurried from star to terrazzo star, bags tucked tightly under their arms, evading the tour guides, who often doubled as dealers and pimps.

"What the hell are we doing here?" Quentin's voice was still hoarse from the nylon. I was almost sorry but I remembered the pieces of Shawna's pretty skin and suddenly wished I had given him a few more seconds under the belt. "What else do you come to the Boulevard for? We're here to buy drugs."

"This is bullshit," he muttered. I understood the irony, but I wasn't sure if he was just annoyed that he had to babysit me or if this represented some strange professional discourtesy. "I'm not buying, man, uh-uh. I'm not buying shit on the strip."

Discourtesy, then. "Suit yourself." I wasn't planning on buying either, but Quentin didn't need to know that. I parked and went over to the telephone booth at the corner.

"What the hell do you think you're doing?"

"Phoning a friend."

"You know, that's where the junkies make out after they shoot up. Sometimes they take the mouthpiece and shove it down their-"

"Here." I pressed the phone in his face. "It's Jamal."

"Shit!" He was staring at the cord, like I was planning on choking him with it again. "No, it ain't. Nobody calls Jamal. He calls you."

"Okay." I pressed the receiver back to my head, hoping he couldn't hear the beeping. "He's too busy to come to the phone so just-"

"No. Wait." He came forward, within striking distance.

I flung the handle at him. The dial tone was audible as it slammed him in the chest.

"Why the hell do you have to be such a bitch?"

"Why the hell did you have to hurt Shawna, huh?" I grabbed the dangling phone and swung it at him again, trying to take his head off. "She never did anything to you. You were the big guy. You got good grades. A basketball scholarship. You could've gone to college. Gotten a good job. And you screwed that up because you couldn't keep your hands to yourself."

He grabbed the receiver and raised it like he was about to strike me with it. He stopped mid-air and slammed it onto the hook. "I told you. I never touched her."

"Then where is she? Stuffed in a refrigerator in your basement? Stuck in crawl space under your back porch? Dumped in a canyon?"

"I swear. I didn't hurt her."

I turned and stormed down the pavement. "Just shut up. You do your job and you'll never see me again. You don't, and I promise you'll end up in a freezer too."

There was a busker at the corner rocking back and forth on a worn-out stool, a vintage maple and rosewood Rickenbacker cradled in his lap like a nesting child. He had the yellow, worn out look of an addict, but there were no traces of needle tracks or welts on his skin.

If he was on junk, it wasn't an injectable. Few users make it more than a week or two on snorting. The economics of narcotics alone make the intravenous route the only option for lifers. I approached cautiously. There's a lot of shit on the street worse than heroin, and the last thing I needed was to stir up trouble.

The busker was playing the open string intro to *Nothing Else Matters* but when his fingers actually started plucking, it was obvious that he was terrible. I dropped a twenty into his empty case and he stopped mid-intro.

"I ain't selling, lady."

"Well, you ain't making any money playing either."

He looked up, offended. There was little of his face visible beneath the grey beanie and overgrown red beard. It was one of those stupid cuts that ended at the corners of the lips, leaving an inch of philtrum bare. A reverse Adolph.

"Sure is a nice tip for someone who doesn't like the playing," he said.

"Sure is a nice guitar for a busker."

"Hey, I used to play all over, man. The Go-Go. Palladium. Sunset Rocks. City chewed me up and spit me out."

The down on your luck musician story wasn't an oddity around here but the lack of talent was. Most of the buskers in Hollywood are pretty good. "Look, I don't want drugs. I want Vincent."

He looked up at me, mouth open, as if he was about to answer, then his fingers went back to the strings, plucking an equally horrendous version of Megadeth's *Symphony of Destruction*. The guy wasn't looking at me anymore. His eyes were shifty, staring out of the corner of his eye. I followed his squint to the far wall.

Quentin was pacing at the corner, slouching like most oversized people do when they're trying to look inconspicuous. He was still wearing his sunglasses, dressed in all black, a Raiders baseball cap, and gold chains. I slammed him against the wall. "Q, what the hell are you doing?"

"Nothing."

"You're acting all weird. You're freaking people out."

"Told you, I'm doing nothing."

"Exactly. You look like you're up to no good. Like I brought you along as muscle."

"I am the muscle, remember?"

"Well, you sure aren't the brains. Here." I pushed him around the corner, into the next store. The plastic shelves were adorned with tiny gold humanoids that said *Greatest Dad* or *Best Teacher* or other little lies. The counter was piled high with penlights and keychains, trash that would be bought and venerated in distant little towns like Kenosha and Savannah. I dropped a bill onto the table and pulled a t-shirt and hat off the racks. "Take your shirt off."

"Hell, no."

"Don't get your knickers in a twist. It's hard enough to look at you with your clothes on. But you dress like a dealer and you're out here buying? On the boulevard? You're either the dumbest dealer in the world or you're a cop. Just wear the shirt, drop the gold and the rest of the crap in the van and meet me back here in five minutes."

I watched as he stomped off before I returned over to the busker. An extended Japanese family had gathered around him, graciously paying attention on one side, holding their bags tightly under their arms on the other. The busker was claiming to be Dave Mustaine now, pulling at the red beard for emphasis. I waited patiently for the spiel to be done, but the family was too polite to move on and the guy was too persistent to end. I tapped him on the shoulder. "Okay, the weirdo's gone. How about you make me a deal?"

"I told you, girl, I'm not selling. And I don't know any Vincent."

"Okay." I grabbed the twenty from his case. "You play like shit." The family tittered to each other, shocked and amused.

"Wait!" He grabbed the bill by the corner, tugging it back. "Edith would know him."

The name struck me like a bumbling fly. "Edith who?"

"I don't know her last name. But she runs the show here, and she knows everyone. If he's ever been here, she'll find him."

"So why don't I give her the money instead?"

"Because she doesn't need it and you just cost me money."

The family was halfway down the street discreetly taking pictures. I relented and let the twenty go.

"Okay," I said. "Where is she?"

CHAPTER 18

Arthur Zahn sat at his white lab table dissecting the specimen with a sterile handpiece. The process of isolating and amplifying stem cells from any donor tissue was arduous -some thought it mind-numbing- but Zahn, a lab rat, loved every moment of it.

He'd been a clinician for years, a damn fine one at that, but day after brutal day of patients bitching and nurses moaning had left him drained, and there was nothing more Zahn loved than to get into the solitude of his lab. Now he could do it all day long, and no matter how painstaking the procedure, or low the remuneration, he hadn't lost any of the love.

Zahn had reached the lab at five a.m., driving the two hundred and seventy miles to L.A. in just under four hours. In a solution of hypotonic buffered phosphate maintained at hypothermic temperatures, stem cell specimens could survive up to forty hours, but Zahn knew that every hour brought a lower yield count, and he wasn't about to drive back to Vegas for another stab at collection. He had to get them out and cultured *now*.

Two hours passed as he worked. It was just after seven. Zahn sat back in his swivel chair, breathing hard. He desperately needed a drink. A cask strength bourbon would do nicely, but he would take anything, vodka, gin, even one of those wretched malt coolers that disguised themselves as real liquor.

An old picture on the table stared at him accusingly. It had been a long time since he had last seen his daughter. Three years, two months, and seventeen days old to be exact. The girl was a dark-haired beauty with a short pony-tail and a ready post-orthodontic smile. She wore a red t-shirt with the *Badgers* logo on it. Day one of fall semester, senior year. He remembered it well.

Five months later she had disappeared into the middle of a Wisconsin winter with five milligrams of Rohypnol in her system. She was found in a snowbank, two miles away from the bar, her body face-down in the slush, in full view of the passing traffic.

The morning she had been found, Zahn, ironically, had received his first advance from Hunter. Seventy-five thousand dollars. He re-wired the electronic transfer directly to the University of Wisconsin where it was going to cover both the spring and summer tuition bills.

Zahn hadn't spoken to his daughter in almost three years, but when the deposit credited, he was sure she would finally call. Maybe he could invite her over. Buy her a plane ticket, show her the sights, mend some fences. This would be a fresh start for both.

And then the phone had rung. The sheriff's office outside Madison. Zahn remembered sitting there, numb. And now all this time later, that feeling had never quite left. That's what he was now. Numb.

He snapped off his gloves and threw them into the trash can. He stared at the soap-bitten hands. He had just as much blood on them as the bastard who had left his girl in the snow. It was fine when it was just for ransom. The parents always paid up and no one got hurt.

But this Portia girl had no money. And the girl Hunter had kidnapped had no money either. He had no idea what Hunter was planning and it made him nervous. But he knew there was only one way this was going to end, and Zahn didn't want to be around when the credits rolled.

He picked up the phone and dialed. He disconnected at first ring. Maybe he should be a little more prepared. Get papers ready. Book a flight. Buy a gun? No, he was getting paranoid.

The phone buzzed in his hand.

What do you want, Hunter? he thought.

A text bubble popped up on the screen. Then another. He tapped one, watched it blow up. The phone dropped like a hot knife. The specimens, sitting in a centrifuge of Dulbecco's shuddered. For a man used to slicing people up for a cure, he had a weak stomach for unnecessary violence. And this was very unnecessary.

Zahn wasn't numb anymore. His skin was on fire. He felt like he was going to throw up.

Bait, Hunter had said. *That's how we get her. Real live bait.*

CHAPTER 19

I stepped into the small, musty office stacked high with brochures. There was a broken neon sign above the door that said Grayline Tours. The walls were covered with glossy prints of cine-vision sights that were soon to be compressed into the grimy two by twos of a tour bus window. Like most movies, the previews were always better.

A woman sat under the posters, behind a small Walmart card table squeezed into the corner.

"I'm out, honey," she said without looking up. Her hand slid under the particle board, out of sight, hidden beneath the privacy divider.

Same old Edith.

I'd seen this entire movie before. There was probably a handgun duct-taped to the underside of the false bottom and a stash of twenty-dollar bags of heroin and PCP.

One false move and the table would end up flipped over in the middle of the room and the gun would be clawing its way up my ribs. I moved slowly and talked slower.

"Out of what?"

"Whatever that fool over there sent you here for."

"I'm not looking for a score. I'm looking for Vincent."

"You're not looking for drugs. You're looking for a druggie." She took a puff on her cigarette, the smoke clouding the halide lamp. She paused as the smoke cleared. "Portia?"

She swooped around the desk and bear hugged me, lifting me clear off the ground.

I've often forgotten how strong a five-foot woman could be. Edith stuck the cigarette back into her mouth, chewing on it with excitement. "Where the hell have you been, sister? Wait, don't tell me. Mr. Hunter?"

"Shit, you know too?"

"Oh, everybody knows that bastard, honey. He's really been fucking our business up on the street. Selling the shit he sells. And now that he's moving out he can do it bigger and better without even worrying about getting caught. It's called operating with *impunity*."

"What do you mean, moving out?"

"Going global, honey. Taking his shitty underground lab, packing it up, and moving south somewhere. Out of state. Out of country. I don't know. Bye, Felicia. Gone. But who am I to gossip? Vincent is the one who could tell you all you need to know. Problem is getting that boy to shut up. Come on, come on."

She locked the door and led me to an empty tour van around the corner. "I should warn you, though. Vincent's in bad shape, girl. Ever since you left, you know? I'm not blaming you, honey, but you'll see. Come on, let's go find that freak-show for you."

The bus rolled off down the boulevard, barely slowing at the traffic light. Edith took a hard left on the red, spinning the steering wheel like a boatswain. An old woman with a grocery cart filled high with household items and pieces of cardboard skittered out of the way as the bus blew past.

"Jesus, you don't usually drive this bus, do you?"

"Oh God, no. Drive around a bunch of whiny snot-nosers all day long? And their kids? Ziggy does that. Aunt Edie is a legitimate business-woman now." She stepped on the gas and the engine belched. "Like your rich boyfriend. Except my junk is good."

"He's not my boyfriend."

"But he's rich. Maybe it wouldn't be a bad thing. You could settle down and-"

"He drugged me and framed me for his murder."

Edith stared at me through her plate black dark glasses. "You could do worse, honey. It *is* L.A."

We were on the corner of Wilcox where a row of seedy shops abutted against a large grey self-storage. A narrow alley ran in between, broken glass and overgrown weeds providing as much deterrent as the bent wire-mesh gate.

"That's where your boy is. He lives in the big mansion at the end. Styrofoam roof, cardboard siding, all asphalt back yard. Lifestyles of the broke and shameless, you know. He should be around somewhere. You know Vincent. He doesn't trust anyone, doesn't ever leave his alley."

The radio crackled. "Yes, yes, oh God, do I have to handle everything?" She put her hand over the walkie-talkie face. It was small and yellow, very Fisher-Pricey.

"Honey, who is this thug you're with? Ziggy says he's acting all strung out, looking for you. You're not in any kind of trouble, are you?"

"No, but if you could keep him off my back for a bit while I find Vin, it would be great."

"Done, honey. I don't need to be asked twice. I'll stick a barrel so far up his ass his tonsils will tickle. And you need anything else, I mean an-y-thing, you just come ask your old Aunt Edie, you hear?"

Most of the shanties were lined up against the wall near the dumpster, jostling for prime position against the green metal cauldron that was often food source and toilet.

The dwellings were mostly cardboard city specials, corrugated fiber, and pallet-wood lined with sections of industrial foam and the occasional soiled mattress. The most exclusive of these were braced by the rarest of commodities, a refrigerator box cut in two or a washer and dryer carton lined with white chipboard and heavy-duty tarpaulin.

I spotted Vincent's white box immediately. The tartan blanket I had bought for him three years ago was neatly folded and an aged copy of

Nietzsche's *Thus Spake Zarathustra* lay on it, protected from the dampness and dirt of the pavement. I checked the dust cover. Memphis Public Library. Rented by Michelle Marks in September of sixteen. I tucked it into my backpack. Only a couple of years overdue.

I half-expected to find a random assortment of technical texts, but Vincent had this habit of giving away everything he wasn't currently using and regretting it later.

The only ones he had kept were weighting down the blackout curtain that served as his front door. I turned them over, a weather-beaten 1950 copy of Turing's *Computer Machinery and Intelligence* and a Merck Manual of indeterminate age and origin, cover missing. Under layers of soggy blankets was a set of ivory chess pieces. I breathed in slowly. Still here. The rest of the box was empty, save for a couple of cans and soiled clothing strewn on the floor.

I crawled out and followed the line of empty boxes to the end of the alley. There was a low moan from around the corner. Behind the recessed stairway that led into the service entrance of a long-closed Walgreen's were two, maybe three, crackheads in a sleeping bag, a random arm and leg sticking out, a kaleidoscope of yellow boils and purple welts writhing and squirming.

There was a scruffy little dog with them, running around in circles. It was leashed to a foot, scampering around, winding itself into an ever-narrowing circle. She - I knew it was a she because she was squatting to pee now - stopped and stared at me. For a moment she was surprised, then she growled, baring teeth that were the canine version of meth-mouth.

"What's the matter, bitch?" The thrusting within the blanket ceased and a large potbellied man emerged. He was quite naked, and his manhood pointed at me accusingly. His eyes were cherry red, and he wiped a trickle of blood that welled at his nose. A large junk blister swelled on the inside of his arm; blue, swollen, bubbly.

The acid burn was a bad sign. A junkie was likely to cut you up and run. Mix in some PCP and he was likely to cut you up and stay for dinner.

"Why you got to mess with me, bitch?" I was still not sure who he was talking to, the bitch who still twisted around his ankle, or me.

"You know how long it takes for me to get there? To come?" I was not unaware of the phenomenon. Heroin numbed more than your brain. This is why junkies could fuck for hours, days even, filling the boredom of a listless high with zombie sex, pausing only when the dark thunderstorm of a junk craving re-emerged.

The man was closer now, his belly jiggling precariously, a wide tribal tattoo ringing the navel that peered through like a white fishy eye. "And I'll be fucked if some bony-ass bitch-"

He attempted to kick the dog that still whipped around his ankle. "Get lost, get lost!" On the third try he made contact and the dog rolled over, whimpering. Its jaw was hanging, lopsided, condyle snapped in half, the tongue hanging like a red snake. He dragged the limp creature as he stumbled along, like a ball on a chain. The dog left a dark trail of blood on the concrete.

A red mist crossed my eyes. "Leave her alone."

"Leave her alone? You should see what I'd do to a little scrawny chick like you. Wouldn't waste my dick on you, but you'd be surprised what I could do with a piece of rebar."

Dr. Jenny Ott, the court-appointed psychiatrist whom I hadn't seen since my foster years, the one who insisted I call her Jenny, not Doctor Ott or Doctor Jenny, warned me about trigger words after my sixth foster home had ended with a set of brass knuckles imprinted on someone's face.

About how I was supposed to take a trigger word and bury it. Literally imagine digging a hole and dropping the word in, letter by letter, in random order so it made no sense anymore. Drop it in, shovel dirt back onto the grave, and stomp on the dirt. She said it would save more pervs from broken noses and more Portias from juvenile. It didn't.

"Rebar," he kept saying, "I'd stick it right up…"

I was ripping the letters apart, mixing them up. B-A-R-R-E. E-B-R-A-R. R-A-B-E-R. I was digging a hole so deep and wide the letters would never see the light of day but as soon as I'd filled the hole, a little gray sprout appeared. It was the spike of the R, followed soon by the e, then the b, a, and r.

The man hadn't stopped. He was still dragging the wounded animal, his imaginations of rape getting wilder and harsher but still involving some ferrous implement.

"…then I'd take it out and stick it back in so far you'd taste iron in your mouth."

That was when I cut him. I didn't plan it, so I can't say I was happy with the results. I'm a perfectionist with my cuts after all, but even a good surgeon has bad days.

All I could remember was a pretty little girl named Sarah

Nickerson and an ugly brute with an affinity for rebar, and the box cutter was out and lashing. The slice went neatly across the pendulous belly. If he hadn't been so fat, the cut would have disemboweled him, but at this depth it was just a peek of yellowish drippy visceral fat.

The man stared at the fat bubble, pressing it back in like a yolk that was bulging. Like most addicts, the blood flow had sucked into the vital organs, and the blood in the periphery was sluggish, oozing instead of spurting.

"What the fuck?" he yelled, still not quite sure what was happening. In the corner I could see the junkie in the bag clambering out, blood dripping down his legs, trying to staunch it with his underwear. He grabbed at a large pair of dirty jeans and tore through a wallet until he found a flutter of bills. He looked at me, his face bruised and ghost-like. I'd recognize Vincent anywhere.

"Here." I sliced off strips of the blanket and pressed it against the man's stomach, instantly back to the role of caregiver. I suddenly realized I had no reason to keep him alive, no client I had to wait for. "You know what?" I spat at him. "I hope you die."

There was a clattering behind me. Vincent was off like a jackrabbit, scrambling up the steps, hands and feet working in unison as he scurried across the cement.

"Wait, Vin!"

It was no use. He was hurt, spooked, and still very high. I took the stairs three at a time and swung around the steel railing. He was nowhere to be seen.

I checked his box, hoping that he'd taken refuge there, curled up under a blanket or crouched behind a plywood board, but there was no one in the alley. I walked down, checking every alcove and corner. Except for a low moaning, there was no sign of life anywhere.

I clambered over the gate and looked down the almost empty avenue. No sign of an underwear-clad junkie streaked with blood. Even with all the crazy shit that happened around here, I was sure that would be noticed.

Suddenly, it hit me. *Shit.* I turned back to the green mechanical dumpster in the alley. The drop lids didn't seal, and the container reeked of garbage and excrement in fifty different ways.

"Come on, Vin, get out." I kicked the container and the smell only got worse. "Come on, man. Before I pass out." I wondered if Vincent himself had passed out in there. "I have a bag of K, two whole ounces. It's yours if you come out."

There was a splinter of glass, the sound of cardboard smashing as Vincent peered out. He smelled as bad as the garbage inside and looked worse. He craned his neck scoping out the escape routes at either end of the alley.

"Is he dead?" he asked.

"No."

"Shit!" He jumped out of the container and scrambled again, hiding behind his box house.

"No, wait, Vin!" But Vincent was junkie fast. He skittered over from box to box. Now he was at the gate, looking like he was going to vault over.

There was a large man at the end of the alley wearing tourist trap sunglasses and an oversized Hollywood sweatshirt.

"Where the hell were you, Q?"

Vincent darted one way, then the other, like he was evading a tackle and Quentin wasn't quite ready to take him on. He spread his long arms out, trying to corral him as he sized up the blood patches. He wrinkled his nose at the smell.

"Some goddamn woman," Quentin said. "Acting like a crazy bitch. Tried to clock me with an umbrella."

"Q, goddamn it, I'll clock you if you don't stop him."

There was a roar from the other end of the alley. The brute had found himself a tire iron, and he stumbled as he approached. It wasn't rebar, but it was close enough.

Vincent ran and Q lunged, grabbing him by an ankle. It was an old football play, the shoestring tackle, barely effective on a man without shoes.

I picked up a rock sized piece of asphalt and swung it above my head. I was a terrible shot, but I didn't need to be perfect. Just close enough. The rock left a quarter-sized indentation on the brute's forehead and a stream of dark purple blood trickled down his nose. The iron fell from his hand, and the big man dropped to his knees. He was bubbling and foaming at the mouth.

I walked around him and found the little dog under him, still locked like a prison ball, still wheezing and panting as she choked on her blood. I thought of Dog and wondered if this would have been her fate is she hadn't met me.

"Sorry kid," I whispered. I stroked her and she soothed, her little black eyes soft and trusting. "You're a good little dog, aren't you?" The puppy was quiet now, but her breath was hoarse, and I could feel the bubbling of a collapsed lung. "Yes, you're a good kid. You don't deserve this."

I took my cutter out and sliced quickly through her windpipe. I felt no regret. Some of us weren't meant to live long anyway. I wrapped her in the blanket and put her away. I left the man alone, hoping he would lie there for a long time.

Quentin was straddling Vincent, trying to avoid touching him. "Who the hell is he?"

"None of your business." I grabbed Vincent by the neck, pulling him to his feet.

"If you're going around cutting people up, then it is my business," Quentin said.

I looked at Vincent. He shivered, his scrawny frame all knobs and bumps expanding and contracting like an accordion.

"Shut up, Q. Give him your sweatshirt."

"You just made be buy this," Quentin protested.

"Well, he can't go around like this."

"I can't go around like this either."

I flicked my cutter open and pointed it at him. A drop of blood flew through the air and landed on the pavement between us. "If you don't take it off, I'll cut it off."

Quentin ripped the sweatshirt off and whipped it over Vincent's head. It hung over him like an oversized Christmas sweater, shoulders at his elbows, hems down to his knees.

"Now what?" Quentin asked.

"We need to get off the street. We need a hotel."

Quentin frowned at me. We were standing in the middle of the boulevard with a half-naked smack whore covered with blood and excrement.

"We don't need a hotel," he said, "we need an asylum."

The beast behind us had clambered to his feet. He stared at his dead dog, his mouth wide open. He took a step and dropped onto a cardboard hovel. This time he was out completely.

Vincent pushed a fistful of bloody bills between us. He finally had his breath caught up enough to speak. "I know a place," he said, "that's both."

Chapter 20

The driver pulled up at the gated compound on the outskirts of the Long Beach shipyards. His blue work-shirt was stained with engine grease and mustard. The embroidered white nametag that said *Lenny* was frayed in a fuzz of white cotton.

He looked around nervously, this wouldn't be the first time he had been jumped on a delivery and Lenny kept his phone on 911 speed dial. He had been hired by a guy in Los Angeles the night before. The call came into his auto shop at nine just as he was about to leave for the night.

The instructions were simple. Pick up a car from the shipyard, take it out to the desert, and wait for further instructions. Lenny had almost hung up when the offer was made, but truth be told, he was two months behind on rent and barely anyone was knocking on the doors anymore.

The gate rolled open slowly, a man pointed him to the large bay with the double wide rollers. The shutters raised and Lenny stared at the car inside. It was a beautiful vehicle, diamond white, close to brand new. He hadn't seen the model before and made the assumption that, unless there had been some serious internal damage, it could still fetch close to six figures.

"You want me to junk this?"

"No, not junk it. Just take it out to this GPS location."

"It's in the middle of the desert."

"Not my call, man. I was just paid to store it." The man pointed at his watch. "And I was paid till five, so you might want to rig it up unless you want to pay me for my time."

Lenny pulled into the spot fifteen minutes before he was scheduled. He pulled the tarp off the car and lowered the ramp. He took a look around and checked the loaded pistol in his back, ready for anything. The phone rang and he jumped. Except for that.

"Did you bring the gasoline?"

"Yeah, Mr. Hunter. You want me to fill the tank?"

"No, I want you to light it up."

Lenny laughed. "Oh." He paused. "You're serious?"

"Dead serious," Hunter said. "You want to get the second half of your money?"

"Yeah," Lenny said. He was way more nervous than he had been on the drive out here. This wasn't right, he thought. He should never have said yes.

"Then light it up. Don't forget the phone either."

The call ended.

Lenny walked around the car slowly. This was what it was like getting in with the mob. You didn't know until you were in and when you were in, it was already too late. Maybe he should have been thankful there was no one in the trunk. Lenny stopped. Or was there?

He knocked on the hood, then around the trunk. Did it sound empty? What does an empty trunk sound like? He pulled a DeWalt from his toolbox and drilled a hole into the back. He shone a flashlight in and peered from the corner.

It was empty. Lenny breathed easier. It could still be a felony, but at least there was no body involved. Maybe it wasn't even a felony. Maybe it was a joke. He took a last look at the car, at the pouncing jaguar on the hood. A real expensive joke.

Lenny pulled the gas tank out and sloshed it over the roof and hood. He lit the trail and watched the whoosh of flame roar up into the dark sky.

He waited a minute, expecting something terrible, something he couldn't imagine. Except for the roaring fire, nothing happened. He watched, mesmerized. Finally he ambled down the slope and tossed the cellphone under some bushes.

Lenny hauled himself into his cab and drove off. When he got to his garage he made sure to wipe the entire surface of his truck down.

Then, just to be safe, he took a bath. Nowadays, you could never be careful enough.

CHAPTER 21

Ibought Vincent a room in the Hollywood Hotel. It was a roach motel on the corner of Wilshire and La Brea, but at least the water ran warm and the doors locked.

The woman behind the bullet-proof glass passed a guest form through the slide tray. "Forty a night, twenty an hour," she said. "Twenty for half an hour too, so take your time."

Her voice sounded like rocks rattling around in a can. She was huffing on a cheap cigarette under a large red no smoking sign. A sticker on the window said *No Pets*. An image of Dog came up, floppy ear and hanging tongue. I missed her terribly but I knew she was better off where she was.

"Stinks," Vincent said.

"What?"

"Your cancer stick. Stinks to hell and high heaven."

She stared at the small man with his oversized sweatshirt and no pants. Even in a hotel frequented almost exclusively by junkies and prostitutes, Vincent looked out of place.

"Hell and high *heaven*? This junkie for real?" The paper was halfway under the slider, held back by a chubby, tobacco-stained finger.

"You know they flavor cigarettes with urea? Don't know what that is? Sounds like urine, right? Smells like it too. And you're sucking on it."

"You talking to me about smell?"

"It's not just smell. They've got Benzene. You know what that is? It's pesticide. And cadmium. Like in battery acid, cadmium."

The woman's face was red, her small yellow teeth sticking out through her pursed lips. "I see the commercials, freak."

"And arsenic."

"Arsenic?"

"Not the elemental stuff. I'm talking about white arsenic. Aqua Tofani. Trioxide. Inheritor's powder."

If he got into it with her, we'd be back out on the street. I grabbed the paper, signed it, and returned it through the slider with a fistful of bills. "He's okay. I'll take care of him."

"You better. Or I'll kick both you out on your arsenic." The woman's hands worked slowly, counting the bills from one hand to the other, staring us down as I shoved Vincent down the hallway.

"Formaldehyde," he said, struggling from my grasp. "I didn't get to tell her. It's a morgue preservative." Once Vincent got onto something, he stayed on. I pushed him toward the elevator.

"Vin, the arsenic in smoke is inorganic. And you know urea's not urine. And it's in a lot of things. Skin cream, deodorizers."

"I know. But she doesn't. Maybe she'll quit. Then she'll thank me."

The idea of a junkie getting a smoker to quit was far-fetched, and I was smiling in spite of myself.

"Don't laugh. Junk doesn't give you cancer."

"No, you just drop dead."

"You don't-" He stopped when he saw the open steel doors. "I'm not going in there. When was the inspection done last?"

"How should I know? Just get in before you get us kicked out of here."

"I don't see any paperwork. Does it comply with the ESO? With California A17?" He grabbed me by the shoulders frantically. "You know an elevator is the only place you can fall *up* to your death?"

"Fall up?"

"The counterweight weighs more than the cab. If the rope brake is deactivated and the overspeed governor fails, the cab falls upwards. You fall to your death. But you're going upwards. It's not a Schindler, is it?"

"It's an Otis," the woman piped in. "And don't worry your frizzy little brain, honey. The elevator's broke."

"Great," I muttered. I pushed him to the rickety staircase.

"There has to be a law against this," he called out. "You can't call this place the Hollywood Hotel just because it's a hotel in Hollywood." It was hard to keep up with Vincent. His junkie brain spun like it had been caught in a revolving door. "You know when the real Hollywood Hotel was built?"

"Nineteen oh two," I said. I'd heard this story before. "Eighty-four rooms, three acres of cultured gardens. Lemon groves, for God's sakes, Portia; lemons."

I finally got him into the dank stairwell. "Doesn't smell like lemons. Smells like urea."

Vincent looked at me blankly. "No, it's urine. Definitely urine. Let's leave."

"We can't, Vin. I've already paid. Besides, we've no other place to go." The building may not have been up to code, but there weren't any other rooms at this rate, and I needed to get Vincent sobered up fast. Getting him up six flights of stairs was a good start. I pushed him, ignoring his complaints.

"Hollywood, man. You don't know what it was like. Jane Russell. Rita Hayworth. Betty Grable."

"Belladonnas," I said.

"And Cora Marie Frye. Oh, she was on the patio all the time-"

"Never heard of her." I finally managed to get him down the dank corridor. I unlocked the door as he slumped against the wall.

"They called her Marie McDonald. The Body. She could have been bigger than all the others. Fucking Seconal. When I saw her-"

"Vin," I interrupted. "You're thirty-five." I knew this would probably break him but there was a chance this would go on forever. "The Hollywood Hotel was demolished in the fifties. You weren't around for any of this."

We were finally at the room and I struggled with the old fashioned keyed lock.

"Come on, Vincent, get in."

He was glued to the door jamb, his eyes wide and mournful. Like the words to an old song, I could mouth them all before the music played.

"They put up a shopping center. On the Hollywood Hotel. On the damn lemon groves. The lemon groves, Portia. All that history. Gone."

"Yeah, well, it's the Kodak Theatre now. It's new history."

"No such thing." He put his face in his hands. The whiskers bunched out from his splayed fingers. "No such thing as new history. It's a sin."

I thought it was a sin that forty bucks a night wouldn't get you clean sheets. The yellow duvet was sun-bleached white, and the white sheets were stained yellow. I bundled up the bedding and threw it into the corner.

Quentin finally arrived, panting, hanging onto the door frame. He was carrying two large bags of groceries from the corner CVS.

"Did you get the sheets? Lemon air-freshener?"

"Didn't have lemon. I got vanilla."

"It has to be lemon, Q. I told you. Lemon groves smell like lemon. This won't work with vanilla. Go back and get it."

"This is crazy," he said. "Bat-shit crazy. I could die on those stairs and no one would know."

"Guano." Vincent was at the window, pulling at his collar frantically like he was trying to force out a bug. It was a crank bug, and soon Vincent would be clawing through his skin to get at it.

"What?"

"Guano," I said. "It's the Quechua word for bat shit."

"Does it matter?" Quentin had finally regained his breath but not his temper.

"The Chincha war was fought over guano," I said. "So yes, it does matter."

Vincent was pulling at his hair and grinding his teeth.

"What the hell is Chincha?" Quentin asked.

"Isla Chincha is an archipelago off the coast of Peru. It's where the Spanish-South American war happened-" I stopped. I was beginning to sound like Vincent. "Why the hell does it matter, Q?"

Vincent's eyes were darting across the room, his head following, turning in circles. "Is there a bat in here?" He flapped his arms and made cawing sounds.

"Bats don't do that," Quentin said.

"Shut up, Q," I said.

"Yeah, shut up, Q," Vincent repeated. His arms had stopped flapping, but his head still whipped from side to side, following the imaginary bat around the room. Soon there would be the random face slapping and the extremity tics. We'd gone through excitement, despair, and now paranoia. I needed to get him settled before he really started going south.

I grabbed the bags from Quentin and ripped open the fresh sheets. They smelled of lemony plastic, and I hoped it would help. Too late. Vincent was clawing at his face with his fingernails, drawing little blebs of blood. It had to be now.

I filled the syringe with downer and crept up behind him. As he turned, I hooked his leg and he plopped, face-first, onto the pillow. His buttock, as corrugated and thick as tire-rubber was exposed by a rip in his underwear. I took my chance and stabbed hard, pushing through the scarred tough flesh until I could drive the barrel home.

"You okay, Vin?"

"What happened?"

"You fell."

"I think I got bit. I think I have rabies."

"You don't have rabies. You're just junk-sick." I dragged him into the bathroom and seated him on the edge of the stained tub while I got the water going. It helped that Vincent was just about eighty-five pounds. Any bigger and my ninety-five-pound frame would be no match.

I picked through the second plastic bag. Disposable razor, shave foam, comb, toothbrush, soap, scissors, vinyl gloves. He'd forgotten the shampoo, but it was too late. Scissors and Irish Spring would have to do for now.

"Let's get you washed up, Vin. I need something from you. But you've got to get clean first."

I started peeling off his clothes as the water ran. I finally got to a sticking point and had to use the cutter to rip off the last few shards. The skin was so indurated, the clothes so entrenched, the fabric had knotted into the skin and both peeled off in clumps of clot and pus.

"Hey, Q! Help me get him into the tub, I'll get his hair cut."

Quentin looked like he was ready to puke. "I ain't touching him. He's a smack-whore. Probably has an asshole the size of a quarter. I don't know what he's got."

"Probably the same shit you do." I pointed the scissors at him. "Glove up if you want."

I began working on the hair, cutting it close to the scalp in even strokes above the comb. I'd pulled a lot of different shifts in my life but hairdressing wasn't one. I gave up and got the razor. "You okay going bald, Vin?"

He nodded, the warm water already soothing him. His eyes were steely blue and calm as ice. Five milligrams of diazepam was usually enough to calm an amphetamine addict down, but I know it would only last for so long. The tremors and agitation would be back soon, and I got the razor working quickly before I was onto his beard.

"What the hell is this? Oh God, I'm going to be sick." This time Quentin wasn't kidding. He turned, grabbed the toilet, and puked, the flow grey and stringy.

I saw a knot of small white worms wriggling in the soapy water. I pulled his feet out of the water one by one, examining the likely spots. Most heroin addicts start by injecting in the spots that doctors find most convenient. The radial on the back of the wrist, the ulna on the inside of the arm. As the tracks start building up and the veins begin to collapse, most tweakers find novel ports hidden under knees and thighs, between fingers and toes, in the buttocks and, occasionally, the genitals.

Old story on the street? You can spot new addicts because they won't sit, you can spot old ones because they *can't* sit.

I found the abscess, thankfully under a knee, a nasty red welt with a yellow iris bulging like a yolk. It was pointing and indurated, the crusty edges soft and furrowed. More worms were fighting their way out and plopping in thick scrums into the water. At least I knew now where the smell was coming from.

"Oh hell, no, that's disgusting."

I took the scissors and pressed it against the abscess, watching the pus swell.

"You might want to get out of the firing line."

Quentin scrambled like a bomb was about to go off. I pressed the abscess and watched it squirt, a yellow infected stream that smelled like spoiled yogurt. I mopped up the pus with a hand towel. The streaks had reached as far as the wall and down the commode. Live maggots wriggled all over the slick floor.

I went back to the abscess and scoured it out, undercutting the connective tissue with the scissors, dragging out the last few worms.

"Here." I threw a roll of bandage at Quentin. "Dry him up and bandage it."

"What if he shits the tub? I'm not getting back in there."

"You're not going to do that, Vin, are you?"

Vincent wouldn't respond. The depressant had kicked in way too fast. "Shit, he's going to need an upper. What do you have?"

"Nothing." He pulled out his pockets, stained yellow from tobacco, as if to prove his point.

"Q, you're a goddamned drug dealer. Go find some."

"Uh-uh. Brother walks these streets picking dope, he goes into the slammer real quick."

"Then why the hell do I have you here?"

"Been asking myself the same damn question."

"Okay." I tossed the plastic bag at him. "You get him wiped up and in bed, I'll get the dope. And for God's sake, don't let him sleep."

CHAPTER 22

There were no dealers on the boulevard anymore. All the good drugs were with the tour guides, the exchanges handled at random pickups in the Hollywood Hills, far from the prying eyes of the police. They waved their stacks of brightly colored flyers, slapping them against hands and hips, ruffling the sheets like over-sized decks of cards.

I approached one, saw him size me up like a bartender. Local blitzer? Molly, maybe some heroin. Power suit? High grade coke. Frat kid? MDMA laced with PCP. Tourist? K2.

"Got some uppers?" I asked the first one.

"No drugs, ma'am," he said, his eyes small and squinty in his sun-burned face. "Just tours."

"No drugs?" I repeated. I was standing, appropriately, on a vomit-tarnished star framed by bronze lettering. A hypodermic was crushed into the ceramic like a used cigarette. "What about that?"

"No drugs, just star tours. Brad Pitt, Johnny Depp." Well-rehearsed. He stared at a black SUV that idled at a curb two blocks down.

"I'm looking for Belushi, if you know what I mean. Morrison. Hendrix."

"Hollywood Hills, madam. Star homes." His eyes wandered, scanning the street.

"Cut the shit. I need a stim. Dex, adderall, whatever you have." The guy was getting shifty and I changed tactics. "You Ziggy? Edith set me."

"I don't know no Edith."

"Aunt Edie, Zig. She told me. Anything I want, ask for ol' Auntie Edie, she said. She's going to be mighty pissed if you don't give me the one little thing I need."

He looked toward Edith's office.

"You want me to call her? Because it's not going to go well."

"Fifty for some dex," he said, finally. We shook hands without a second glance at the product or cash, an honor among junkies that I've never quite understood. I learned a long time ago that the last person to trust was a junkie. The second last was a dealer. Especially if the junkie was a dealer too.

But I didn't have time to worry about details now. The truck idling on the corner was closer now. The blinkers were on, like it was ready to merge out.

I tucked the ampoules in my shirt seam and got off the main drag up north for two blocks. Quentin had used most of my remaining cash at the CVS and now I was running out of time too.

I trawled the filthy public bathrooms on the streets off Vine, putting together an impressive arsenal of drug supplies. Burned spoons, half-empty lighters were littered around the back of the amber-stained toilets, and in the overflowing trash I finally struck gold, a factory-sealed hypodermic. I added it to the stash in my pockets and exited through the back door into the alley.

I exited and crossed the street. The truck was blocking the exit. It was a Suburban. I could see the grill markings now, California plates, obsidian black. The automatic start clicked on and the engine rumbled to life.

I turned, ran down to the main road, dropped behind a mailbox. I had a boxcutter in my sleeve, the blade popped and ready. Extra sharp blade. Could cut through tire rubber. Or an ACL. Their pick. But the truck was gone. Time to get back to Vincent. I hoped he hadn't dozed off. It was going to be hell to wake him, even with an eight ball of Dex.

I walked another block, away from the hotel. No sign of the truck. I crossed Wilcox. Then Franklin. I began breathing a little easier. Then there it was, trawling its way up the road, hazards on, following me like a shark sniffing blood in murky waters. This was no random trolling. I tucked away the cutter. In a close quarter fight, chemicals trump blades any day.

I ducked into a store and waited for it to pass. Time to take care of business. I slipped up behind it, rapped on the right back window, and crossed to the other side to the driver's side. If a driver's carrying, it's almost always holstered. I had the syringe in my hand, my thumb triggered on the barrel.

The window rolled down. "We've been looking for you, young lady," Guerrero said.

I hate to say it, but I was relieved. The syringe was for Vin, and I didn't want to leave the needle broken in some stranger's neck. I definitely didn't want to leave it stuck in Guerrero.

"Shit, I said. "I almost stuck you, G!"

"I'm glad you didn't," he said.

"I'm sure you are. What's the matter, found another finger?"

"Better." Medina leaned over from the passenger seat. "We think we found your boyfriend's car."

"Now I have a finger for you." I grimaced. "How do you know it's his?"

"It's a white Jaguar torched in the middle of Death Valley," she said. "I'm willing to take a shot. Do you want to see it or not?"

"Aren't you supposed to call the cops first?"

"It was the local cops that found it. Which gives us a couple of hours to get a first peek before they start making some calls. You in or not?"

"I'd like to. But I'm busy."

"Really? You got something else that's more, I don't know?" She stared me up and down, her eyes lingering at the bulge around my stomach. "Pressing?"

I tucked the pouch further into my waistband. I knew she wasn't a cop, but the last thing I needed was for her to go squealing to her boss if I dropped a bag of rocks onto the pavement. The rear door swung open silently.

"Now?" I asked.

"I told you, we have an hour, maybe two, before they find out who this car belongs to and the window closes. Hop in."

The syringe rolled around under my fingers. I tried to convince myself that Vincent was in capable hands, but the more I thought about it, the more I was sure Quentin was out at a bodega scoring a quart of brandy. Forget it. Vincent was going to have to wait. Whoever popped Nathan also dumped his car. And whoever dumped the car-

"Last chance, Portia."

I hopped in and the truck plowed its way down the strip and took a sharp right onto Highland. There were three of us, but the plush, cavernous interior swallowed our bodies up enough that we could be in separate vehicles. I settled in and closed my eyes.

The ride out of L.A. was silent, filled with the hum of tires and tired radio. Medina kept switching the channels. CNN live. Limbaugh. ESPN. The Rams were losing. The Chargers were winning. Nobody really cared. L.A. wasn't a political city. It wasn't a sports city. L.A. was an L.A. city and its utter lack of self-awareness was suffocating.

Medina finally settled on a smooth jazz station, mostly clarinet and piano, the occasional belch and screech of a trumpet. The music was sickly sweet, but it seemed to fit the mood better.

After about an hour of driving into the Simi Canyon, we finally broke into the flat, salty deserts of eastern California. The vast scrubland of Death Valley brought the taste of acid to my throat. Dirt always made me think of death and there were plenty of dead bodies around these parts. Conservative estimates? Probably one every fifteen square miles. Now there was probably one more, in the trunk of a car. I closed my eyes and tried to put it out of mind.

The truck pulled off and rumbled into the flats, a plume of salinated dirt spitting as wide and fine as a wake. A few miles down the trail, two police cruisers were parked in Vee. The engines were humming, the shimmer of desert heat radiating off the hood.

"Looks like it's still the rubes," Medina said. "You better get dressed."

"I am dressed."

"Well, get undressed then. Here." She tossed a plastic bag into the back seat. "Put it on."

"What's wrong with what I'm wearing?"

"Everything." She sliced a hand through the air to cut off any protest. "But mostly because nobody's taking you seriously as an insurance adjuster like that."

"Insurance adjuster?" I peeled through the clothes, standard black jacket and skirt, white shirt. "Class D felony," I said.

"It's a wobbler, actually. It'll get dumbed down to a misdemeanor-"

"I was talking about the clothes."

Guerrero laughed and made it way worse.

"Just put them on," Medina snapped. She slung a camera over her neck. "And leave your stash under the mat. Don't need the cops arresting you for possession in the desert."

She slammed the door and went over to the policemen. In moments she disappeared around the corner, behind the cruisers. I pulled at the door handle. The lever moved, but the door wouldn't budge.

"Don't piss her off," Guerrero said. "She gets mad at you, she gets mad at me." He switched the dial on the radio to a pre-set. It was Sam Kinison in the midst of a screaming foul-mouthed rant that involved hippies and midgets. "And then we have to listen to Jazz one-oh-six. You like smooth jazz?"

"No."

"Then wait till she gets back."

I felt around my pockets for a weapon. I turned up with a tarnished penny and a couple of old bills. I pressed the cold face of the coin against his neck with my thumb. I had to be plenty desperate to resort to this, but it had worked before.

"Open the door or I'll blow a hole into that fat neck of yours."

The radio finally turned down. "I'll give you points for trying, honey. But the whole point of a barrel is that it *has* a hole." He shifted in his seat.

I could see his face in the rear-view. His eyes were covered by black Wayfarers that disappeared into the folds of his massive neck.

"You should listen to Medina and change. If you want to see that car, that is." He turned the volume up a notch and I threw the coin at him.

It plunked off his head and bounced onto his lap. He fished the coin out, licked it and scrubbed its face with the lining of his jacket. "*Jeez*, you're either really smart or really lucky."

"You call any of this lucky?"

Guerrero squinted at the coin. "Nineteen-oh-nine Lincoln Wheat. S-VDB. Only about four hundred thousand were ever made. In this condition, I'd say seven, maybe seven-fifty. How many of these do you have?"

I stared out of the window. Medina was still with the cops.

"That many, huh?"

I remained silent.

"No bank accounts, no electronic tagging. No bundles of cash in a safe. You can cross state lines and no cop would ever know. No thief would ever think of making off with the pennies in your change holder, either." He pushed the coin back across the console. "You know, Portia, I think I like you."

In the distance I could see Medina come back with the one of the officers. I gave up and struggled into the perfectly fitted clothes.

"Car's empty," she said. "Plates were stripped. The locals ran the VIN. Luckily the car doesn't belong to Nathan Hunter so they haven't made that connection yet."

"Who does it belong to?"

"It's registered to a Marcia Hunter."

"Mother or sister?" Guerrero asked.

I looked at him, then at Medina. "You don't know which is which?"

Medina ignored the barb. "They think the family sent us. It's only a matter of time before they realize Hunter's missing and I don't need to tell you they're not going to look kindly on this." She pushed a tablet into my hands. "Remember, we're the insurance adjusters, so make sure you play along."

"Like I'd admit to killing him and dumping his car in the desert to the first cop I see."

"That's not funny. You're still the only suspect. So you better not touch anything either."

Around the corner a white sports sedan straddled the dirt road. The smell of burnt leather and rubber mingled with the musty smell of dry salt. "You were right about the special order. Portfolio edition. Sold in Coventry and shipped to Boston. Nothing in the glove compartment. Trunk. No papers. No other tracks. No cars, bikes, feet. Not even a lizard print within a hundred feet."

I turned around and looked at the dirt. There was the random shrub, glasswort and pickleweed, salt tolerant greens that were hardy enough to survive the hundred and thirty-degree days.

"So, he comes down here, lights his hundred and twenty-thousand-dollar car up, and just disappears without a trace?"

"Looks like it." She was staring at the driver's seat. The ribs had blistered and puffed out like scales. "How tall is Hunter?"

"I don't know? Five-ten. Eleven?"

Medina measured me by eye and looked back in. "Seat position seems about right. The steering wheel and the rear view are a little low though. Maybe you were right about not driving. You don't remember this at all?"

"No."

"Okay." Medina sounded disappointed. She circled the car, taking pictures. "If you see something, let me know."

"There's nothing to see here."

"What do you mean?"

I walked around the car, tracing the scorch pattern with my finger. "Fire burns hottest at its fuel source, in this case the gas tank or the engine. It burns outward because it sucks in the oxygen. The compression in the tank causes an explosion under the car like an IED. The paint on the roof doesn't have enough time to blister, let alone vaporize."

I kicked the fascia under the floorboard.

"Tank's still in one piece," I said.

"You're saying the fuel was poured over the top and the car was lit from the outside."

"What I'm saying is this didn't happen going down the freeway at a hundred and twenty miles an hour. The tank was drained, the car was placed out of sight from the highway but close enough that it would be found. Whoever went to the trouble of doing this won't have left any evidence in the car."

I walked down onto the pebbled area below the road. The stones ran along the embankment, smooth and shiny, stranded by the stream that once carried them. A lizard skittered across the dirt leaving a white furrow that filled in as the winds picked up. On top of the hill Medina was still working the camera. I imagine she was hot under her fitted silk jacket, but her hair was still perfect. She tilted her head, motioning me back up.

No way, sister, I thought. Not yet.

On the side of the incline I found what I was looking for, a scuff mark under the scrub, a boot scrape where an errant footprint might have been hastily erased. Under a shrub, a dark shimmer. It was probably a broken beer bottle, but this was no time to take chances. I slid down the dirt and kicked it with my boot. My pulse slowed to a trickle. There was only a light film of dust on the black glass.

There was a scorpion among the stones, baring it's claws at me. Its tail curled up, the stinger glossy in the sun. It was daring me to approach. Bad omen. I went for it anyway.

"What did you find?" I turned and saw her staring down at me. Her sunglasses were raised and she was squinting.

"Nothing."

"You sure?"

"Yep." I was walking awkwardly. The pants were fitted and the phone I'd just found was tucked into the only place I could hide it without arousing suspicion. I felt like a drug mule with a bag full of coke up my nether regions waiting my turn at customs.

"So, did that help? I mean, you sat in that car. You still can't remember anything?"

"Not a thing."

"Well, that's a bust, isn't it?"

"What did you expect?"

"I don't know. I've learned not to expect anything." She got into the truck and stared at me as I dropped into the back seat. She was looking right at my crotch, struggling with a host of obvious questions.

"Like the view?" I asked.

Medina turned to the front and settled in. If she was embarrassed, she didn't show it. "Your vagina's ringing," she said.

She settled in and pressed her sunglasses up the bridge of her nose. I ran my hand under my belt and pulled out the slender phone, not much larger than a deck of cards and about half as thick. I pressed the button on the bottom, and watched the picture load incrementally.

"You know what's funny, Guerrero?" Medina asked. "There were no tire tracks. Not any that would match that car at least. Our truck left tracks. The cops left tracks. But there were no tracks that would match that size of car anywhere. Somebody picked that car up and dropped it right in the middle of Death Valley. Probably drove it out all the way from L.A. Just to set it on fire. Think that's weird, Guerrero?"

Guerrero dropped the truck into gear. "It's all weird."

"What do you think, Portia? Do you think someone's having fun with us? Playing a game? Portia?"

"Huh?" I was a million miles away at the moment.

"Think it's just a game?"

"Sure."

"Pretty sick game, right?"

I didn't answer. My fingers were as cold as glass. The picture was only half-loaded, but I clicked the phone off. I'd seen enough.

"Yeah," I said finally. "Sick." I closed my eyes, but I could still see the picture. A young woman with flame-red hair that curled down to her shoulders. She was sitting on a couch, naked under a single white robe.

There was a strip of red cloth tied around her neck. On the bed next to her was a Sawzall and a Dremel.

CHAPTER 23

Zahn stared at the text under magnification. The text on the top of the state-issued Oregon driver's license was in clear blue, laser-etched print. The license wasn't real-ID compliant, but it was the newer upgraded version, less than six months old. The holograms of Mouth Hood and the imprints of the state capitol were close to perfect.

"It's good," Zahn said. "Fake, but good. Why are you sending it to me?" The license showed a young woman with a messy ponytail, silver with purple streaks through her crown. the black glasses were oversized, and the nose and ears were heavily pierced.

"It's Portia Black."

He squinted, raised the magnification on his surgical loupes. The name on the license was Regan Simon. The address was outside of Salem, about an hour south of Portland. Both were printed in black, and the print here didn't hold up.

"You sure?"

"If you don't believe me, run a DNA analysis. There should be some on the license. Definitely some on the knife handle."

Zahn pulled out the knife from the package with a tweezer. It was an orange Home Depot box-cutter with the slide latch, the kind a kid might tuck into the bottom of her backpack just in case.

"What do you want?"

"I heard Miss Black has left the Winter household. Makes it a little harder to keep track of her. I think it's time to turn the screws, Doc."

Zahn shook his head. There were way too many screws already. He swiveled around in his chair. The refrigerators were all in programmed functions, controlled freezing or thawing of tissue samples accurate to the fraction of a degree.

He switched on the infra-red backlights and took a survey of the petri dishes. There was a toe in one, fragments of jawbone in the other. The bottom row was the bread and butter of the operation: pieces of flesh, neatly labelled and arranged like a butcher's cabinet.

"I don't really know what you want."

"I want to keep our girl from getting too comfortable."

"I think she's already-"

"You make bad decisions when you're uncomfortable, Zahn. Remember when you said it was time to throw a bone out there? Maybe you weren't wrong. Give her an idea that she's not getting away this time."

A cryo-cyl with a liquid nitrogen pump sat next to a laboratory Dewar that held most of his specimens at minus one hundred fifty degrees.

"I have a thigh bone."

"Excellent. Have it ready for delivery."

"Who's picking it up?"

"Nobody," Hunter said. "You're doing the drop off."

"You can't be serious."

"Fryman Canyon. I want it there tonight. Make sure it isn't too far out. I don't want the dogs to get too exhausted looking for it. Not like last time."

"I'm not doing it, Hunter. I'm a scientist, not one of your-"

The phone turned off, the screen black and glossy. He could see the reflection of his face. Tired. Beaten down. A seventy five year-old in a fifty five year-old body.

The phone lit up and began to buzz. "What?"

"Are we ready to do our jobs, *Doc*-tor Zahn? Or do I have to remind you who pays the bills around here?"

"I'm not walking around with a backpack of bones in the middle of the day."

"Alright, but not tonight. This evening. Not too late. You get stung by a scorpion or a brown recluse, I don't want your cells anywhere close to our bones."

"I'll be sure to drag my body far away enough so I don't contaminate anything with my DNA."

"Good boy. I knew you'd come around."

The phone clicked again. Zahn threw it across the room, hoping he would hear the screen crack, the plastic pop. Something satisfying. Nothing. Zahn winced. He couldn't even break things right. He looked around the lab, at the trays of bone and gristle nestled in their cool blue and red growth containers.

There was a printout of an itinerary on his desk. American Airlines from San Diego to Juan Santa Maria in Costa Rica. A forty-four sat unloaded on the paper. Zahn sunk his face into his hands. Who was he kidding? A gun? A plane ticket? He was too far in for that. He was way too deep to call the cops either. Even if he turned state, he would still be facing real time.

He scrolled through the list of missed calls. There was one from that private security firm in West L.A.. What was her name? Jacqueline Medina? She had been snooping around when the Kreiner girl had been found. Hunter had found a way to get her off their backs. Now, Zahn realized, she might come in handy.

Zahn went over and picked up his phone.

CHAPTER 24

Guerrero rolled up to the curb and clicked off the safety locks. He turned to me and gave me the thumbs up like a parent at the school drop-off.

I stuck my tongue out at him. "Screw you, Guerrero."

"Boy," Medina said. "Talk about the other side of the tracks." She rolled down the window and wrinkled up her nose. "Smells like someone just plunged the toilet."

Across the street a crackhead was stringing out on a fire escape, screaming and rattling the metal bars like a monkey in a cage.

"Think he's going to start flinging poop?" Guerrero asked. "Because then you're comping me a Delta Sonic. I'm not washing that by hand."

My stomach squeezed, and a gush of acid coated the inside of my throat leaving its hot fingers trailing down my chest. The crackhead was Vincent. I jumped out of the truck, waiting for a moving car to pass.

Medina was staring at me. "You know it would make life a lot easier if you just came back. At least until this all blows over. You'd be a lot safer with Miss Winters."

"And she's not flinging poop either," Guerrero added.

"Not literally."

"I know she might seem a little self-centered, but she really does care about you."

"She owes me. If she could get that monkey off her back, she'd disappear in a second." I got out and stared at her across the half-drawn glass. "And the moment she stops paying you, you'd disappear too."

"Welcome to L.A.." Medina's lips were turned upwards, but the smile was as dark as the window that rolled over it. I could see my face in the black glass as the truck rolled off. I looked like shit. And I felt worse.

The woman behind the counter was pulled up to the window, her nose smearing the glass, leaving a trail of sweat and oil. "Hey, you! You better shut those two up or I'm calling the cops, you hear?"

I was already halfway up the first flight, but I could still hear her voice clawing up the stairwell.

"Knew I didn't like your face, you and your junkie boyfriends. Goddamn freaks."

I stopped halfway up the flight, blinded by a wall of anger. Vincent could wait. The old woman couldn't. I stormed back into the lobby. The glass was bullet-proof, but the door was the old-fashioned single bolt. Despite what the movies would have you believe, the fastest way through a door is through metal, not wood. I slammed the heel of my boot against the faceplate and it sheared off in two pieces, nails and pins clinking and rattling in the lockset.

I was across the room and on the old woman before she could get up. The chair rolled out from under her and spun lazily across the room. Her mouth was an open red doughnut, the lips split and treacly with blood. Her limp frame plopped onto the floor like a margarine out of a tub.

"You have a damn elevator that's not up to code. You have open electrical boxes in the landing. And your exit signs aren't marked. That's three strikes and you're shut so fast, you won't even have time to flush the toilets. Which, by the way, don't work either."

"I- uh-"

"Now take your time and think, God damn it. Think carefully before you answer. Who's staying in room six-eleven?"

"I, uh, no one, I think."

I pulled her up by the collar. She was dangling off the ground, her breath raspy and fetid.

"You think?"

"No one. No one at all."

"What's your policy on dogs?"

"What size?"

I tightened my grip on her collar. I'm small but my forearms are braided like twisted steel.

"We don't have a policy," she wheezed. "Dogs are fine."

I dropped her back into the chair.

"Good." I grabbed the telephone and threw it at her. It struck her in the middle of her forehead. "Now call the damn cops if you want."

I took the stairs three at a time, my breath sharp like paper cuts, as I made it to the sixth floor. The door to the room was wide open and a crowd had gathered. I peeled them away one by one. Like layers of tape, they stuck to each other as they dispersed, still trying to maintain their front row seats. I kicked the last one out and slammed the door shut.

"What the hell is going on, Q?"

"He's crazy!" Quentin said. "He's fucking crazy." His shirt was ripped, and his sunglasses were askew, his breath smelled like licorice. "He tried to kill me."

"He's not crazy. And he didn't try to kill you. If he tried, you'd probably be dead by now."

"You think I didn't try?" Quentin bared both arms, pink and bloody.

Vincent paced the cage like a feral cat looking for an escape. He clanged a broken beer bottle against the bars as he stomped up and down.

"How the hell did he get a bottle of Bud?"

"It's not his. It's mine."

I knew it. "You went on a goddamn beer run? Seriously, Q, I could kill you."

"Me? I'm not the one who left for four hours and expected someone else to babysit."

He had a point there. I pushed him aside and stuck my head out the window. "Vincent, you need to come in. Now."

"I'll jump. I swear, I'll jump," he screamed. "Then I'll be dead, and you did it."

"It's fifty feet down, Vin. Onto an awning. Worst you'll do is break a leg." I switched the stim in the syringe for a downer.

The metal balcony was pinging. It sounded like the screws were pulling out. Vincent clambered onto the sliding ladder and hung there. "I'm not coming in. I won't-" He stopped, his eyes suddenly focused. "Where did you get that?"

I had Jamal's disk out, the sunlight catching fire in the translucent red plastic.

He crept closer, his movements wary and cat-like. When he was in striking distance I grabbed his wrist and stuck him between the radial and ulna.

It took a few minutes but Vincent was finally calm enough to coax into the room. I put him on the bed and covered him with a blanket.

"I need your help, Vin. You know what this is?"

He took it, and turned it over. "It's a lucent key. I haven't seen one of those in years."

"What's it for?"

"Allows you to get into a web directory. Something secure. Like a bl- black directory. You need…"

"Stay awake, Vincent, what do you need?"

"You need an onion browser. And you need a password."

"I don't have the password."

"Neither do I," Vincent said. His eyes blinked, the sedative pulling him deeper into the mattress.

"Great," Quentin muttered. "He's useless. Now can we kick this bum out?"

"You have a password?" Vincent asked drowsily.

"No."

"Then maybe we should kick you out." He popped the drive into his mouth and swallowed.

"What the hell!" Q said. "You crazy mother-"

"It's safe now," Vincent said. "You get me a computer. i5 chip, two-fifty megs, an internet connection. Sixty mbps or more. I can get-get you in." He looked at me. "We need money, too. Bitcoin. Etherium. Digicash."

I turned to Quentin. "You're a dealer, Q. You have a stash somewhere."

"Hell, no. I don't."

"Oh, come on, this isn't the nineties. You don't keep it all bundled up in rubber bands. Or do you want me to call Jamal and ask him?"

Quentin's shoulders dropped. "How much do you need?"

"Five hundred."

"No way."

"I'm not borrowing it, Q." I took the coin out of my pocket and spun it over. "It's an S-VDB. It's worth at least five."

"I know what it is. Jeez, I'm not an idiot." He turned the coin over in his hands. "How many of these do you have?"

"Last one," I lied.

"It'll cover the crypto. How do we pay for the computer? Downloads. Internet connection."

"I know a place that has lots of computers." Vincent voice floated over dreamily. "And they're free."

"And what then?" Quentin asked. "Even if you get a computer. And wi-fi. You still don't have a password."

"You only need a password if you don't know where the trapdoor is."

Quentin crossed his arms over his chest, frustrated. "And you do?"

"I should." Vincent looked at Quentin, then at me. His eyes were pinpoints, blue and dead. "I programmed it," he said. He pulled the covers over his head and disappeared.

CHAPTER 25

The computer section at the Cerritos Walmart was tucked in between the DVDs and the kids toys, a single row of entry-level processors and low-lumen displays. Vincent was on the floor, his knees drawn up, a base model Acer cradled in his lap. The glass locks of the case were strewn across the floor, the glint of their teeth sharp and silver, little crocodiles floating against the patterned vinyl.

"You sure you're allowed to do this?" Quentin asked. It was a stupid question, even for him.

"It's Walmart," Vincent said as he ripped through the plastic wrap with his teeth.

"What the hell does that mean?"

"Means exactly what he said. I worked janitorial at a Wally World in Topeka. Guy came in with an Easter bunny costume on. It was June. Took a pit stop in the middle of housewares. Unzipped his costume and dropped an egg in the Tupperware. And when I say egg, I meant-"

"You're shitting me," Quentin says.

"Shit you not. I lived in a Walmart in Paducah for most of September of sixteen. And I mean *actually* lived in it. There would be junkies shooting up in the stalls, hookers taking their *Johns* into the, well, johns."

"Red light special," Vincent interrupted.

"You know," I said. "Like K-mart has a bluc light special?"

"Yeah, I get it," Quentin said. "Is he done yet?"

Vincent had a finger in the air. The computer was running, the processor whirring and the screen fading colors in and out. He plugged the drive into the USB port. The boot-up process aborted almost immediately, and the screen began rolling line after line of code before it went glass black.

"God damn it!" Quentin said. "You broke it. Let's get out of here before they call the cops."

"You're supposed to be the lookout, Q, so just go."

Quentin slouched back to the head of the aisle, peeking around the metal dividers. Out on the streets he played the OG, walking two steps too slow, chewing on an imaginary toothpick but in here he was pacing up and down, nervous, peeking around the Formica shelves like a little boy asked to be the watch while his dad stuffed dollar mickeys up his sleeve.

A middle-aged woman with two toddlers in tow stopped with a cart loaded with groceries. She stared at Vincent, slouched on the floor in a pile of styrofoam and cardboard.

"Are the DVDs down here?"

"Next aisle," Quentin said gruffly. His shoulders were squared, hands in his pockets. There was something studied about his performance, the street theatre of gangsters working their roles.

"I'm looking for *Snow White.* Or *Cinderella.* Something classic, you know. For my grandkids."

"That's still in the next aisle."

She was persistent, this one. "You know, I hate to be that grandma, the one who just puts the kids in front of the TV. But this wasn't my plan for my golden years, you know? Maybe *Frozen.* You think *Frozen?*"

Quentin finally lost his patience. "You see a blue jacket, biddy?" That was uncalled for. The woman was a grandma, but she was far from old. "I don't work here. Get whatever the hell you want, just get out of here."

Quentin pushed the cart out of the aisle and sent it rolling over to the rack of paperbacks. He sauntered back, and I finally got it.

He was Pacino in *Scarface,* full of braggadocio and neediness. It was the persona every two-bit thug with no real game aimed to imitate. Not Frank

Lucas in *American Gangster*. Or Frank White in *The King of New York*. It was Tony Montana, lisp and slouch and ill-fitting clothes and all. It was all I could do not to beat the crap out of him.

"Goddamn it, Q," I said. "If security wasn't coming over before, they sure are now."

"I don't care. This shit's crazy. Jamal's been running three guys on this for months. Exit node assaults, zero-net monitoring, SQL viruses. They haven't even gotten past the outer firewall. This fool doesn't even have a Tor download. He's never getting into the dark web. Forget about finding a damn trapdoor."

"Done," Vincent said. He got up and stretched. I hadn't had time to shop for him and he was wearing yellow crocs with plaid pajama drawstrings that fit precariously around his bony hips.

"You said I could get candy." I handed him a couple of crumpled bills and watched him amble off to the checkout.

"Jeez," Q muttered. "Don't do drugs, kids."

"Yeah," I replied. "Just sell it to them."

"You never let it go, do you?" He stomped off down the aisle. "Just find what you need and let's get out of here."

I stared at the screen, dark and forbidding as a black pool of water. Vincent once described the web as a city. You walked on its streets, looked up at the shiny buildings, bought products from the pretty stores. Every once in a while, you could step down into the subway, full of its rancid smells and awkward tastes and think you've seen it all.

You haven't. There was way more under that first layer of the onion than you'd imagine. Power grids. Gas lines. Water. Utility tunnels. Places no one wanted to go. And below that, Vincent always said, flowed a river of shit.

I was knee-deep in it now and about to go wading. The friendly marketers peddling purified ecstasy and grade coke were behind me. The pages ahead were drab and utilitarian. The promises were not.

A cooking website listed epicurean recipes made with human flesh. The reviewer recommended an adolescent male, describing the meat as tart but tender. Veal but with more acid, and especially suited for grilling.

Another poster had stocks of weaponized Marburg virus obtained from a nineties era *Biopreparat* laboratory. Marbug, he or she patiently explained, was a little town in Germany near Frankfurt where Grivet monkeys imported from Lake Victoria in Tanzania first transmitted a filoviridae pathogen to their human caretakers. Following this little tidbit, the poster explained that the virus caused a hemorrhagic fever much like Ebola and similar outcomes could be expected on dissemination.

Beyond these outliers, it was the darknet staples that were the big sellers. I clicked through the site, past the pedophilia, bondage, torture, and automatic weapons and went straight to the hardcore synth-drugs.

The listings were alphabetical. My heart sunk. There were none under B. *Belladonna.*

"Can I help you?" A bespectacled young man with a pointed beard and large grommet-like earrings stood at the end of the aisle. He wore a blue Walmart vest that hung limply over his narrow shoulders.

"Yeah, does this run DOS?" Vincent stood behind him, his mouth rolling with nerds like clothes tossed in a washing machine. He had a supersize Pixy-stix and a double pack of Gobstoppers under his arms.

I hit *G. Grable.* No entries.

"What's DOS?"

"You know. Eighty-six DOS? QDOS? Quick and dirty operating system. Like CPM 86 but built for an eighty-eight Intel micro?"

H. Hayworth. Nothing.

R. Russell. Still nothing.

The man stared at the cardboard and packing on the floor. "I don't know what the heck it runs. I just know you can't-" His eyes drifted to the lockset in pieces on the floor. "Did you just open this? Did you break into the case?"

He pulled the radio off his belt loop and waved it like a gun. Vincent shuffled off, a trail of pixy dust behind him.

"Hey you! You wait right here!" He pointed a finger at me. "And you put that back right now."

He looked like the typical Walmart employee, a little too smart for this job but not quite ready for a regular nine-to-five grind.

"You got bigger problems than that, buddy." I pointed at the head of the aisle. Vincent was by the floatie cage, untying his pants. The waistband dropped all the way to his ankles and he started working on the underwear, zigging it down on the left, zagging it down on the right.

I had to buy him the Pokémon briefs because he wouldn't fit into the adult sizes, and I could see yellow hamster-like creatures on his cheek wiggle as he climbed up the metal enclosure. He was finally at the top, peering into the cage.

I turned back to the computer and scrolled through the listings. I was running out of time and options. I looked at Vincent hanging off the cage and it suddenly came to me. *McDonald.* I clicked the M. Nothing.

I looked at Vincent. What had he said? McDonald wasn't her birth name. He had called her something else. *Cora Marie.* Think, goddamn it. *Cora Marie what?*

I hit *F. Frye.* The screen went blank, then reloaded. A single listing. I clicked the wallet and watched the bar timer creep. The employee was still screaming in the background, tugging at Vincent's ankle, calling for help all at the same time.

"Get off, asshole, get… yes, it's an emergency, in the toy section… the guy's pissing in the pool toys… get the hell off…"

The man finally had a hold of Vin and they tumbled to the ground. Quentin scrambled around the aisle, his eyes blazing. "What the hell's going on? What is he doing?"

"Buying me time." I snapped the case closed and pulled out the disk. We ran across the breadth of the store, down to the grocery exit. The old-man greeter made only the faintest attempt to slow us down.

The warning on the loudspeaker went off and a stream of security and managers were hoofing it toward the toy-section. Almost in response there were dozens of people flying out of the doors with unpaid rolls of toilet paper and AA batteries under their arms.

"What about freakshow?" Quentin huffed as we sprinted down the parking lot to the van.

"Don't worry about Vincent," I said. I had known the kid for eight, maybe nine years, and he was about as slippery as a fish in a tank.

I revved the van and laid on the horn, weaving through a throng of pedestrians. I clipped one dragging a fifty-inch flatscreen on a baby carriage. We were past the service exit, then the main entrance.

Vincent screamed out of the garden exit on cue, his pants still half-up, six or seven employees on the chase. Q slid open the door and he rolled in. I jammed on the accelerator, and we peeled out of the parking lot like a bank robbery gone very wrong.

"Well, that was a disaster," Quentin said. "What the hell did you think you were doing?"

"You can't spell pool without a little pee." Vincent laughed hysterically.

"Your brains are fried, you know that? I'm going to come back there and kick the pee out of you."

"Relax, Q, I told you. He was just buying me some time."

"Time for what? It's the deep web. There's no customer service, no live chat assistance. It's not like you can ask for an address. Or a phone number."

"No, you can't," I said. "But you can place an order."

"And every order can be tracked," Vincent said.

I took the turn onto La Cienega. There were no cars following us, no sirens nor flashers in the distance. The pain in my jaw had finally simmered down.

I had just begun to feel better when the phone started to buzz.

CHAPTER 26

Zahn pulled up onto the dirt embankment at the point. A large sign prohibited use after six p.m., but there were two other cars parked in the corners, windows thick with steam. Zahn grinned. They were going nowhere anytime soon.

He always found it strange that a popular lovers' lane would be perched off such a morbid sounding stretch of road, but the area of Mulholland Drive, known locally as Dead Man's Curve, was a ninety degree, almost hairpin above the Fryman Canyon that had claimed more than its share of automobiles and virginities.

Zahn opened his trunk, unclasped the cooler, and pulled out the package wrapped in a double thickness of butcher paper. He peeled the sheets apart and stared at the contents. There was a set of bones approximately the size and shape of a complete fibula and tibia and a shattered femur with fragments of cortex.

The latter was courtesy of a ball-pein hammer and a toss around with one of Hunter's pit-bulls. The result was an approximation of a corpse torn up in the wild, pulled apart by coyotes, perhaps a bobcat, the meat stripped, the bones chewed into and scored by sharp teeth.

Zahn couldn't imagine the medical examiner would think any different. A ziplocked cutter sat underneath, open and crusted with dried blood, a melding of two different blood types, an O-positive and a

B-negative. The driver's license was tucked in with some moldy bills into a worn billfold.

Zahn tucked the packages into his jacket and zipped up. He found his way down the winding path that made its way into the canyon, past the creeping foliage that clung to the steep slope. He was aware that there were rattlers in the underbrush as well as other unsavory critters and he had worn a double set of copper-lined socks and a pair of heavy, shin-high work boots.

He wore insulated gloves to push aside the sharp branches, but also to prevent any chance of DNA transfer. Like most of his workwear, the gloves were incinerated on a regular basis to prevent cross-contamination.

At the very bottom was a hulk of rusting metal, a car lying on its back like a dead beetle, its undercarriage split open by its sudden descent down the slope, a spray of green moss and shrubs regurgitating from its belly. Zahn put his flashlight down and turned on his phone.

"You're five hundred feet off," Hunter said.

"The undergrowth is too dense. I'm here to drop off a body, not join it." He looked up the slope at a car's low beams, shattered and glassy in the mist. "Besides, it's not where it would land when dropped; it's where the bones would be taken by a scavenger."

"Fine. But if some animal gets to it before the police do, you're the one pulling all-nighters to get me new bone. And tissue."

"I've got a safe place for her." Zahn peered into the rusting hulk of the car. He clicked off the phone, clambered over the doorframe, and dropped through the rotten vinyl.

A milk thistle grew out from the floor, its sharp flowers grabbing and tearing at Zahn's sleeves. Zahn unwrapped the package and scattered the bones. He clambered out and trailed his way twenty feet back and dropped the knife and license under the brush.

In the distance, a coyote whined. Zahn gathered his kit and hurried back up to his car.

Chapter 27

I spent the rest of the evening pacing the room, watching the neon lights flicker and burn on the boulevard. The tourists started to flood out at sundown, and that was when the squabbles started, petty tiffs over tips; knock-down, drag-out fights over drugs or sex. By the time the cops got there, the instigators were long gone, broken bottles and the occasional tooth in a puddle the only remnants of the crime.

The flashing cherries and berries on the street kept Vincent entranced at the window like a child at a candy counter. Quentin dozed in the armchair while I sat on the bed replaying the new video.

The screen on the flip phone was only three by five, a midget by today's standards, and the blurriness in the corners kept much of the room obscure. There was one man in this video, large and hairy. He was wearing a plastic bib over his shoulders but nothing around his waist, and his genitals were excited. His face was blurred, but the knife was not.

The girl was blanched and blue, like she'd been bled out slowly. I saw the drugs in her eyes, keeping her compliant but awake. The torture was over. There was little else that could be done without tearing her apart enough to be rendered useless.

I turned off the phone and fell into a dark, dreamless sleep, Dog's head on my lap, the phone on my chest, dreading the next buzz.

I woke with the sound of a crashing garbage truck. Through glued eyes I saw the alarm clock blinking.

"Is it really nine?"

Vincent sat on the edge of the bed, his ankles crossing and uncrossing as they swung in lazy arcs. He hadn't slept. In his lap he held a brown carboard box, his fingers running across its edges like he was petting a cat. Dog paced around him, sniffing at the seal.

"Where's Q?"

"Gone." He tapped the box. "It came in this morning. Can I?" He ripped through the packing tape and dipped his hands in, churning through the packing peanuts. He pulled out a glass jar and placed it onto the table.

The wrapping label was understated, no oversized lettering, anthropomorphic nuts, nor animated characters embracing the label. Carissa's Best. It had a homemade, granola-mom feel to it, perhaps a whole group of moms who started out with the aim of sponsoring the local travel soccer team and hit it big.

The label was imprinted with the words *all-natural* and *organic* ringing the paper in alternating sequence.

"That's what you got?" Quentin was at the door, a forty ounce of Silver Thunder in his grip. "Fucking Skippy?" He was laughing out loud, malt liquor foaming at his lips.

"Sniffers."

"What?"

"The smell," Vincent said. "It's for dogs. Right?"

Dog bobbed up and down, her snout trying to find the closest access to the table.

Vincent unscrewed the cap, stuck his finger in and swirled it around. It popped back out, covered in peanut butter. He stuck it at Quentin. "Want a try?"

"Hell no, get that shit out of my face."

"Suit yourself." He scooped the butter out on the table. In the middle of the cream was a small plastic tube, the size of a triple-A battery. I scraped the transparent coating with a knife until I could see the gel bleed through the score and popped it into the microwave.

Quentin watched the tube rotate on the plate. "How do we know it works?"

"There's one way." I popped open the door, shoved Quentin's head in and slammed the door back down. He was pinned like a fighter wrestled into submission, the microwave door a headlock he couldn't get free from. His face bulged, turned red, then blue.

"Cherries and berries," Vincent squealed.

I pulled him back out, slammed the door closed, and straightened him up. Vincent had the flashlight in his eyes. "That's good, Q. You did good."

"Bitch," he muttered.

"You're okay, Q."

He took a step forward, his expression angry, then confused. We grabbed him by the arms and frog marched him down to the easy chair.

"You bitch." His mouth struggled to form the words.

"Easy, boy." Vincent pushed the cushions up under his neck.

"You're good, Q, you'll be fine. You won't remember any of this to-morrow."

"Like hell I won't, like hell…" His eyes were glazed over, his words slurred.

Vincent looked up. "It's the real stuff." He reached in for the patch, moving it with the fork. "That's how he got you?"

"Stop touching it, Vin."

"It's not hot anymore."

"You get it on your hands, it'll absorb. I need you awake."

"Okay." Vincent shut the microwave door and ambled over to the table. He flipped over the box. There was a white UPS label affixed to the cardboard.

"What do we do now?"

"QR code it. We can track the delivery signature back to the origina-tion stamp." He picked up the phone and snapped a picture of the code. "Looks like it came from…" His eyes went wide. "Wait, what is this video?"

"Leave that alone, Vincent. Just find the delivery address."

"UPS store." The reverse tracking showed the location and date stamp. Clinton Drive. Barstow. 2:00 p.m.

"What time did we leave Wally World? About eleven?"

"He's quick." Vincent dropped down onto the bed and twirled his finger in the jar.

"Which would make it easier for us, I guess."

"You been to Barstow?"

"Just passing through. You?"

"We were somewhere around Barstow on the edge of the desert when the drugs began to take hold." Vincent stopped. "You okay?" he asked. "You need a dentist."

I was holding my jaw. The pain was back, like a knife up my jaw. I could feel the heat leach out into my palms, red and virulent. "We don't have time for that."

"We have time," Vincent said. He nodded at Q. "And we have money."

"I'm not stealing from a guy I just doped."

"Then borrow it. A loan."

"No."

"We have to test it. I mean, if it's a lucid drug, you know? How do we know if we haven't tested it?"

The pain had burrowed into my shoulder now, nesting in the little cove under my collar bone.

"Okay," I said. "But only as a test."

Vincent grinned. He slipped Quentin's wallet out. "Hey Q, what's your ATM pin?"

CHAPTER 28

He hovered over me, humorless eyes magnified by the thick plate-glass lenses. The eyes were a weathered blue, the iris sliced in thick, uneven chunks, like a ripped sail. He held a curved instrument in his hand, its point sharp and wicked, glinting in the florescent overhead lights.

His pupils constricted as he came in closer, his face just inches from mine. It was all I could do not to squirm. I've been held hostage by a man on plenty of occasions but never by choice.

"Am I making you uncomfortable?" he asked.

"Anyone actually says no to that?"

"Yes, quite a few."

"They're lying." The instrument he was wielding found the worst spot, and an electric shock lashed across to the corner of my lip. The ache burrowing under my jaw squirmed its way out and crawled up into my ear. "Jeez, whatever it is, you found it."

"I'm sorry." Doctor Harmon pulled back, laid his instruments on the table, and turned the light off. He did sound genuinely sorry and, strangely enough, that made the pain a little more tolerable.

He was pushing sixty, gray-haired, with the scalloped balding pattern that left enough hair in the center to feather up and over like a comb. The hair flopped back and forth as he talked, and I could see the brown age spots that gathered underneath.

I'd been a regular at the dentist till seven and never needed more than the occasional cleaning before or since. Then I went into foster care and was introduced to the glories of fraudulent Medicaid claims and parent kickbacks. Three years. Twelve cavities, four stainless crowns. The whine of a high-speed handpiece still raised the hair on my neck. I've always been grateful I'd skipped town before my permanents came in.

"Your teeth, young lady," Doctor Harmon said, "are perfect. Your extraction site, however, not so much."

"Extraction site?"

"Yep, the third molar on your bottom right side-"

"What extraction?"

"Number thirty-two was extracted, looks like a couple of days ago? Number thirty-two, Universal, not FDI. That would be that wisdom tooth." He tapped my cheek where the dull throb still danced up to my lip and back. "You've developed alveolar osteitis. A dry socket."

"That can't be."

"It isn't that uncommon. Especially in mandibular molar areas where a significant amount of trauma has occurred."

"No. I mean, it *can't* be. I've never had an extraction."

Doctor Harmon nodded at his assistant. She turned on the computer mounted on the handle and traced the cursor along the screen, behind the white squiggly blocks of teeth to the black dip in the bone.

"That's a bony crypt. There's a wisdom tooth sleeping on the other side. But this one's gone. See how the crest dips as it's healing? Most of the time the socket fills with blood that forms a clot. Osteoblasts, bone cells, migrate in and form new bone on that clot scaffold. Sometimes the clot breaks down and now you have exposed bone. Very painful exposed bone, I might add. The symptoms and timeline are pretty consistent with what you're presenting with."

"I've never had an extraction. Ever. I definitely didn't have one in the last couple of weeks."

Doctor Harmon rolled back in his chair, his gloved hands up defensively. "I'm sure you'd know if you did. But the scan is pretty convincing.

Look, I could send you for a second opinion, to an oral surgeon. Maybe to a maxillofacial radiologist. But you'd be wasting your money. It's healing, and you've been through the worst of it. Painkillers as needed, some irrigation, a little packing, and you'll be good as gold. Pity though about the banking."

"What banking?"

"We like to bank primordial crypt tissue. Amazing stuff. Like a second shot at cord blood. But you can get more than just blood cells. Bone, tissue, cartilage. There's some research showing how you can nudge these cells into totipotentiality."

"Dr. Harmon," the assistant admonished him, "I don't think she speaks dental."

Harmon chuckled loudly. "Oh yeah, right. *Toti*, like everything. Potentiality, like, well you get it, right? We can take a cell and create other cells of any type. Someday you'll get into an accident, need surgery, treatment for cancer and they'll piece you back together with a tooth that's still sleeping in your mouth."

"What kind of body parts can they make?"

"Practically anything. They're making scleral tissue from DPSCs; that's dental pulp stem cells. Gingival mesenchymal stem cells are being used for brain neurons. A classmate of mine, Artie Zahn, does some crazy stuff with just a few cells.

"A finger?"

"Yeah." He looked at me quizzically. "Sure. I mean, you would have to scaffold and grow the phalanges. But then you have the framework to seed any kind of tissue, connective tissue, muscle, skin. I think it could be done."

"How do I get in touch with him?"

"He doesn't see patients if that's what you're asking. But next time I see him I could pass along a question or two if you have something specific."

I paused, thinking. "No, that's fine."

"Okay," Dr. Harmon said. "Lie back, open wide, you know the drill." He laughed.

Dental humor. It's terrible. Like the plaque on his operatory: *Dentists make great impressions.* Or the one that says: *You don't have to floss all your teeth. Just the ones you want to keep.*

"Time to get you numb. Margie, can you get me a carp of Articaine and some Alvogyl? Let's get that socket packed and get you going."

The Suburban was idling across the street, the windows tinted as black as the powdered rims. It was wedged in between a beaten-up Geo Metro and a rust-stained Sienna minivan.

"If you're trying to blend in, it's not working."

"Get in," Medina said.

"Uh-uh. I got my own team."

She pulled off her sunglasses and squinted. "A dealer and an addict. Both with extensive criminal histories. Not the team you want to be assembling. Especially after that, well, I don't know what the hell that was at Walmart yesterday."

"Boy, you're spending a lot of time on me."

"I don't get paid the big bucks not to know what's going on."

"Well, you don't know much. You certainly don't know *them.*"

"Krysinski, Vincent Valerian. Twenty-six. Born in Brooklyn. Nice parents. Don't speak a word of English. They were proud as hell when he got a full ride to Mellon. Could have been a Silicon Valley superstar if he hadn't started shooting up. Now he lives in a box and gets paid for sex. Supplements his lifestyle by writing lucent code for deep web developers. I mean seriously deep web. Calls himself a crypto-anarchist. He has a Pandora's Box of STDs, chief of which is untreated HIV which, of course, matters little because his speedball habit is probably going to kill him first."

"Thanks for the Wikipedia page."

"Your other friend. Quentin Michaels. AKA San Quentin. Born and raised in Long Beach. Woodrow Wilson High School valedictorian. Pretty decent ball player too. Not pro-good, but enough talent to see him into a decent college on scholarship and enough brains to see him graduate early. People said he was a good kid, got into trouble with a senior prank that involved stealing a rival high school's mascot."

"A goat," Guerrero said.

"A goat, yes. Stole it and released it in the Bruins locker room. Got him kicked off graduation ceremonies. But no charges. He stayed out of trouble for pretty much the rest of his time. Could have gone to college, broken the cycle, as they say. Yet he chose to stay in the hood, get arrested, and become a statistic."

"What about me? What kind of statistic do I turn up as?"

Medina opened the door. "Who said you were a statistic? I'm trying to make sure you don't become one. Come on, get in. I hate talking through a window."

I slipped in. "Do you get paid full time while you're idling or is it a half rate?"

"It's not a cab service."

"I forgot," I said. "You're investigators. So, tell me, what did you find out?"

"You first."

"Get lost, Medina." I turned and pulled the door latch. "I'm not here to do your job for you."

"Nathan Hunter's parents are both dead," she said quickly.

I turned back. "Keep going."

"He has one sibling, a younger sister, Marcia. Only family member as far as we can tell. I'm assuming they're close."

I paused for a moment. "Like, let you borrow the car and light it up in the desert close?"

"Imagine your only brother is missing, possibly dead. No trace, no leads. Your car, the one your brother's been driving, turns up totaled in the desert. What's your move? I mean, really, your worst possible move?"

I ruminated over the words. Worst possible move was something I was well acquainted with. "Punch out the only suspect?"

I saw Guerrero smile in the rear view.

Medina jerked a finger at him. "That's what he said. No, that's forgivable. But, obviously, it hasn't happened. Yet."

I winced.

"But I'm talking *real* bad. Casey Anthony bad."

"Throw a party. Turn up at a strip club. Get drunk in a bar?"

"How about going on vacation?" Medina tapped the end of her nose. She passed over a photograph, a telephoto black and white of a young blonde with dramatic highlights. At that distance she could pass for Steph.

"Where was this taken?"

"Plaza Coronado."

"Tijuana? Isn't it a warzone?"

"HQ of the Arellano-Felix cartel. There's been seventeen hundred murders this year at last count."

"I thought the Felix brothers were in jail."

"That's the problem, really. There are some remnants of the original Tijuana cartel, but most of them banded together with the Beltran Leyva brothers. Other joined forces with some of the Zetas factions to stop the Sinaloans from moving back in. Since then it's been mayhem. Kidnappings have gone through the roof."

"Not the best place to sip a margarita on the beach."

"No." Medina said. "But it might be the perfect place to pay a ransom."

Ransom, I thought. I'd just been demoted from manslaughter to kidnapping. I wasn't sure why I didn't feel better.

"So how about asking her?"

"Wish I could. But until I can, this is good news, right? I mean, there's been no ransom note that we know of. But it's quite possible that the terms were such that she's refused to report it. Or…"

"Or what?"

"Or maybe this isn't ransom at all. Either way, don't get any ideas. You try to cross the border, they'll put you into the slammer so fast."

"I know, they told me, don't cross state lines."

"I wouldn't cross county lines either."

"What do you mean?"

"You haven't heard?" Medina turned to Guerrero. He put an iPad on the console and swiped to the day's edition of the *L.A. Times*. In the corner of the third page was a half-column, likely added just prior to print cut-off. *Human remains found at Canyon Drive.*

"So what?" I shrugged. "That's the preferred dumping ground for every two-bit serial killer in-"

"I just got an interesting call. There was a driver's license found nearby. The name was Reagan Simons."

"Who tipped you off?"

"It was anonymous."

"Anonymous tip," I scoffed. "Either you won't tell me or it's bullshit."

"Could be. Except it came with a couple of pictures." She swiped a finger across the screen. "Recognize this knife? Looks like one of yours? It's got blood on it. It would be a shame if they put it into the system, got a cold hit."

"Not likely-"

"And this license? Regan Simon? They can match it to your intake records."

"I was booked as Mackenzie Bricker. Twenty-five. Straight shoulder length black hair. Mixed race. Regan Simons is white. Twenty-two. Got a confused punk-goth thing going on."

"They'll tie the two together eventually. That's a start. Then they'll have biometric software that will out the rest of your identities. And one other thing my source told me. There was a piece of bone found. It had your cells on it but the bone itself? The bone belonged to someone else. You can fudge a lot of things, Portia, but you can't fudge DNA."

"You know something Medina?" I got out the door and scowled at her. "Just when I think you know what you're doing, you go and say something stupid like that."

I turned and stomped off. In the middle of the street, I heard her voice trailing behind me.

"Hey, Portia," she called. "Fudged or not, the bone fragments we found? We have a name. You want to know?"

I stopped, turned slowly.

"Shawna Cole," she said. The black window rolled up and the truck pulled out.

Chapter 29

We sat outside the UPS store in Barstow for almost five hours, Vincent lounging in the back among the piles of books. He'd read eleven by noon, flipping pages like he was shuffling a deck of cards, then turned his attention to the jar of peanut butter, twirling large gobs into his mouth and licking his fingers clean one by one.

"You're going to be sick. You're not going to eat that all, are you?"

"You want some?

I wrinkled my nose at him. "Now I think *I'm* going to be sick."

"Girls," he said. "Swap spit with a guy you never met. Then won't take a bite from my finger."

"I didn't swap spit with anyone."

"Wouldn't be-be here if you hadn't"

"Shut up, Vin. God, you're worse than Quentin."

"Fine," he said. He turned and proffered the container to Dog.

"Jeez, that's even worse, Vin."

Vincent raised his hand sharply. A grey, powder-coated Jeep pulled in at an angle, straddling two parking spots. A boy hopped out and left the engine running.

"That him?" Vincent asked.

"Hard to say," I said. "He doesn't look very darknet."

The boy circled the Jeep, reached across the passenger's scat, and piled three small brown boxes under each arm.

"Guess we're about to find out."

I crossed the road, swung the double doors open and cut in to the desk. I saw the boy on his phone, fourth in line, the boxes on the counter as he scrolled thorough his phone.

"Hey," an older lady said, "there's a line here, kid."

I ignored her and shoved my way to the balding man who manned the desk. He was at the scanner, measuring packages and he barely looked up. "She's right," he said, "there's a line. In case you didn't notice."

"You know the guy who comes here selling the nut butters?"

"Line," he said, pointing. He was leaning forward trying to get his wand over an oversized box, and at this angle I was concerned that too much leverage might break something; the bridge of his nose, the malar process. Grab him too fast, too hard and I could shatter his orbit.

I did it anyway, pulling him by the collar and twisting his head down sideways so his head popped off the counter with barely any contact. Perfection. I pressed him down.

"The nut butters," I repeated. "Were supposed to be almond. It was peanut. I'm allergic to peanut." I was ad-libbing here, but I was just trying to repeat the word nut as many times as I could. It had the desired effect. The boy pulled his boxes closer and took a step back toward the door.

"You know what a nut allergy can do to you? A bad one? Anaphylaxis. Know what that means? It closes up your throat so you can't breathe. Then you go into cardiac arrest. Your brain cells start dying. If you don't get a shot of adrenaline you're looking at fifteen minutes. If you're lucky."

The door swung wide and the boy was out, diving for his Jeep. I missed the handle by seconds as he peeled out of the parking lot. My van pulled to halt beside me, the sliding door gaping. Vincent was behind the wheel, his eyes blazing.

This could only end badly, I told myself, but I was vaulting into the back seat and we were screeching down Rimrock toward the Mojave Freeway. The Jeep skipped the ramp, took a hard right and barreled its way out onto the open road that ran straight into the desert.

Bad move, I thought. My van only looked like junk. I'd saved money on the baubles and put it where it meant something. The engine had been recently upgraded and I could take on anything without a supercharger. After five minutes at a hundred miles an hour, the desert run became a crawl.

The Jeep sat in the brush where the pavement bloated above the culvert. It was parked awkwardly, the extra wide tires clawing at the dirt as the hood leant into the embankment. A body hung over the railing, dumping the contents of the boxes into the dry marsh.

Vincent was out and running before I could get out. Dog tore past him, tackling the kid as he threw the last box over. Vincent grabbed him by the ankles and had him upended him over the rail bars. The kid was in danger of dropping on his neck twenty feet below. I knew Vincent was junkie strong, but it still amazed me how much leverage a hundred-pound body could manage.

"Vin, goddamnit, what the hell are you doing?"

"Interrogating him."

"*Interrogate*, Vincent. Not Suge Knight him." I pulled the boy back over and dropped him on the pavement. He cowered against the railing, his eyes beet-red. "You want to tell us something, kid?"

"I'll tell you, goddamnit man, I'll tell you. Just get this freak away from me."

Vincent threw his hands into the air, and walked toward the car. He passed it, kept going.

"Vin, where the hell are you going?"

I looked up and down the road. There was a single black truck approaching from the North, black fender glinting in the reflection from the asphalt. I had to make this quick.

"Who runs it?"

"Runs what?"

I grabbed his phone. It had been opened recently and the screen hadn't yet locked. It was open to the keyboard, like he was trying to make a call. I swiped through recent numbers. "You better start talking. Or you want me to start making some calls?"

"Look, I don't know who runs it. I just deliver. Someone else sets up the game. The systems. The software. The product gets dropped off. I get a cut of what I sell. It's like any business."

"Except it's drugs."

"That's all I'd get involved with."

"What do you mean all? What else is he running?" I stopped. The boy had said *game*. "It's not about the drugs, is it? It's about the girls." I shoved my phone into his face. "Girls like this?"

"Shit," he said. "I told you I don't get involved with-"

"But you knew it was happening." I pulled up a picture of Hunter. "This the guy?"

"No, man. That's not him. He's..." He was looking past me, but I didn't need to turn. I could hear the tires cut into the pavement, spitting gravel all around.

"What? What is he?"

"Let him go," Medina said.

"They've got her. The girl."

"Relax, Portia. It's not real. Let him go."

I released hold and the boy scrambled back to his Jeep. The spray of dirt was wide and red as he fishtailed back onto the road.

"Damn you, Medina. Let me do what I do."

"I know what you do. But this isn't it. You're blinded because you're sitting in a well. It's not real. None of it's real." Medina stuck her forefinger and thumb in my face, a fraction of an inch apart. "And you're this close to screwing it all up. Leave it to a professional."

"Professional? A professional would have known that Marcia Hunter transferred a half-million dollars to Schroder Cayman in Georgetown. I'm talking United States dollars. Greenbacks. The money sat there for a few months, but two weeks ago half of it was withdrawn and transferred to and outfit called *Estructura Azteca* in Rosarito."

"How did you find-"

I nodded at Vincent's receding figure. "I have someone who actually knows his way around a computer. Anyway, that's not the point.

We're sitting the largest exit point on the western drug corridor. Walking right in through the door. Brugmansia comes up with the cocaine from Colombia. It lands at Lazaro Cardenas or Acapulco, the Michaocans send it up the coast to Culiacan. Then the Sinaloans take over, truck it to Mexicali or Tijuana, pack it into the seat cushions, and drive it right thorough the border."

"Portia, I know where the drug corridors are."

"Why would anyone treat Belladonna here? Bring the Brugmansia up to Mexico. Powder it, and chemically treat it over there. Then you can export it as pharmaceutical product with no oversight. No FDA. No DEA. No state board reviews. Know why you can't find a trace of Hunter's pharmaceutical dealings here?"

"Because he doesn't have any?"

"Because he knew he couldn't get what he wanted here. So, he threw in the towel, poured the money into loss leaders like his clubs. Once the money was clean, he could funnel it straight out to the Caymans. Now he gets to start-up without anyone even looking at him. Vincent!"

I pushed her off and stormed back to the van. I could see his figure blurry in the blazing sun. He was already halfway to town.

"Portia! Don't do anything stupid," Medina called.

Her voice was lost in the squealing of tires as I screeched across the road to the opposing side. My phone was blinking on the car seat. It was another picture. The girl had a red satin belt around her neck. There was a large, serrated knife on the table next to her. In the corner, through the window, I could see the reflection of a face. And I knew exactly who it was.

CHAPTER 30

Marcus spun the phone back across the table and rubbed his eyes wearily.

"Well?" I asked.

"Should've shown me this shit after breakfast." He pushed his plate of steaming eggs and hash browns to the side.

"Seriously? This is sin city. This doesn't happen every day?"

He looked out of the window, the deep furrows in his face accentuated by the golden tint of the glass. In the reflection, he was a tired sixty-something man, one beaten down by an average life. An accountant, an insurance salesman perhaps, someone with a comfortable lifestyle but no excitement. The reflection was wrong. There hadn't been a hit, a kidnapping, an old-fashioned rough-up or shake-down in Vegas that Marcus hadn't had a hand in. More often than not, it was two hands wrapped around some unfortunate's neck.

"I'm sick of this shit," he said. "It's the advertising, isn't it? These people come to my town and think it's a free for all. Like they can take a shit on the lawn without asking permission first." The image of defecation in the open caused me to lose my appetite just as his returned. He dug into the plate, packing away the scrambled eggs in three bites. His mouth was mealy and yellow as he spoke. "You know, I've seen some pretty fucked up stuff. When I first came here there were nurses in a hospital placing bets on the next patient to die. I mean, this is a gambling town but-"

"That's messed up."

"Gets worse. One day one of them got the bright idea of stacking the odds in her favor." He picked up the pepper for a third time and dunked it over the plate. "Look, this whole damn town was a gamble. It still is. And when you're gambling, you win some, you lose some. Sometimes it's luck, sometimes you make your luck. Vegas is a stacked win. Against all odds. It's a fucking meadow in the middle of a desert. That doesn't just happen. It happens because someone cleans shit up before it stinks."

"So you'll help me?"

"No." He doused his hash browns with salt and ketchup. His second order received the same treatment, and he stacked them carefully like a rustic Napoleon. This was the kind of man who expected to die from a coil of piano wire, not the narrowed lumen of an artery.

"Why not?"

"Because this isn't the old days. This kind of shit?" He pointed at the phone. "It isn't costing the casinos a dime. And if they don't see as much as a nickel rolling out of the door, they don't care. You're better off filing a report at Metro."

"You know I can't do that."

"I know," he said. "But I can. Anonymously, of course." He took a sorrowful look at his left-over hash browns before he slid out. "I'll see that it gets to the right hands. It was good to see you again, Portia. I really mean it. Breakfast is on me."

I watched him pull himself out of the booth, his arms wide, pushup style. He was older, maybe slower but the hands that gripped the tabletop still could probably rip it in half.

"Hey, Marcus. Remember Melissa Crawford?"

He stopped mid-turn, his shoulders slumping, his polyester suit sticking to the vinyl like a conscience.

"Ashley Thompson. How about Blaze-"

"Stop!" He dropped back into the booth. "Just…" He placed a thumb on his lip, trying to stop it from trembling. "Just stop. God, you're a pest, you know. I should never have come."

"You know they stiffed me."

"Nobody stiffed you. The casinos said they would pay if you found them alive."

"I did."

"Portia, what you found was barely still human, let alone alive."

This time I was wincing. The girls had been found ripped up in an abandoned home in the Sun City district. Trailing out into the yard were multiple sets of dog prints. "If the cops hadn't dropped word on the street it wouldn't have happened. But somebody leaked info, and somebody got scared and shit happened." By shit, I meant the dogs. Two local pitbull mixes were found shot in another abandoned house. The little one had two toes in her intestines.

"Look, I know what you do," Marcus said. "And you do it well. But this? This isn't your thing. Let the cops handle it, huh?"

"God, you sound like someone I know." I dropped a set of photographs onto the table. They were a mix of casual pics and professional shots. Melissa was the redhead with the baby face and impish smile.

"Remember her? She bartended at the Irish pub at New York, New York. Tried out for the stage show at the Luxor. They said she was too pale. Breasts were too small." I shuffled through the pictures. Ashley was darker skinned, prettier, with full lips and a pouty smile.

"You knew her too. Hostess at the Mirage. Same casino. Same show. Breasts were too big. So was her butt. God, this town is picky. You think five hundred drunks packed into a sweaty auditorium would care?" There was a promo pic of both of them under the Vegas sign, dressed in sequins and feathers.

"Know how we told them apart after? One was a redhead. The other, brunette. The pathologist told me. That was the only way. But he had to wash the blood out of the hair first to be sure. And they probably thought Hollywood was the boulevard of broken dreams."

"Paris," he said. He gathered up the pictures and flipped them over so he wouldn't be reminded. He pulled a sleeve of Rolaids from his pocket and popped three at a time.

"The casino?" A whiplash of hope burned.

"No, the city. The boulevard of broken dreams was Paris-"

I cut him off. "I know. Sidney Lanfield. *Moulin Rouge.* How about this? You find me the room. And give me a head start. Then you call the cops."

"Jesus, Portia, you're killing me."

"Yeah, Marcus." I flipped the photos back up again. "You're never the one getting killed."

Marcus looked up. "Okay, let's go ask Edgar. If he says no then I'm going home and you're going…" He paused. "Wherever you go when you're not being a pain in my butt."

CHAPTER 31

"Is she serious?"

We were in a dingy second floor office above the Grand Bazaar shops, behind a sign on the door that said A&M Storage. The rooms were piled high with discarded electronics, mostly late eighties and early nineties vintage. He urged us to sit but there were no chairs, except for the one in front of the rickety computer desk where he was lounging. I found a cracked oversized Peavy and made it my chair. Marcus, likewise, found another dilapidated piece of equipment much too small for his ample girth, and settled gingerly onto it.

"I think she *is* serious," Marcus said.

Edgar Alvares flipped through the images on my phone. "Holy shit!" His fingers were long and spidery, the knuckles thickened and protruding. The fingernails which were not bitten down were sharp, like little screwdrivers. He seemed like someone who should be repairing clocks or vintage stereo systems. In the corner of the window, behind the drapes, was a blurry green face, a single arm extended to the sky. He pulled up images on his computer. The green, stone-cut eyes were a perfect match. "Lady Liberty? That's who you're looking for? Don't you have Google?"

"She needs the room it was taken from," Marcus said.

"Ah, the plot thickens." Edgar grinned, a missing front tooth leaving a dark hole in the center of his face. "There are more rooms in the Bellagio Hotel than there are people in the town of Bellagio, Italy. See what I'm saying?" He pointed a skinny fore-finger at the window behind him, tracing a quarter-sized circle of smudge.

A crowd was already lining up at the roadside to watch the cannons of water that shot up regularly from the man-made lake in front of the Bellagio. A man in a Mickey Mouse costume conversed with another in sunglasses, shaggy hair, a doll with matching shades in a baby carrier. A third sweltered in green foam muscles and a painted-on snarl.

"One hundred and fifty thousand. That's the number of hotel rooms in Vegas. Fifty million tourists. Seventy thousand bars. Six million vodka shots a night. All you have is the reflection of a statue. Which, by the way, can be seen from at least eight different hotels on the boulevard."

He ducked behind a desk and retrieved monorail map that outlined the resorts. Luxor. Excalibur. Aria. Monte Carlo. MGM. Paris. Cosmo. New York New York. "Okay, maybe not quite eight, but you get the point. You're not just trying to find a hotel. You're trying to find a hotel room. It would be like dropping a penny at the beach and expecting to come back a week later to find it."

"But you could. I mean, if you had a metal detector. If you weren't just using your eyes."

"She *is* serious," he said. He turned to Marcus. "Where did you find this girl."

"She found me." Marcus was sitting in a corner now, his large chin braced on his fist. "Unfortunately. Just give her what she wants so I can call it even."

"Okay. I'll try. But this isn't a metal detector."

"Excuse me?"

"You said metal detector. This isn't a metal detector. It's a bullshit detector. There are thirty thousand cameras in every casino, but even they can't tell a five from a fifty or a club from a spade."

"Then what's the point of a camera?"

"It's not the camera, it's the guy behind it." Marcus sounded bored, like he had heard this speech before. "It's about emotion. About feeling. Blah-de-blah blah-"

"Every time you look at a picture," Edgar interrupted, "your eyes take a mental photograph. It's not the same as a real photograph because it's not a representation of what you *actually* see. It's a representation of what your mind *wants* to see. Sometimes it sees more because you wanted to see something. Sometimes, it sees less because any information your mind thinks is unnecessary gets discarded."

He plugged the phone into the computer and began running multiple programs.

"Cellphone pixels do the same thing. They block out areas in the photo that are unnecessary because they choose not to see them. Blurs out little blocks and makes them one so that all that information can fit into one frame. Little pieces of bullshit to make you feel that there's some consistency. This takes some of the bullshit away but I'm not promising anything."

Edgar scrolled through the photos to the one of the torch. The pixels started flipping like a deck of cards in a shuffle.

"The statue faces southeast," he said, "like the original. The torch is in the right hand. If you were at the Tropicana, you'd see it head on. But it's the left side you see. And the fingers. Should be four. But you only see two. That means you're looking down. It's a wraparound window. High roller floor. From the angle I would say it's the southeast corner. Tropicana Avenue and Las Vegas Boulevard."

"MGM Grand," Marcus said. "You see the checkerboard carpet?"

"And the red flowers? Has to be the Skylofts."

"You know the carpet?" I asked.

"What do you think I do here, sell junk on Craigslist? I get paid to know everything that happens in every room in Vegas, missy. It's like a fucking peepshow, except without having to load a damn quarter every minute. Here." He pointed at the screen. "There's a glint on the window. Is that gold?"

"Looks like gold to me," Marcus said. He sat back, looking pleased.

"What?"

"The MGM was built around a Wizard of Oz theme. The glass is all Emerald City green. The interior furnishings are gilt, but the only gold on the building face is the signage."

"High roller floor," Edgar said. "Probably a three bedroom. Number twelve to eighteen." He pulled up the registration database and scrolled through. "You got the first picture two days ago? We're looking for a check-in date on the weekend or earlier." He stopped. Looks like the corner loft was booked on Friday. For a whole week. Butler service was discontinued. No-entry policy was requested."

"That's legal?"

"Sure. The hotels don't like it. But it's more about making sure some-one doesn't die in a room. Not that they care about a couple of dead tour-ists. They've got a whole clean up team that turns around splattered guts and nuts in under twenty-four hours. No, the problem is suicides tend to stop paying their bill. And that really pisses people off. Believe me, happens all the time. It's like Disneyworld. Lots of people come here to die."

"I thought there was a twenty-four hour entry policy for all hotels since the Mandalay shooting."

"Some have two days, others three. MGM doesn't have an official policy," Marcus said. "Apparently their guests' privacy is more important than safety."

"How do I get in?"

"Now that's the squeeze, isn't it? You really think someone who's gone to all this trouble would just let you in? I mean, if you're going to do some-thing like this, there are a hundred foreclosed homes in the city. No one would ever know. Why send you a video where you can see exactly where they are?"

"Because the video was meant for someone else," I said.

"And when you knock on the door and you're not someone else, then what?"

"Portia," Marcus said. "What Edgar's trying to say is there's a rea-son why they chose this location. Three thousand bucks a night. Private entrance. Top level security. It's a three-room apartment, not like a single hotel room. You can't just bust in and get her out. It's going to need a whole Swat team. Snipers on the roof. Forced window entry. It's time to call the cops."

"What the hell happened to you, Marcus? You went all corporate. Now you trust the cops?"

Marcus looked at Edgar. "What do you think?"

"Remember what happened to those girls, man. And the police wouldn't move a finger until it was too late. I say fuck the pigs. Let her at 'em."

Marcus knocked the back of his head on the wall behind him, like he was trying to loosen up a bad idea. "Okay, I'll give you a shot. There's only one way for you to poke around without arousing suspicion," he said. "How are you at cleaning up shit?"

"It's what I do every day."

"I thought you'd say that. You have till tonight. Then I'm calling it in… and Portia?" He reached into his pocket and pulled out a small black case. "I know you're partial to blades, but you might need this."

CHAPTER 32

Hunter was almost halfway through the eighteen-course degustation menu at Joel Robuchon when the phone rang, the intro to Wu-Tang's *Once Upon A Time In Shaolin*. He excused himself and took the call in the concourse.

"I have a girl for you to look at," the voice said.

"Now?" Hunter asked. "I'm in the middle of a five-hundred-dollar meal."

"I'm sure you've had better. Shit, I've had better. And I didn't drop six zeroes on a ring-tone."

Hunter relented. "Where is she?"

"She's outside the MGM. Literally a thousand feet away from you." Hunter swiped through screens until he found the tracker. The dot blinked on the corner of Sahara and Tropicana.

"Don't get too close. The software is only accurate to twenty feet. If it buffers, you're likely to run right into her."

Hunter looked at the woman at his table. She wouldn't miss him for a few minutes, would she? And this was a golden opportunity. He slipped out, past the marble and gold of the stores, through the dinging and clattering of the casino floor. He exited through the front door, met by a wall of heat. Hunter sucked it in, following the tracker as it weaved through the traffic. It stopped, then moved slowly to the crosswalk. Hunter was behind her now, close enough to touch.

Portia Black. And she had no clue she was right there for the taking. The light turned and he watched her disappear into the crowd.

Hunter was back at the restaurant moments later, his face flushed, a line of sweat beading at his eyebrows. The woman across from him held a champagne flute in her hand daintily, like she was planning on dropping it at an opportune moment. The liquid in the glass was pink, the bubbles rushing up the bowl and exploding on the surface.

"Are you enjoying the Armand de Brignac?"

She ignored him. "Who is she?" The plate of food in front of her was untouched. Sea-urchin corals on a bed of pureed fennel. He wasn't sure if she was doing it to spite him or if she knew that *corals* was a euphemism for gonads.

"How did you know it's a woman?"

"It's always a woman with you." She leaned back. The crus rosacea around her neck glinted in the ivory light. Hunter winced. They had gone a little overboard with the garotte but she hadn't complained. The girl was a trooper. "Who is she?"

"Portia Black."

The girl tipped back her flute and smiled. "And suddenly my night gets a little more interesting."

"You always said you wanted to be an actress, Alexa. A Belladonna." Hunter stood up and extended his hand. "Well, honey, your big audition is tonight."

CHAPTER 33

"Have you worked the strip before? Because this isn't the Red Roof. Or the Ho Jo." The woman was obviously annoyed to have me around. I got it. Even housekeeping on the strip was cutthroat and every new maid was competition.

"I do Mandalay," I said. "Three month. Then, you know…" The broken English seemed to put her at ease. Language skills were a must for the premium jobs. And my accent was dead-on.

"You know there's no bay."

"No bay?"

"In Mandalay, I mean. Mandalay is a city in Burma. My Burma. The city is five hundred miles inland. No bay. And yet five thousand miles away, this monstrosity has the gall to call itself the Mandalay Bay. Why? Because it rhymes?"

"It's Vegas, yes?"

"Cynic. You'll fit right in." She crooked a finger and guided me into the locker room. "Come on, walk and talk."

"You are from Mandalay, yes?"

"My grandmother was born in Rangoon. Now it's Yangon. New name. Same shit. She worked in a quarry breaking rocks. No tools. Take one rock and break another. Her hands were like this." She tightened her fists into claws. "Finally got two of her children to Calcutta. Found a job in a hotel, cleaning bathrooms. It was better. From the outhouse to the toilet, you know what I'm saying? A shithole's a shithole, but some are better than others."

I nodded. The world over, the stories were always the same.

The service elevator opened and we pushed the carts in into the aluminum hull. It was the only place in the hotel that wasn't lined with gold plating.

"Anyway, my mother made it to L.A.. She did the same as her mother. Scrubbed floors and toilets until she had no knees left. Doctor said she should have an operation. She gave the money to me instead. Thought I would be a doctor. An engineer. You know, the American dream. All I got was student loans and bad credit. I had to leave Los Angeles so she wouldn't know that this what I was doing. Scrubbing toilets. It's in the blood."

"Sorry."

"Vegas," she said. "She's a bitch, don't forget it." The elevator stopped on the twenty-fourth floor and I pushed the cart into the empty hallway. "Okay we're here. You can start on that end and work your way back up here."

"What's up stair?"

"Not for you, honey. You've got to be here at least three years before you even sniff those floors."

"Good tips?"

"Tips?" She snorted. "You sure you worked in Vegas before? Nobody tips. Every penny gets sucked into those slot machines. No, sometimes those fuckers get so damn drunk they forget shit in their rooms. Fly back to Ohio or Alabama and forget a Breitling or a Patek under the beds. Gold cigar cases, bottles of Dom."

"They don't claim?"

"Sometimes. But mostly they don't really know where they lost it. They're either drinking so much or drugged so far out of their minds that they can barely remember which hotel to come back to, let alone which room. Fifty thousand people waking up in someone else's room and things disappear."

She stopped, her face red. I knew she had said too much and now she was about to take it out on me.

"You okay? Are you listening to me? This is your floor. You've got thirty minutes. You get everything done on time and to my satisfaction and I'll pass that on to the house manager. You don't and your trial's over. You got it?" She stomped off and left me alone in the corner. I looked at my watch. Marcus had given me till seven. It was already six-fifteen.

A woman stumbled out of her room, clutching at her nightgown with one hand and an empty ice-bucket in the other. "You know you people are never here when we need you." I asked for service at eleven. It's one. It's *past* one."

I felt the stench of vodka approach before she did. Whoever said vodka doesn't smell hadn't taken a whiff of it after an all-night bender. She waved a pale hand in front of my face. "What? Don't you speak English? Why don't any of you people speak English? You want to come here, you learn how to talk. Eng-lish."

Her hand dropped and she grabbed at her robe again, trying in vain to contain a set of overinflated breasts. "Never seen a boob either?" She stared at my chest, humble in the face of her surgical wonders and pushed me aside. "Make sure you have the bathroom done by the time I'm back."

I could have hit her right there but I couldn't move. The phone was buzzing in my pocket. It was new video.

The room smelled worse than its occupant. The sheets were stained with what looked like crusty brown vomit. Boxes of food littered the floor. I kicked them to the corner, shut the commode with the last clean towel, and sat on it.

The video was sharper this time. The girl was in the recliner, arms trussed up and strapped behind her to the backrest. The robe was folded down to her breastbone where the burn marks had turned an ashy, swollen purple. Her eyes, still bruised and lumpy, were open as the large man approached, a tree pruner in his hands. He touched her outstretched feet, flicking at the toes one by one. He turned and walked the fingers back like he was playing *this little piggy*. He finally latched the beaks around one, pumping the handles as the ratchet tightened.

The girl was screaming, the duct tape stretching and peeling as a trail of blood began leaking down her nose. I stumbled out of the bathroom and threw up over the bed. My head was swimming but the adrenaline was rushing back in.

From the window I could just see the southeast corner of the New York hotel. The coaster was screaming into its first loop. Lady Liberty was looking away. It had to be close. Through the plaster and cement above me I could hear it, I could hear *her*, faint and muffled. Or was I just imagining it?

"What the fuck are you doing?"

The woman was behind me, still clutching at her soiled robe. "I thought I told you to clean. And you're here watching videos on your phone. And oh, my fucking God, did you just puke on my sheets?"

The phone dinged again and everything went red. I grabbed the ice bucket, still half-full of melted ice water, went over and dunked it on her head.

"Feel cleaner now?" I pushed the bucket into her arms, dropping her into the bed. Her mouth was moving, but no words would come out. "I know what you're thinking. You're going to get me fired. Get me deported. Well, I don't work here, sister. And I sure as hell ain't going anywhere." I picked up a lipstick from the floor and scrawled on her forehead. "You, however, you keep going the way you are and you'll need my number."

I stormed out, leaving her sputtering on the bed.

I hoped I'd timed this right. She was probably calling the front desk right now and security would be up in minutes. I took the stairs of the emergency stairwell three at a time, up to the thirtieth floor. The door had a silent alarm, but I wouldn't need more than a minute. Maybe two.

The phone dinged again. I ignored it. Straightened my dress. Walked through the hallway to the very end. A large man in a well-pressed blue sat at the concierge desk, talking a bored young couple through the amenities.

"Show tickets, anytime, anywhere," he said. "*Zumanity. Criss Angel. Penn and Teller.* Even if they're sold out. You come to me, I'll find you a seat. And we offer limo service to and from."

"Is it the Bentley?" The woman perked up. She was well dressed, a large, glittering diamond around her neck but she wore it uncomfortably. Like it was the only one she had.

"Sure is. Two thousand sixteen Bentley Mulsanne. You book it, we take you anywhere on the strip. Now that's an entrance." He stopped short. "Ma'am?

"Two thousand sixteen," the man said derisively. He was propped up in his chair, chambray suit cut high on the collars. "I thought we were getting the Maybach."

The concierge wasn't paying attention to him. His eyes cut across the hallway, following me.

"Ma'am?" he asked again. He was getting up and swiveling out from behind his desk. I walked faster, pretending not to hear. "Ma'am," he repeated, louder. "This floor has already been done."

I turned but didn't stop.

"They asked for extra towels," I said.

I wasn't carrying any, but it didn't matter. I was ten steps away from the suite. He was on me, bear-like fist around my arm. The couple were tittering to each other. I noticed the bulge at his waist. He was armed. So was I.

"Look." I flashed the phone at him, a last desperate attempt.

"The hell is this?" His grip loosened, his face going from the phone to me and back. I looked at the screen. It was the new message. A photograph. It wasn't the girl. It was me. The one Medina had received. Me on the bed. My robe open.

"I said, what the hell is this?"

I was thinking the exact same thing but I was too far gone now. I pulled away and popped the taser Marcus had given me from my pocket. He was close enough that I felt the sting. He doubled over and I kicked him, grabbing the Ruger from his waist belt.

The couple at the desk were scrambling for the elevators. The active shooter sequence would be activated in less than a minute.

I grabbed the master keycard from his belt and waved it over the lock. The door opened soundlessly. The entryway was quiet and dark, the panorama curtains drawn. It should have been my second clue, but I was already in the abyss now.

I edged my way to the end of the privacy wall. I had memorized the floor plans Marcus had procured. Beyond the wall, I knew the room stretched out into an elongated L, an expanse of windows that looked out onto the entire south strip.

The granite and maple of the breakfast bar was protection, but I had six steps before I could get under its cover. I threw a porcelain statue across the room, a black and white cat, watched it shatter against the glass as I slid out across the floor. I was around the plaster buttress of the bar before the noise dissipated.

"God, she's good," a voice said. "Like a movie. All you're missing is the slow-motion bullets."

There were two of them, sitting across from each other in dark suits and discreet ties. There were briefcases by their sides, the leather rich and shiny, matching the quality shoes. One of them pressed his horn-rimmed glasses back up the bridge of his nose, crossed his arms like an accountant ready to deliver some bad news. Profits were down. Money was missing. The feds were knocking.

But he said nothing. Neither moved. They just sat there and watched. The bad news came from behind. In the form of a safety click.

It was the concierge, still heaving from the effects of the taser. "Just give me a reason, bitch."

I stood up slowly, hands wide. I un-cocked and laid the pistol on the table.

"They have her," I said. "Call security. Call the cops. Ambulance."

There was a noise from upstairs. A slender pair of legs appeared through the slits in the circular stairway. Heels clicked as she turned at the bottom of the steps. It was her. Her feet were exposed. Intact. All ten toes. The calves were sculpted and unblemished. She was wearing a sundress that exposed her sunburned chest. No cuts, no bruises. The only mark was a small tattoo on her neck. She looked at me like a bug caught in a trap.

"What the hell is going on?"

The woman walked by, her eyes never leaving me as she passed. The tattoo was tiny and blue, a flower. A Belladonna.

Before I could stop her, security was tumbling into the room, and the cuffs were snapping on tightly, so tight I thought my wrists were about to break. One of the men was reciting the Miranda while the other recorded the whole thing.

The girl turned once. Flame-red hair. Mastro's. The club. It was the same girl.

"Wait! What the hell is going on?" I demanded as they dragged me out.

"Don't worry, honey," one of them whispered. "Where you're going, you'll have plenty of time to figure it out."

SIX MONTHS LATER

CHAPTER 34

I was standing outside the Central California Women's Facility, a single plastic grocery bag in hand, waiting for the Chiller express, the Trans-metro bus that ran from Chowchilla to nearby Merced. There was a man next to me sitting on an unwieldy pile of boxes, his legs wrapped protectively around them. He had probably just been released from Valley State, the prison, not the college, that sprawled across the road.

If this were a movie, we'd both have someone waiting for us, a running car, a hot meal, the promise of a stiff drink and a warm bed. This wasn't. When the gates slammed shut there was just an empty road and just enough cash for bus fare to Madera in the south or Merced in the north.

"How long?" the man finally asked. His eyeballs were yellow and the pupils darted around like a he was following a buzzing fly. He didn't look at me once.

"Six months," I said.

"No, how long before you're back?" He chuckled.

"Don't intend on it."

"Nuh-huh. Maybe, maybe." He bit his lip and craned his neck, looking for the bus. "Got any money?"

"Nope," I said. That was half a lie. I had a stash in a safe deposit in Oregon. A couple across the Midwest. One in Georgia. People I could call on in almost any state with IOUs. The other half, however, was also true. I had used all my pennies getting to Vegas and I had five dollars and twenty cents beyond the bus fare. Four-fifty if I decided to go all the way to Merced.

"You got a job?"

"Nope." I said. Entirely true.

"Got any skills?"

"Plenty."

The man laughed. His teeth were as yellow as his eyes. "Not the kind of skills that put you in the pokey, honey; the ones that can keep you out. Waitressing. Landscaping. Pole dancing."

I laughed with him. I'd waitressed a couple of times and mowed lawns to make ends meet. I wasn't built for erotic dancing. Which sucked because it paid the best of the three. "No, I guess I'm only good at making messes, not cleaning up."

"Well, you'll be back, honey. Recidivism. That's a fancy word I learned in the guesthouse. That word means taking ordinary folks like you and me, folks who have done wrong and now are trying to do right. And dropping us right into life again. No money, no jobs, no support."

The old man was right. The current rate was just over sixty percent. He had the additional double-strike of being a black and a male, so he was probably pushing eighty. "Had a friend who got out last year. Had been in for eighteen years. Came out and couldn't work a phone no more. Couldn't figure out how to swipe a bus card. You know there's this thing called in-stant chat? People walking around all day chatting into their phones and sending pictures to people they never even met? Shit, he liked prison better. The world he knew? Our world? It's gone."

"Should've just left your boxes in the prison then," I said, half-joking.

"Should've. But there's some valuable stuff here. I could pawn shit off for a hundred, maybe a hundred fifty. Buy myself some real good liquor. Maybe a woman. Some smokes. A hit of coke. Not street. Real dominos. The good stuff. Stare at it long enough, your face goes numb."

"And then?"

"Matter of time. I'll be back here pretty soon. So will you. Hey, here it is."

The bus rumbled to a stop and the driver swung the door open with a grunt. There were two types of people who took the bus here. Ex-cons and future cons. The driver treated us appropriately. I helped the man with his boxes but refused his offer to sit with him. I took the back seat and watched the prison disappear.

The ride to town was about fifteen minutes, and when I got out I headed over to the only pawn shop to sell what I had. I emptied the prison bag onto the counter. Two t-shirts. Dirty. A belt. Worthless. The black flip-phone. Dead. I needed about fifty bucks for a bus ticket to Oregon and all I had left was my grandmother's gold chain.

The man behind the counter was Hispanic, handlebar mustache and flat-topped hair. He had at least three gold chains around his neck, another two on his wrists. I knew I was going to vomit when he valued it. Gold, like diamonds, sold for a fraction of what you bought it for. It was a fucking scam and he and I both knew it.

He went to the back room. He was probably coming back with some ridiculous low-ball offer. Or he was calling the cops. I thought of the old guy at the bus stop and his pile of boxes. *Ree-cee-dee-vi-see-um*, he had said. Phonetically. Like the person who had first taught him the term had never expected him to remember it.

The man behind the counter was back in a few minutes with another who looked the same but twenty, maybe thirty years older. He proffered a card.

"I don't do lawn and I drop plates," I said. "And I don't dance."

"It's not a job offer," he said. The card hung there between us and I finally took it.

"Best Western?" There was a number on the back, twelve digits. Not a telephone number.

"It's down the road and on your left. You can't miss it."

I jangled the chain in his face. "I don't have bus money. Forget about hotel money."

"Oh, yeah, almost forgot." He pushed a Visa debit card across the glass table. "Two hundred bucks. For incidentals."

"You're kidding."

"I just do what I'm told, honey."

"And apparently I don't." I clasped the chain back around my neck and apologized to Grams. I could see her tsk-tsking in her tattered easy chair, her eyes narrow behind the Coke-bottle glasses.

I sat at the Krispy Kreme across the road from the Best Western, crushing a whole box that had just dropped out of the fryer and run through a river of melted sugar. I was sufficiently carbed up enough to cross the street and enter the leafy driveway that led me to the shiny paneled desk. The woman looked at me expectantly.

"Reservation?"

"You tell me," I said.

I handed her the card and the driver's license I checked into jail with. It said Renee Miller. Date of Birth: May fourth, nineteen ninety-four. The issuing state was Arizona and I was listed as an organ donor. I was sure the pathologist would have fun with that. The woman typed in the numbers from the card, looked at the license, then at me. If the name on her list didn't match, she didn't show it.

"Room four-four-one." She swiped and handed me a room key.

"That's it? What about room charges? No deposit?"

"Taken care of."

"By whom?"

"Wasn't given a name, ma'am. Have a nice stay."

"I'm sure I will," I said but as the elevator doors closed, I was certain I wouldn't. A weapon would make me feel better. I made a mental note to order a steak on room service so I could at least have a knife.

Room four forty-one was on a middle floor near the elevators, and its location calmed me. A pro hit would have put me closer to the outer edges, a window to nowhere, easy access to a stairwell, near the rumble of the ice machine. I was still taking no chances. I called maintenance for a non-working faucet and hid out behind the vending machine. The maintenance guy, a burly older man with a belt full of tools and keys came up in ten minutes. He left a few minutes later shaking his head. All clear.

I searched the modest room for cameras. There was usually one hiding with the electronics bundle under the television but the room was clear. The covers actually looked clean but I still didn't trust them. I dropped the sheets onto the floor and rolled them up inside out. I knew plenty of people who dropped trouser as soon as they entered a hotel room, then spent the rest of their stay acquainting the furniture with their colon.

I piled up the rolled bedding on the bathroom floor and locked the door. The sugar crash was pulling at my limbs, melting them, and I took a final precaution. I rolled the desk chair up and wedged it under the latch. Done. I was out before my head hit the tub.

I woke up with a start. It could have been twenty minutes. It could have been two hours. Every last trace of donut high was long gone. I was starving, and the lack of sugar had me fuzzy. I undid the barricade, opened the door, and walked into the room without thinking.

There was a man sitting in the easy chair, spinning a duct-taped switchblade on the table. My stomach wrenched. The ivory handle looked as shiny and inviting as a line of coke. "Good sleep?" he asked.

I looked at Jamal, dumbfounded.

"Don't worry, the knife's not for you. I mean, it's for you if you want it. Just not *for* you."

"What time is it?"

"Two-thirty."

"In the afternoon?" I did the quick math. Five and a half hours. That was longer than I'd slept straight in years. I looked out at the sun. He wasn't kidding. "What do you want?"

The knife stopped spinning. "I wanted to catch you before you disappeared, *bint.*"

"And the question remains, what do you want?"

"Always business. Six months in prison and you don't want a hot meal? A nice bed?"

"Only once I know what it's going to cost me."

Jamal tossed a brown paper bag across the room. There was money inside, tens and twenties, most of them crumpled and worn. "Your payment," he said.

"For what?"

"I see prison hasn't changed you. Still the same hard-ass, belligerent little-"

"Payment for what?" I repeated.

"The kid you found in Barstow. I had Quentin keep a finger on him. That led us to a young man named Michael Duncan. Mickey *Deez*. Worked for me once or twice. Nice kid. Pity. He's gone now. But-"

"Okay, I get the idea. You got the distribution. I'm happy for you."

"You're not happy. You're never happy."

"When I can get out of here, I'll be happy."

"No, you won't. You'll be hiding out in New Mexico. Or Tennessee. Or Alabama. You'll be holed up. And things will settle down. And everyone here will forget about you. And you think you'll be happy. But you won't be happy. You know why? Because you know that cutting out the middleman is just that. Like crimping a pipe and leaving the faucet on. You know Hunter's still out there. He'll always be out there until you get him."

Jamal opened the large duffel by his chair and laid a black plastic folder on the table. A diagram stretched across both pages, a flowchart of chemical formulas that started with ornithine on the upper left and ended with scopolamine on the lower right.

"What is this?"

"FDA filings for a little outfit called Neogen Pharmaceuticals from about two, three years back. Generic etofosfamide. Dapsone. Ritonavir. You know the scam. Buy up rights to generics that have limited use and remarket at astronomical markups. The M.O. for most of their filings are the same."

I stood and stretched. "I have a bus to catch." I tried to feign disinterest but I couldn't hide it.

"But not for this one. This, *bint*, is a paragraph IV filing for an abbreviated new drug application." He stared at me, waiting for me to jump in. "Notice how the chemical formula looks different? It's non-stoichiometric."

"What does that mean?"

"That means that we might have found our drug. And guess what else I found? Wire transfer to Neogen Pharmaceuticals. In United States funds."

He held it up like a proud parent. The check line was scrawled in hand. Five million dollars. In the signature line was scrawled the name: *Nathan Hunter.*

"Now, *bint*, what time was that bus you had to catch?"

CHAPTER 35

Jamal drove a black Escalade with suicide doors and Pirellis so skinny they looked like bicycle tires.

"What do you think, *bint?*"

"Looks like a Penny Farthing."

"Is that good?"

"Sure." I shrugged. It was ridiculous, actually. Fifty-eight hundred pounds of curb weight on four Fatlip Dropstars.

"Cool," he said as he vaulted in. He had a set of Bose headphones on, DJ style, one cupping his left ear, the other twisted around so he could hear. "You know, I can get you into one of these. Big upgrade from your Chevy."

"Dodge." I tried to explain to him the value of being inconspicuous, but Jamal was pumping up the fourteen speakers and singing along. I looked at the row of CDs in the tray. I was expecting something old school, Busta or DMX, but the tray was filled with *old* old school: Hafez, Farid, Al-Atrash. Jamal flipped the dial. It was Oum Kulthum singing *Betfakar fi Meen*. Jamal began humming along.

I was suddenly in Dearborn, Michigan, in a little Lebanese restaurant that served little more than greasy falafel and overcooked shawarma. The boy at the counter was singing along to the cassette player tucked above the grill. I translated the words roughly as, "You who have enjoyed my tears."

The boy was slicing off meat as the rotisserie turned. He paused the music, sung it loudly into the vent, and laughed. I waited for him to enter the swing doors into the kitchen and followed. There was a cook chopping mutton on the stainless slab. His apron was spattered pink with blood, and he didn't pay me any attention.

The boy had gone down into the cellar, still singing. I followed him down, through the slabs of meat, each one hanging from the ceiling on its own iron hook. The set-up was Rocky-ish, and I half expected him to pound one. It was dead quiet in the chiller. He was at the very end, still singing, caressing one that didn't look like a goat carcass.

"Bint?"

I could see her face, streaked with red, her eyes open, dead. Hanging like meat.

"Bint!"

"Yes?"

"Seatbelt. Don't want you getting hurt."

"Too late."

Boulder City was a half hour from Vegas at three in the morning. Most other times of the day it was two hours of bumper stops and endless lefts. It made it worse that Jamal had to stop at every fast food joint and greasy spoon for lunch. There was a pile of bags on the center console, only half of which had been tucked into. Most were leaking oil onto the leather but Jamal didn't seem to notice.

"You know Boulder is the only city in Nevada that doesn't allow gambling?"

I knew this wasn't true, but the music was still on and Salma's vacant stare still bit at me. She was still swiveling there on a hook. When you're dead, you're meat. If that doesn't convince you to go vegan, nothing will.

Jamal kept rambling. "You know why it's the only town that doesn't allow gambling? Because it was built for the workers constructing the Boulder Dam and they wanted to keep their workers away from Vegas. No gambling. No womanizing. No drinking. All-American family men.

A place they could bring their wives and children. Like a little oasis in the Mojave."

"Boulder City has fifteen thousand people. Las Vegas has half a mil. No one picks water when there's booze."

"Exactly."

"Exactly, what?"

Jamal turned onto a leafy driveway with a large stone sign that said Neogen Pharma in block granite lettering. "You don't go to a place like Boulder City to hide your smelly garbage. You want to do something seedy, there are plenty of other places to hide it."

"What are you rambling on about?"

"What I'm trying to say is don't expect anything. This isn't a movie. Just be cool."

I stepped out of the truck and watched Jamal struggle out of his car seat. I'd just pulled in with a three hundred-pound drug dealer driving a purple Escalade with suicide doors and he wanted *me* to be cool.

I looked at my crumpled jeans and stenciled muscle shirt, the same ones that had been tucked into a prison locker for six months. I smelled like Dial and camphor.

"Shouldn't we be wearing suits?"

"You want to look like one of them?"

I saw a woman cross the glass bridge above us. She was wearing a sleek gray jacket, the skirt and shirt matching black silk. It was a look Medina could have pulled off effortlessly. "No," I said. "I just don't want to look like one of us."

If the woman at the front desk had the same reaction, she didn't show it. She was a middle-aged blonde with the best part of her life behind her, and it leached through in her tone.

"Welcome to Neogen Pharmaceuticals. Can I help you?" She spat the line out without looking up, so fast and tempered it might have all been one word.

"You sure can, lady," Jamal said. He dropped a Black and Decker duffel onto the counter. It sounded like a bag of cement. "I'm looking for Nathan Hunter."

The woman finally looked up, her lips pursed. "We don't have anyone here by that name."

"Sure you do. Isn't this Neopharma?"

"Neogen Pharmaceuticals."

"Then Nathan Hunter owns this place."

"No." She smiled, but she was working hard at it, covering the frown that sat behind her eyes. "We have a board of directors, but we have no Hunter on the board."

"Well, how do you explain this?" Jamal tossed the paper over the counter. It landed on her desk perfectly, like a paper airplane.

"I have no idea who this is. And I really have no idea who you are either."

Jamal pulled himself up to his full height, all five feet six. He was about as wide as he was tall. "I'm your friendly neighborhood pharmaceutical liaison."

There were at least seven attractive young men and women in the lobby, fitted shirts and skirts, moisturized faces and polished briefcases. They looked nothing like Jamal.

"Pharmaceutical liaison?"

"Yeah. Drug rep."

"You mean drug dealer."

"Cocaine," Jamal said. "Fentanyl, methamphetamine-"

"Drugs."

"No, don't say that like it's a dirty word. I sell drugs. You sell drugs. We're in the same business."

"Illegal drugs. I wouldn't say we were even in the same ballpark."

Jamal opened the bag and dropped a series of zip-locks onto the table. Each contained a set of blister packs, European and Asian markings emblazoned on the silver foil. "All legally prescribed. Legally sold. Cocaine hydrochloride. Made by Roxane labs. Desbutal. Made by Abbott. Five milligrams meth, thirty milligrams pento. Very hard to find nowadays. See, what I'm trying to say is, I know the game. I play it too. Except that I'm upfront about what I'm selling to my patients. You, on the other hand, you just find a way to make a buck, then you move on to the next designer drug."

"I see," the woman said. She reached over to the panel under the desk.

"No, don't do that."

"Do what?"

"The security button. This isn't a bank. I'm not trying to hold you up. I don't even have a gun. I just have a couple of questions."

The glass doors slid open and a tall man with a comb-like mustache and little other hair stood in the corridor. "You better come on in."

Jamal zipped up his bag and winked at me. "Bet you thought I was going to get you arrested again."

I shrugged. "You've still got time."

CHAPTER 36

We got ushered down a milk-glass corridor with pearl accents on the doors. The man pushed open a door into a modern stainless office, the white corduroy carpet puffy and ribbed, like packed snow. The bronze plate on the desk said: Martin Murphy. Chief Scientific Officer.

The man behind the desk was young, his face warped and bean-like. His glasses fit awkwardly over his undersized ears, the stems askew to hold the lenses even. I recognized the classic signs of craniofacial dysostosis right away.

"I understand you're looking for Nathan Hunter," he said.

"Yes." Jamal plunked into a white rolling chair and dropped his bag on the table.

"Would you please?" Murphy pressed his pencil against the bag like a fly that had crawled onto his desk. "Mr. Hunter has no relationship with this company."

"I disagree." Jamal unfolded the paper and dropped it onto the table.

Murphy looked at it, folded the paper, and handed it back. "Nathan Hunter is a shark," he said. "He smells blood in the water, he comes and takes a bite. He doesn't stick around."

Jamal tapped on the paper. "He stuck around long enough to get a project off the ground. Neo-Scopolamine?"

Murphy sighed. "Is this about Neo-Scopolamine or about Hunter?"

"I think it's about both."

"It's about neither. Because neither Scopolamine products nor Mr. Hunter are relevant to Neogen."

"Relevant enough that you would invite me in, instead of calling the cops."

Murphy glanced at his watch. "Mr. Siyad, would you get to the point? I'm late for a lunch meeting."

The name-drop took me aback. I looked at the man, then at Jamal. "You know him?"

"We're business associates," Jamal said.

"Oh hell, no." The man seemed a little perturbed by his profanity and sat up tighter in his chair. "I mean, no. I'm acquainted with his enterprise but we're not in a business relation."

"I offered him a job two years ago," Jamal interrupted. "He declined."

"I have a doctorate from Emory. I wasn't about to sell marijuana."

"Look at the pot calling the ketamine black." Jamal sat back, pleased with himself.

"I'm not calling anyone anything. And I'm not here for a paycheck. I just wanted to make a difference in someone's life."

"You did." Jamal jabbed a backwards thumb at me. "Hers."

"Oh?" He paused. His face dropped. "Oh." His voice was suddenly reverential, like he was looking at a corpse. "You think he used our Scopolamine on you."

"Thank you," I said.

"For what?"

"Everyone else assumes I used it on him."

"Either way, it's impossible. N-Scopolamine was never approved. All trial doses were destroyed. Whatever Mr. Hunter used on you, he didn't get from us."

"Unless he made it on his own. Just used your lab as the crucible. It's been done before. Get all the permits, do all the testing, then junk the whole thing before FDA approvals. But the formulas? That's the gold, man."

"It's a pharmaceutical laboratory. You can't just open one in your basement."

"You'd be surprised," Jamal said.

"I wouldn't trust Hunter as far as I could throw him." Murphy raised his arms. The web in his neck made it hard for him to get past shoulder level. "Obviously that's not far. But Hunter didn't come here *for* Scopolamine. He came here *because* of Scopolamine."

"What's that supposed to mean?"

"As a hydrobromide, low dosage scopolamine works on post-op nausea. Gastro-intestinal or biliary spasms. Bowel colic. There's a behind-the-ear patch for motion sickness called Transdermascop. We thought we could expand the indications by hacking the chemistry but it didn't do anything. It just potentiated the side-effects."

"You spent a lot of money on a worthless drug. Isn't that part of your business?"

"For Chiron or Amgen, yes. We don't have quite the same leeway. It almost ruined us financially. Hunter came along and gave us some breathing room. But that was six months after the trials ceased. The trial doses were incinerated, RCRA forms were filed, there was nothing left." He stopped and turned to Jamal. "Are you okay?"

Jamal was doubled over, wincing. "Something I ate."

"Can't imagine what," I said.

Jamal flashed me that stare. He turned his back to the man. "Do you have a restroom?"

"Down the hall, on your left."

The man's eyes followed Jamal all the way to the door, then they locked on me, small and fierce. He stared, unblinking. Just when I finally decided to let go, he leant back, steepled his fingers, and closed his eyes tightly. "You sure you know what you're doing?"

"No."

"Of course not. None of you do. You play poker?"

"No."

"I didn't think so. Probably the most popular card game in the world. Except for Go Fish. But it's only the fifth most popular game in Vegas. Craps. Blackjack. Roulette. They all beat poker in popularity. You know why? Because poker is just as much in here." His fingers pulsed at his heart. "As it is up in your head. It takes a lot of trust. You know the old Kenny Rogers song. Gotta know when to hold 'em? Because you have to know when to quit, even when you think you have all the cards. And quitting a game you *think* you can win is the one thing no one ever masters."

"Why don't you just tell me what's going on?"

"House rules, honey. A dealer can politely tell you to step away from the table if he sees you're in over your head. But he can't ever show you the cards. The one thing I can tell you. Forget Scopolamine. It's a dead end. Hunter didn't throw millions onto the table for some stupid street drug."

"So, what does ten mil buy you?"

Murphy chewed on his lip, biting back a secret. "Talent," he said. The phone rang and he picked it up immediately. His eyes remained glued shut, almost like he couldn't bear to look at me anymore. He swiveled in his chair, a wide bald spot facing me like a third eyeball, daring me to move.

"Where did you find him?" Murphy turned, looked at me carefully. "Have him escorted out. I'll make sure she joins him." He pulled his glasses off and rubbed his eyes in concentric circles. "It appears as if your friend missed his turn to the bathroom and ended up in one of our restricted areas. I'm sure it was quite an honest mistake. However, you'll understand if I have to ask both of you to leave immediately."

He pointed a crooked finger behind me. "The exit is on your left, down the hallway. If you see a door marked restricted, I'd beg you to turn and walk in the opposite direction. I would hate to have to call security for you too."

I stood. "Don't worry about me. I just got out of Sing-Sing. I'm not about to go back in." I raised my hands and walked toward the door.

"If you knew what was out there," Murphy said, "you might have wished you never got out."

I stopped, the door-handle cold and hard in my palm.

"So, if you were the dealer? Would you suggest I fold and walk away?"

"No," he said. "I'd suggest you fold and run."

CHAPTER 37

I was waiting by the Escalade two minutes later, watching Jamal being escorted by two large men in crisp black suits. His pink jumpsuit made the trio appear like an ice cream sandwich melting in the sun. They pushed him off at the curb and waited, arms crossed, lips pursed.

"You know what? Screw you guys. Work for the man. I used to. Now I am the man." He slammed the door to the truck. Another three bags of food slid off into the well between the seats. He picked one up and thumbed through it. The guards waited.

"I think they want us to leave."

"They're stupid rent-a-cops. They don't know I have a three -oh-five under the seat. And if I wanted I could just put the car in forward instead of reverse. Oops. Didn't mean it. Creamed you all over the pavement."

The guards finally gave up and took a position behind the sliding doors.

"See?" Jamal started the truck and put it into reverse. "So, what did Murphy say?"

"Nothing."

"Come on, you know he's got beef with me. Why do you think I left the room? He must've said something."

"We talked poker."

"Texas or Omaha?"

"I'm not sure. I think he was about to tell me something, then you decided to go all rage against the machine. What the hell were you up to?"

"Getting a little down-low on the competition. You know, you can't trust the advertising anymore. They make a lot more than pharmaceuticals. In fact, you know what their most interesting product was? Not a drug. Ever heard of Miracle meat?"

"Like Memphis meat?"

"It's cultured bio-protein. Grown in a test-tube. Take some cells and myoglobin, put them in a broth, and you have any kind of meat you need. Chuck to filet, any kind of poultry, seafood, whatever."

"Are they in production?"

"Initial testing was done about two years ago, but the production costs were coming out to about thirty or forty thousand bucks a pound. Kind of hard to get funding at that price point."

"And?"

"They sold the tech."

"How much do you think tech like that would value at?"

"I don't know. Ten, twenty million, maybe? But it's worthless, of course. Unless you have the talent to go with it."

"That's what Murphy said."

"What?"

"Hunter wasn't here for the drugs. He was here for talent."

Jamal shifted in his seat, pulled a crumpled piece of paper from his back pocket, and dropped it onto the console. I peeled the paper open and stared at it. It was an A4 bulletin board flyer. Pluripotential stem cell extraction therapy from dental pulp tissue. The lecturer was Dr. Arthur Zahn.

Zahn. Where had I heard that name before?

"Zahn was a former consultant." He tapped a finger on the paper. "What do you think? Pluripotential. Sounds like talent to me."

It was not the title I was worried about. It was the sponsoring organization at the bottom of the announcement. It was Belladonna Laboratories.

"So, when you going to join that poker game, *bint?*"

I stared out of the window. The road was glazed and sticky in the mid-day sun. It finally came to me. Dr. Harmon's office. *A classmate of mine, Artie Zahn, does some crazy stuff with just a few cells.*

"I told you. I have a bus to catch. I'm not playing anything."

Jamal smiled. "On the contrary, *bint*, I think you've been playing all along. You just haven't anted up yet."

CHAPTER 38

I heard the click of the safety before I felt the cold steel bore into my neck. "Turn," the voice said. "Very slowly. You don't want my finger to slip."

I followed the command, hands raised halfway, eyes squinting in the flashlight. "Shalom," I said.

"Oh, for God's sakes!" Shimon picked me up in a bear hug. "Why didn't you call me? Tell me you were out?"

"Didn't have a phone, Shimon. Please put me down."

He did, embarrassed. His kind of affection was old school, a wink, a nod, the occasional growl. Men from Tel Aviv were not avid huggers. "You should have called. Really."

"I just came for Dog, Shimon. I'm not staying."

"Yes, you're staying. Miss Stephanie would kill me if she knew you came by and I never told her."

"Nah, she'd fire you at worst. Now, Frida? That woman would probably kill you."

Shimon laughed. "Come on. I'm not in the mood for getting fired today." He pulled me around the side of the garage, through the shrubs to the main driveway. "I'm less in the mood for getting killed."

The twin entry lights were on, and sitting on the flagstone steps, her snout nuzzled between her paws, was a mottled old black Labrador. My heart leapt. Dog was old, and I'd been afraid to ask.

"You think she remembers me?"

"Miss Winter?"

"Shimon!" I laughed, but I wasn't quite sure if he was joking. "I meant Dog."

"Argos waited twenty years for Odysseus to come home. And he remembered him."

"Didn't he drop dead right after?"

"Odysseus or the dog?"

"Both, I think."

"That was Agamemnon. And he was murdered."

Dog stirred, her head darting rapidly from side to side. Her vision wasn't great, but I saw her nostrils flare as my scent picked up around her. For a moment she was uncertain, then her ears pricked up and she charged down the steps, sliding to a crumpled heap at my feet.

"Well, at least you're happy to see me."

"Make it two." Frida was standing in the doorway, her arms crossed. "Come on, I bring you something little to eat. Then we get you into a shower and bed."

"I'm just here for Dog. Besides, Steph-"

"Miss Winter will do nothing. Come now, I'm not asking twice." Her voice was stern, but her eyes were glossy with tears. If I made her cry, I knew I'd never hear the end of it.

I made my way into the kitchen as Shimon and Frida bustled around. Frida's version of a bite to eat was closer to a three-course dinner, although she swore it was a beggar's meal back in the old country. I tried to make myself helpful and worked on the dishes in the sink but was soon chased out with a soup ladle. "How a girl can take soap and water and make a dish dirtier is beyond me," she complained. "What kind of man marries a girl like that?"

"Kind of man who can cook and clean," I heard Shimon say. A clang, a rattle of dishes, and Shimon was expelled from the kitchen too. He winked at me as he passed. "She shows love in mysterious ways," he said.

I found a safe haven in the library. The boardroom table was gone, and Mr. Winter's Queen Anne desk was back in its position by the window. I'd never been in here alone and I felt like an intruder, a kid sneaking into a forbidden room, aware that the alarm might go off at any moment. There was a leather couch near the desk and a large pedestal globe next to it. I pressed the axis rod and it swung back, revealing a butler's pantry of alcohol.

I hadn't had a drink in six months and my mouth went dry looking at the amber-filled bottles. There were ten thousand-dollar bottles of Karuizawa Samurai and fifteen thousand-dollar editions of Delamain Le Voyage. In the center island was a sixty-two-year-old vintage Lalique that I wouldn't even dare estimate. And at the very end was a bottle of eighteen-year-old Sazerac. I poured out a double into my open mouth. I'm not pretentious, but I'm a sucker for a well-aged American rye. I tossed my head back, feeling its warm tentacles claw their way down my throat. I reloaded and closed the latches, erasing all evidence of my crime.

I moved onto the long bookcase that served as the west wall. It was covered with an entire collection of Encyclopedias. The crunch of the pages told me that they were bought and shelved without ever being opened.

The lower section was composed of two rows of black leather-bound books with gold lettering. I opened one and realized it was blank. Like so many other things in the Winter household, the entire library was just a prop, a façade. I was glad that at least the liquor was real. As I returned to the globe I noticed a hardbound book on the desk with three steel binding rings down the spine. I opened it and peeled through the laminated pages.

It was an old-fashioned photo album from back in the days when people took everything in film and preserved the bleached paper stills in folds of cellophane. There were photos of Steph from childhood through her teenage years. School pictures from Brentwood. Vacations in the Riviera Maya. Piano recitals in Manhattan. Ski trips to Jackson Hole-

"Portia, you coming?" I could hear Frida clicking her way to the library. I knew I should've put the album back but the last page had me hooked. On the bottom left was a four by six. A quad chairlift ran up a slope patterned with crisp corduroy, the sun brilliant off the white powder. Aspen. Breckenridge. Some place expensive. Mountains towered in the distance, sharp teeth biting into the blue sky. Two girls tried to smile through the oversized helmets, arms around each other, eyes squinting in the glare. I recognized Steph immediately, but the other girl-

Frida was standing in the doorway. "Food's getting cold."

I pointed at the photo. "Who is this, Frida?"

She peered at the album and grimaced. "I don't know. One of Miss Winter's good for nothing friends."

"What's her name?"

"I haven't seen her in years. You expect an old lady to remember these things?"

"You forget nothing, Frida."

"Why does it matter?"

"Matters enough for you to give me a hard time about it. What're you hiding?"

"Nothing. All I remember is that girl got herself into some serious drug trouble when she was fifteen. Mother packed her off to a fancy boarding school in Vermont. Haven't seen her since. Now you leave other people's business alone. And that goes for the liquor too."

Frida was good at plenty of things, but lying wasn't one of them. She went over to the globe and reset the latches.

"If you want to get drunk, you do it in the kitchen like a normal person."

"Do you have an eighteen-year-old Sazerac?"

"I have a bottle of Irish Rose that's been sitting in my closet for twenty." She grabbed my arm and pulled.

"Sounds putrid."

"It tastes worse, believe me."

She shut the book and popped it into the drawer. "I told you, nothing good comes from messing with other people's business."

It was impossible to say no to Frida and, like a child, I was fed, pushed into a drawn bath, and tucked into bed. I never got the promised liquor, but with a heavy cloud of sleep approaching I couldn't find it in me to complain. I even began to forget the album. The snow. The girl.

Frida tucked me in and patted me on the head. I was powerless to resist. I felt six years old again. It was the best night I'd had in years.

CHAPTER 39

It was still dark when I woke up. The projection clock on the ceiling read four thirty-seven. I tossed and turned, knowing that a whole uninterrupted night of sleep was weighing me down. I was used to three, maybe four hours at a time, and eight straight felt like a hangover.

I heard a crackling from the corner of the room, the echo of shattering glass. The sound pierced the room like a gunshot. I rolled off the bed like a frightened cat, taking the pillows and covers with me. The knife tucked into my sock was out and flipped open.

"Jesus, Portia. I guess prison hasn't changed you." Steph settled into the easy chair by the window and peeked out. She dropped another ice cube into her glass and watched it splinter.

"I'm just here for the night, Steph-"

"We starting this again?"

"I have a meeting with the PO in Henderson tomorrow morning. I need to be there by eleven, pretend that I was within the great state of Nevada all night. Unless you want him to turn up here."

Steph dabbed her forehead with the back of her hand. "I so wish I had men chasing me across state lines."

"Get yourself framed for murder and you'll have half the LAPD to pick from."

Steph pointed the glass at me accusingly. "You didn't go to jail for murder. You went to jail because you got set up, flew into some bitch frenzy, and thought you could shoot your way out of Dodge-"

"Okay, I know. I got played."

"You got *more* than played. You got screwed." She laughed. "You think this is over, don't you? You messed up, you paid your dues, now you get to just walk away? Doesn't work like that. You realize that as long as your ex-boyfriend is missing, you'll always be suspect number one. Especially if you just up and disappear."

"One, Nathan Hunter is not my boyfriend. And two, he's not dead."

"Where did you hear that?"

"That's he's alive? Grapevine."

"There a grapevine in prison?"

"Looks like a grapevine, stings like electrified fence."

"And you'll get stung again if you're not careful."

"What's that supposed to mean?"

Steph rummaged for the remote and turned on the television. A spokesman for the California State Patrol leaned in behind her podium, answering questions that seemed well-rehearsed.

"The victim has been identified as Alexandra Cooper, twenty-three of Covington, California."

"Yes, DNA from a possible attacker was found on her remains."

"No, we won't have any positive identification back from the crime laboratory for at least a few weeks."

"No, at this point we have no knowledge if this victim is related to the remains found at Fryman Canyon."

"Interesting." Steph turned off the sound. "They find another body the moment you get out of jail."

Not *any*body, I thought. The girl's face was still on the screen in a freeze-frame. "Let me guess. They already have a name. Something catchy. The Backpack Butcher. Or the Canyon Killer."

"Don't get cute, Portia."

"I've been in the clink for over six months, Steph. One hundred ninety-two days and counting. If they haven't put two and two together by now-"

"Cops? You think I'm worried about the L.A.P-fucking-D?"

Steph plopped the glass against the table hard enough for the drink, amber and thin, to slosh over the counter. She got up and stomped out.

"Steph, wait. Where are you going-"

Her voice was thin through the walls. "Not going anywhere. Neither are you." She was back in a minute carrying a brown, duct-taped box with a UPS label. The packaging looked all too familiar. "This just came in for you."

The box was small but heavy, a block of ice wrapped in brown manila paper. "A welcome-home gift? Well, at least someone cares."

"You think I didn't come because I don't care? Whatever happened to you? It's not over. It's some kind of sick game. And, like it or not, I'm part of it too. I didn't come because I didn't want anyone to know you were getting out. Obviously, that didn't work."

I shook the box. It was well packed, but the weight inside wasn't quite centered. Something heavy rolled around inside. "Peanut butter?"

"Random." She stared at me, hoping perhaps for some elaboration.

"You don't know what it is?" I asked.

"Of course, I don't know. I never opened it. It came in two days ago. The day you got out."

"Why is it cold?"

"Because the note said keep refrigerated." She stared me down. "I assumed it was some sort of food product, but I wasn't taking any chances. I had Medina scan it, run some x-rays, have a sniffer dog check it. It's not a bomb. Or drugs."

"You're still paying her?"

"God, Portia, you're like a disabled kid who would rather stay home behind a curtain than be pushed around the block in the sunshine. Just open it."

I popped the knife and tore through the packing tape. Between the pillows was a plastic container surrounded by a foil freezer bag. I popped open the latches, and unscrewed the lid. Nestled within was a glass specimen case.

Steph turned up the lights. "What the hell is it? Meat?"

I turned the case over. "It's not Omaha Steak, that's for sure." The fillet had a ruby quality and stringiness of fiber that jumped out at me. It had been some time since I'd seen one cut like this.

"I can have Medina test it."

"Don't bother." I packed the container back into the box. "I know what it is."

"Just by looking at it?"

"The redness in meat is from hemoglobin in the blood and oxygenated myoglobin the muscle fibers. White meats? Under two percent. Lamb's eight or nine. Beef is around twelve. A good cut is purplish. Well oxygenated; it's cherry red at best."

"And this-"

"Is the other red meat."

Steph settled back into the chair. "And you thought you were just going to walk away."

I was up at 6:30. Truth is, I never actually got back to sleep. I went back to the library, and thumbed through the book. The girl stared back at me, unapologetic. She was younger, blonder than when I'd seen her last. But it was her.

Alexandra Cooper. Alex from the club. Alex from Mastro's. Alex from the Skylofts. Like a bad penny, she was back. But this time in pieces.

I went back up to the bedroom. Steph was snoring on the couch, open mouth, one arm over the back cushion, legs spread apart, the kind of Instagram photo that would destroy her rep forever. But I had worse pictures of her, the kind you burn after seeing. I placed her strewn limbs back together and covered her with the blanket. There was a glow through the fiber, iridescent and blue. I slipped the phone out and the backlight turned off and the glass went milky dark.

Steph began to stir. She reached out for her drink, knocked the glass over, then rolled face-down into the couch arm. I dropped the phone into my pocket and left with the canister of flesh.

There was a light on in the garage, bleeding yellow through the open bay. Shimon was trying to look busy, tinkering under the hood of a red Range Rover Autobiography, a belated Christmas present that Steph never had the time to unwrap. I snuck out behind the detached garage, feeling my way through the rows of boxwoods that stood like dozing sheep.

The van was parked on the embankment, facing the slope that cut onto the driveway. If I dropped it into neutral I could roll halfway to the gates before anyone noticed me. I hit the clutch and squeezed the shift, the gear crank popping like a gunshot in the early morning. The car began to roll, and as I felt around for the ignition I realized there was nothing there. A face was at the window, head bobbing, keeping pace. A set of keys dangled from Shimon's hand.

"You've got nothing better to do than stay up for me?"

"That's what Miss Winter pays me for. What, you think I just sit around cleaning spark plugs all day?"

I tilted my head toward the Range. "Kind of hard to clean a spark plug on a diesel car."

"Carburetor, then."

"They don't have those either."

"Yours does. And it was filthy. You've got a crunching in your gearbox too, maybe a flywheel. Need to get that fixed. And I fixed your window, though. And your door, since you can't get grease under your pretty fingers."

My fingernails were a scourge of bitten-off ivory, but at least they were clean. But Shimon wasn't staring at my hands. "Since when do you carry a smartphone?"

"Shimon, you know a girl named Alex Cooper?"

"Alexandra? I remember her. I haven't seen her in a few years, though."

"You know where she lives?"

"I know where her parents live. But she doesn't. Live, I mean. She died two, maybe three years ago. Heroin overdose."

"That would make sense. Frida said she was an addict. But it's not true. I saw her. Six months ago."

"Where?" Shimon frowned, then his eyebrows lifted, a look of understanding on his face. "I see. She was the girl in the hotel room. The bait."

"I need to know if she's still alive, Shimon."

He held his hand out and I handed it over reluctantly.

"This is Miss Winter's burner."

"Excuse me?"

"You know, a burner phone, like the drug dealers use. Every girl has one. No screen locks. They leave them around. Leak pictures to the tabloids. Deadspin, Snopes, TMZ."

He thumbed at the screen and passed it over, a selfie of Steph and Alex at a restaurant, heads together, smiling. "Time stamp is three days ago. Malibu."

"They just identified Alexandra Cooper's remains in the San Jacinto Canyon last night. Remains that were disposed a month or two ago."

"I see," he said. "She doesn't look dead at all. How much of her was found?"

"Bits and pieces."

"Like those bits and pieces?" He tilted his head toward the package on the passenger seat. "Where're you taking it to? UCLA? USC? Someplace with a biomedical program, yes? Perhaps some expertise in molecular biology? Tissue engineering? They won't help you. You might as well take it straight to the state crime lab. Have them match your biometrics and fingerprints while they're at it." He put his hand out, and I reluctantly handed it over. "Besides," he said. "You already know what it is."

"Meat."

"No," he said. "The appropriate name is flesh." He passed the package from hand to hand like he was weighing it. "I'd say about a pound."

CHAPTER 40

The University of Southern California's School of Dentistry is Los Angeles' oldest and, if you ask anyone not wearing blue and gold, its finest. But, like most urban universities, USC is caught in the classic conundrum of city schools surrounded by the growing poverty of the city center around it, subsisting on its steady stream of low-income patients, yet, simultaneously, hemmed in from any meaningful expansion.

Parking anywhere in the University Park area was non-existent, and I took the tram that ran across campus from the garage near the 110 to McClintock. It was filled with patients and students hurrying along to early morning seminars and appointments, and there was a distinct smell of sweat and fear among both: needle phobia for some, and a ninety thousand a year tuition bill for others.

The students, dressed in scrubs, had the occasional white coat hanging off shoulders or tucked into bags. Most of them had iPads open, cramming for upcoming tests.

One was flipping through slides on craniofacial anatomy, nerve and blood vessels that traced along the head and neck in white, red, and blue lace. Another was wading deep into histological specimens of taste buds.

I sized them up one at a time. Too tall. Too broad. Too male.

I followed a girl with short-cropped hair and similar build. I waited for her to step off the tram as the crowd squeezed and released like a drop of water. It was a routine I'd pulled often enough for it to be second nature. A bump, a shove, and it was five hundred feet before the girl realized her coat and ID was missing.

I checked my watch. Seven fifty-six. Four hours before the state of Nevada listed me as delinquent.

The inside of the Norris Clinic wasn't the hospital-like warren I expected. Instead of sharp-cornered white walls and small rooms, the building was open, two floors of textured laminate and curved glass with a wide-open atrium reminiscent of a cruise ship. I pulled the coat tighter like a shield, aware that the frayed jeans and sneakers were a dead giveaway amongst the sea of blue scrubs and crocs.

"Are you lost?" A lady in a crimson jacket and the USC logo emblazoned over the pocket came up and peeked at the ID.

"I'm looking for the auditorium."

"Uh-huh?" She was peering closely at the ID. Too closely. "You a student here?"

"Yeah."

"And you still don't know where the aud is."

"Just transferred." Most dental schools were situated near the kind of poverty-stricken neighborhoods I grew up in, and I threw the first name that came to mind. "Case Western."

"You're a long way from Ohio, Miss Yang."

I looked at the badge, dismayed. I really should have scoped the kid out better. I could pass for West Asian, but East Asian was a stretch.

"My fiancée moved here last year so I figured, what the heck." If she called security the nearest exit was a good fifty feet away, and the place was probably swarming with cameras. That would go over great with my parole officer in Henderson. Who, at this point, I was definitely going to be late for. "I guess everything's a long way from Ohio."

"Don't I know it. I'm from Chautauqua County, New York. From a little town called Stockton. Think anyone knows where that is? God, they probably couldn't even find Stockton, California. Come on."

She pulled me to the center of the building. "Stairs are here. Elevators down the hall. I'd take the stairs. Elevators take forever. Aud's on the second floor. Take a left and it's about halfway down. Can't miss it."

I got to the auditorium without attracting any further attention, but I was taking no chances. I found the darkest spot in the back, close access to the rear doors and a miniscule chance of getting called on.

A man leant over in the dark. "You missed all the good stuff." He was heavily bearded with a thick comb of greyish black hair. He looked too old to be a student, but he had a copy of *Mesenchymal Stem Cell Therapy* on his lap and he was highlighting in the dark. I could barely see the yellow marks on the paper, but he was running through it with the speed of someone who had memorized the book.

"You don't look like you're paying much attention anyway."

"Can do two things at once." He pointed in the direction of the podium, then at his book, and me. "Occasionally three."

"What did I miss?"

"Pluripotent stem cells, blah blah. Enzymatic digestion with collagenase, blah blah, sieve-size sorting blah blah. The difference between magnetic and fluorescence activated cell-" He stopped, looked at me carefully. "You don't get any of this, do you?"

"No."

"First year?"

"Yep."

"Want some advice?" He was back at the text, scribbling notes along the margin. "Dental school's way too difficult for you to straddle two canoes at the same time. Before long you've got your foot in neither and you're up the river with no canoe and only a paddle."

"So what do you suggest?"

"Just get your basic sciences out of the way. Anatomy, biochemistry, materials science. You know, doggy paddle before you backstroke. Worry about organ engineering later on. I mean, it's not even a real science yet. And anyone who tells you different is selling you snake juice."

"You're awfully cynical for a what, a fourth year?"

"Twenty-fourth. No, make that twenty-fifth year. And yeah, you'll have plenty of time to get cynical too."

The lights turned up suddenly and the lecturer at the podium was powering down her laptop and greeting the audience.

"Thank you again for bearing with me, but that's just a pre-amble. An amuse bouche, if you will."

There was a titter of polite laughter from the front row.

"I'd like to introduce our main course next, an expert in the field of nanotechnology and regenerative medicine. Someone who actually knows what he's talking about and won't hesitate to make it up if he doesn't."

"Sounds like quite the schmuck," the man whispered.

"Dr. Arthur Zahn comes to us from a certain University across town we won't mention by name."

More laughter.

"Dr. Zahn was the associate director for craniofacial reconstruction at Weintraub and was working on his Master's degree in molecular biology when we were able to steal him. I'm glad to say that, even though he recently retired as our director of biotechnology, he still maintains a close connection with our programs, and it makes me even happier to say that, when he received his PhD, it was in Trojan Red."

There was a hearty round of applause, and the man next to me got up and straightened his ancient tweed jacket.

"Well, I guess it's time to play the monkey." He bashed together a pair of imaginary cymbals. "Remember, one canoe, one paddle."

As he threaded his way down to the stage, heads turned, appreciative faces, hands still patting.

He strode down to the dais, taking the steps two at a time. "Thank you for your kind words, Doctor Ruiz, but unfortunately my lecture will be a slightly larger mouthful than your amuse bouche, so I hope everyone remembered to bring an appetite. And maybe some Pepto."

He flicked his hand, the lights dimmed, and a slide popped up, a young girl, coffee-colored skin, wide-bridged nose, and full red lips. One ear was half the size of the other. Her eyes were blacked out under a privacy bar, but I recognized her instantly.

"Classic presentation of Tanzer type-three microtia. The peanut ear. Traditionally reconstructed with a rib graft and free flap transfer. The Brent technique takes seven to eight separate operations. The Nagata version takes four but the results are far from perfect."

The next picture was the same, but her ear had been reconstructed to a saucer-sized shaped appendage.

"No rib grafts, no cartilage sculpting. No titanium implants. No silicone."

The screen changed again. The healed ear was half-moon shaped, the concha was developed and the helix separated.

"You know, the only problem we had was finding the *right* stem cell. Before 3D printing a matrix, before cultivation, before surgical tissue transfer, you need a cell. A cell that's down the line long enough to be able to be induced into cartilage, or skin, whatever you need. How about an easily accessible place that most everyone has? A throwaway body part that evolution has forgotten. A body part that you're more than likely going to have removed someday."

A phantom pain kicked up the side of my jaw.

He clicked the computer and a video of stem cells being extracted from a transected wisdom tooth played.

"One wisdom tooth. Just one. And all of that is the patient's own cells. With just a little prodding from us." He folded his arms. "Gives you chills, doesn't it?"

He was right. I was getting chills. He continued to speak but I couldn't hear his voice. I knew I definitely wasn't making my parole meeting either. The girl on the screen was staring at me through the blackness of the privacy blocks.

Her name was Shawna Cole.

CHAPTER 41

I cornered Dr. Zahn at the first break. He was at the coffee station wielding a set of plastic tongs, sizing up the meagre assortment of pastries on the table.

"I need to talk to you."

"Ah, the eager young freshman. I thought we already had our conversation. Danish or Croissant?"

"Depends. You want to die of diabetes or heart disease?"

He dropped the tongs onto the table. "You're definitely not going to get an internship with that attitude, missy."

His tone was harsh, but his eyes twinkled.

"I don't want an internship. In fact, I don't know a thing about dentistry or genetics."

"I know it feels that way but it won't last long."

I turned the badge out for him to see the face.

"Oh, you're not…" He squinted. "Not even close. What is this about?"

"I need to talk to you about Shawna Cole."

It was like a spotlight has been turned on. Dr. Zahn's demeanor changed from genial professor to defense witness. "Who?"

I passed a two by two of Shawna over to him. Quentin's arm was over her shoulder, the rest of him had long been cut off. "Shawna Cole. The first patient on your slideshow."

"I can't confirm that. I can't even-"

"You don't have to. I know her. Her name is Shawna. Born in Irvine. Nineteen ninety-two. Makes her twenty-six, if she's still alive. But she disappeared two years ago. Her remains turned up in the Fryman Canyon about six months ago. That last picture? You said it was two months ago."

"Are you law enforcement?"

"No."

"Did you contact the police?"

"I didn't. But you did. Filed a missing person's report when she didn't turn up for her recalls and you couldn't contact her. But you've been seeing her throughout. Surgical evals, post-ops."

Dr. Zahn looked around. There was a crowd milling, waiting patiently. "I'm sorry, but even if we forget the potential HIPAA ramifications here, this entire conversation is inappropriate. Do you have a question about my lecture that doesn't involve me breaking federal law?"

"No."

"Then you might want to return that lab coat before someone calls campus security. And I'd advise you to leave before I make that call myself."

"Doctor Zahn-"

He was gone, shaking hands and answering questions. He turned once, stared at me, then disappeared into the crowd. I slipped out of the jacket and dropped it onto one of the chairs as I took the back exit. There was no need to stay. I had Arthur Zahn's business card in my pocket. And his emergency number. It would take Vincent five minutes to track down his home address.

But first, I had an apology to make.

CHAPTER 42

Quentin was sitting at his usual spot at the Qwik' n Easy, shooting dice with a couple of kids half his size. An overweight brother lounged in a lawn chair nearby. It flexed so deeply under his sizable frame that his butt almost skimmed the ground.

He looked up as I pulled into a spot, his finger tracing an arc toward me. I could see his lips mouth the words *white devil*. I took offense to the term, considering I'm only partly white.

Quentin popped the dice in his pocket and leaned up against the wall, his bony frame like a bent pipe resting against the concrete. "Looky who's here," he said. "Straight out of the pokey. No leg bracelet, nothing."

"I wouldn't be too flippant. Shooting dice is illegal, you know."

"Nope. Betting money on dice is illegal. Shooting dice for fun. That's no crime."

I stepped on the pile of bills on the dirt. "Just because it's green don't mean it's grass."

"Just because it's brown don't mean it's dog-shit either."

I smiled, trying to give a little. If I was going to apologize I might as well make it count. I dropped a twenty onto the ground. "What's the buy in?"

"You crazy? This ain't the Wynn. Ante is a buck. And it's dice. Street craps. Not some fancy casino shit."

"I'm in. Seven elevens, right? Two, three, twelve's a crapper. Points or seven-outs. That it?" I found a dollar and added it to the pile. "I'm shooting."

"Uh-uh. My nuts, my shot." Quentin pulled the dice out, a ruby red pair with glossy white eyes. "Crap," he said. "Lucky twelve." The others dropped their bills and passed. He rolled the come out against the wall like he was trying to break it. A six and one stared up at him.

"Shit." He handed the money out.

"One more," I said. "But not for the penny slots." I dropped a ten-dollar bill. "You can shoot."

He matched the ten. "Crap," he called and rolled. Three and four.

"Shit," he said again. The kids were laughing now.

"Shut up." He stared them into submission and turned back at me. "Okay. You want to play? For reals?"

He pulled out a soiled Benjamin and flattened it against his shoe. It was a classic hustle and I knew it. I counted out ten Jacksons.

"You shoot." He handed me the dice.

I felt every contour of the plastic, rolling them in my fingers. "Pass," I called. The dice spun and settled.

Two sixes.

Q whooped and fist-bumped the kid next to him. "Told you. My money, honey."

"Sure," I said. "In exchange for the dice."

He stretched out his hand, palm open. "Take 'em. I don't need no dollar store dice."

"No. The other ones. The loaded ones."

Q stared at me angrily. "Search me. I don't have any other dice." He pulled the linings from his pockets and flattened them out like bunny ears.

"Hey, little man. Yeah, you." I pointed at the kid who had just fist bumped Q. "Open up."

I grabbed his wrists before he could stuff them into his pockets. A pair of red dice were cupped in his palm. I tossed them at Quentin. "What did you do? Melt 'em? Weight the eyes up?"

"Get lost." Q threw the money at me.

"Hey wait! I don't care about the money. Here. You can have it. I don't want it."

I followed Quentin as he stomped down the street. I peeked over my back, making sure no one was sneaking up on me. The big guy was still in his lounger, staring up at the sun through his black lenses. He looked like he was asleep.

"What do you want? Really? What the goddamn hell do you want? To make my life miserable? Because you're damn good at it."

"It's about Shawna."

"Again? We doing this again? Six months in the slammer and this is all you come up with?"

"I came to apologize, okay?"

For a moment he stopped, stared me down, even more suspicious. "You want to apologize? To me?"

"Shawna's alive."

"How do you know?"

"I know it. I can't prove it. But it's true."

The news hit him like a punch. He slumped against the wall and slid down onto his haunches. His mouth opened, but no sound came out.

"Quentin-"

"Is she okay? I mean, she's good?"

"Yes."

His face sunk into his palms, his breaths were muffled. It sounded like he was trying not to cry.

"Quentin."

"What?"

"She screwed you."

He looked up, his eyes red. "What do you mean?"

"You were set up. And so was I."

I tried to be brief, but it wasn't an easy story to tell. By the time I was done, I wasn't even sure I believed myself.

"I don't..." He stopped and looked away. "I can't do this." He got up and slouched off.

"Quentin!"

"Yeah?"

"You can walk away, but you can't pretend it didn't happen."

"Then what?" He asked. "Tell me. What do you want me to do?"

I knew what I wanted to do. I wanted to run. Disappear. But Steph was right. I wasn't getting away easy this time. "I don't know."

He marched up to me and shoved the dice into my hand. "Well, when you got it figured it out, you let me know."

CHAPTER 43

I saw a white box van behind me, blinkers on, crawling down the boule-vard. I let it pass, peered into the tinted windows, two men in mechanic style uniforms.

A cartoon character with an over-sized handlebar mustache was emblazoned on the side, a wrench and tool case in his hands. I noticed the edges of the sign had curled away from the sheet metal. Magnetic vinyl, not a wrap job.

It was half a block ahead of me now, awkwardly maneuvering itself into a spot that it would barely fit into sideways. I checked out the other side of the street. Two old men sat at undersized chairs next to the fire hydrant. A checkers board was set up on the small plastic table between them. A group of girls played nearby. Hopscotch, double-dutch, or some other game that kids don't play enough of nowadays.

It reminded me of Rochester. Minnesota. Or maybe New York. I was eleven, I remember that, and it was summer.

I had been in the system long enough to realize that the system was going to be long. When you're in the pipeline, the hope of adoption diminishes rapidly from the day you enter. It's like a puppy at the pound. One moment you're lovable and cute, and before you know it they're pointing at you sadly, going: *oh, you don't want her, she has problems.*

Yet, there I was. Rochester. Definitely New York. On a street called Park Avenue no less, taken in by a sweet older couple who had never had kids and were trying their hands at renting one. The best part was Mr. Harris spent most of the afternoon sleeping on the couch while I played out front. Later I would learn that he had contracted a rare form of blood cancer which would end my stint at the Harris household in under six weeks.

But for that short summer I just camped out on the porch and watched old men play cards and dominoes and girls draw lines in the pavement with sidewalk chalk. Occasionally they asked me to join in, but I always refused. I was a rental, not a buy, so I wasn't about to get comfortable.

"Hey, you playing?" The little girl in front of me had an earnest look, drawn tighter by the seashell braids that wrapped over her ears. I smiled at her. "No, I'm not, kiddo."

"Then get off my square."

"Oh." I looked down at the concrete, the chalk a mix of blue suns and yellow moons. It was a game I'd never played before and I stepped off. The girl was still pointing. Past me.

The door to the van was open, and two figures were walking toward us. I grabbed her by the arm and pulled her behind me.

"You kidding me?" The girl pulled her hand away. "They ain't looking for us, dummy. They've been following you."

She was right. The uniforms were making a bee-line in my direction. They approached in opposite directions, hands reaching into their shirts. A knife, perhaps? A taser?

I took the only exit, a stairway leading to a small office suite. An attorney or an accountant down on their luck. Maybe one who never had luck at all.

The door was open, and I found myself in an old corridor of hand scraped wooden floors in dire need of refinishing. There were bulletin boards on all the walls, notices piled on top of each other. I grabbed a couple of silver buttoned push-pins and hid them in my pocket. One of the frosted glass doors was open and I slipped in.

A woman sat behind the desk, phone at her ear, propped against her shoulder with a plastic buttress. She was eating a sandwich, mouth open, a creamy white circle of mayo and turkey. My finger pressed against my lips, and I tucked in under the adjacent desk.

I was crouched in the crawl space under the table when the first pair of legs came through, high-cut gabardine slacks with subtle black argyle. Banker's socks, not a match for the uniforms I had seen outside. The other two had probably taken the front and back exits. It left me with little choice.

There was about a foot of space under the privacy bar, and I had a straight line shot at his ankles. I stuck one of the push pins into the back of his calf, just below the cuff line. He yelped and dropped to his knees. The second pin sunk into the hand that grabbed at his ankles. He was in agony, and it was easy to grab his collar and pull his head under the bar.

I could see his eyes, immediately bloodshot, tiny rivers of red cutting across the white corneas. It was like a magician's trick gone wrong, his body stuck on the outside and his head, beet red and sweaty, in my lap under the box. The woman at the desk was screaming, but she hadn't dialed 911 yet. I had five seconds before this all went to hell. Maybe less.

"What the fuck do you want?" I asked.

"Medina wants to talk." His words sputtered through gritted teeth.

"No shit. Tell her I'm listening."

A pair of black stilettos clicked behind him. "Jesus, Portia, are you always like this?"

I let go and clambered out. I had a knife pointed at her from across the desk. "Spend a couple of months in the big house and you'll get there. What the hell are you doing here?"

"Looking for you," Medina said.

"Next time just send a text."

"Where? You don't have a phone. An email. Mailing address. You just have half a dozen drop boxes in half a dozen cities."

"I meant at Steph's."

"I don't work for Miss Winter anymore."

"Well, I sure as hell can't pay you."

"I know," Medina said. "It's on my own time." She sat on the edge of her desk. "If you won't stab me, I'll go quid pro quo."

I folded up the switchblade and tucked it into my shoe. The man pulled himself up from under the table. His bald head was freckled with perfect bubbles of sweat, the flimsy third eyebrow ruffled. He looked like he was ready to swing at me. I was glad it wasn't Guerrero, a little bummed it wasn't Carlson. "I'm sorry," I said.

"Fuck you," he muttered as he slouched out.

"How much is the daily?" Medina asked the woman at the desk. She was still sitting there, phone cupped to her ear, sandwich still perched perfectly between her fingers.

"What daily?"

"Rent? How much?"

"Three thousand a month."

Medina whistled. She peeled off two bills. "Two hundred. That'll cover rent, electric, and whatever else." She laid another on the table. "And that's for your trouble."

"We have appointments."

Medina peeked at the ledger. "No, you don't. I only need fifteen minutes. Just take a breather. You need one."

The woman crumpled the bills into her pocket and hurried out. Her eyes wouldn't leave me as the door swung closed.

"Looks like you have that kind of effect on a lot of people. Don't you get tired of it?"

Medina dropped into the chair behind the desk and rolled her ankles up on the tabletop. Her shoes, even the undersoles, were spotless. "I mean, don't you ever think it's time to settle down? Get a normal job?"

"I don't do normal. And I'm an ex-con. You know anyone hiring?"

"I'd hire you."

I stared at her, from the perfectly pressed ponytail to the gilt sunglasses to the pointed faux gator Choos. "Do I have to wear the uniform?"

"The clothes again?" Medina grinned. "Okay. I'm sure you'll find something with a less demanding dress code. Are you good with baling hay? Picking berries?"

"I think I'll stick with-"

"Just thought I'd ask." She threw over a padded manila envelope. It landed perfectly in the center of the desk. A pack of neatly arranged eight by tens shot with a telephoto lens.

I shuffled through the pictures, young women in a tropical setting, oversized hats and black dark glasses.

"I thought this was going to be about Nathan Hunter, not his sister."

"You're missing the ocean for the breeze."

"I don't care about your vacation pics." I stopped. The photograph in my hand quivered. The girl was in direct focus, reaching for a drink, pink and frozen. Her eyes were open, vacant. Bored.

"Last one's the money shot, isn't it? I cross-checked with departure and arrival records," Medina said. "Stephanie Winter was in and out three times over a period of a year. Multiple entry visas. Standing accommodations at the Lucerna. Always used the same alias."

"Marcia Hunter."

"Yep," Medina said. "Marcia Hunter. Do you want to see more, or are my vacation pictures boring you?"

I nodded. Medina turned over another photograph. "Kelsey Kreiner. Twenty-two. Parents own Kreiner shipping. Went missing around July of sixteen. Maybe six months after you found Stephanie Winter. Her blood was found all over the backseat of a Chevy Silverado abandoned in the Salinas area. Mr. Kreiner dropped off twenty million in unmarked diamonds in a laundry bag at a Golden Sheets laundry. It went into dryer number three. Cops surveilled the place, had a remote cam hooked up. No one touched up the bag. Yet when they retrieved it, there were just glass beads in it."

"It was an inside job."

"The cops thought so. But they had no leads. Kelsey was found walking CA-198 near Visalia near three days later."

My hands crushed the edges of the paper, leaving grease prints. Medina peeled it out of my hands and put it back into the folder. She dropped another picture onto the table.

"Casey Francke. Heir to the Francke Leasing empire. Twenty- six. Disappeared two, maybe three months after Kelsey. There were two packages sent to her home. The first was her underwear stained with her own blood. The second was a strip of flesh. Probably a section of hamstring."

I winced.

"Grandparents wired twenty-five million to a bank in the Channel Islands. The money was lifted directly from the account. Made its way to Vilnius, then Moscow, then Budapest. All in a matter of minutes. It turned up in Memphis an hour later, then disappeared. Casey was found at a bus-stop in Reno the next week. She was incoherent. Drugged. But strangely enough, she could walk. In spite of her wounds."

"I had no clue."

"No, but you should. You're getting soft, Portia. You've been in the black box so long you don't know which way is up. This was never about drugs. You probably already figured that out, right?"

"It was always about the girls," I said.

"Belladonna. Memphis meat. Your DNA turning up in inconvenient places?" She shook her head. "How did you meet Stephanie?"

"Mr. Winter called me."

"Right after the Harvey Andersen case. They found pieces of him fed to his pigs, right? That was you?"

"He had it coming to him. Look. I got a call. I did my job."

"I'm sure you did. That's how it all got fucked up."

The vulgarity was foreign to Medina's tongue and I could tell whatever was coming next was going to be bad. "You a cutter or a choker?"

"Excuse me?"

"Cutter. The knife in the sock is a dead giveaway. It's always there. Like you're tempting yourself. But then again choking doesn't leave a mark. You know, two thumbs on the jugulars just long enough to get you into hypoglycemic shock. Who needs drugs anymore-"

"What the hell are you talking about, Medina?"

"What I'm talking about? What do you think rich kids do when the doors close? Play some shitty game you can play in a two bedroom in Nebraska? When you have all the money in the world and nothing to spend it on? There are only so many yachts you can buy, parties you can attend. Life is shitty, right?"

"Steph's kidnapping was a game?"

"Not just a game. The *game*. Best game in town. Like Russian Roulette. If the whole politburo was playing it. God, there was a time you couldn't get kidnapped if your life depended on it. No fury like a rich girl scorned."

"There was no payout from the Winters."

"Exactly. You took care of that. Now you owe somebody a lot of money."

"Steph." I got a flashback to the club. The girl with the enema. The one who had called me Nebraska.

Relax, she belongs to Steph.

She's in the game.

You in the game?

"The Winters ransom money was supposed to be the setup money for Nathan and Marcia Hunter. But when life gives you lemons, right?"

"So, they decided to give some other rich friends a chance to suck some money from their parents."

"And all they needed to up the ante was some really convincing DNA. By the way, how was that lecture at USC? What was his name, Dr. Zahn? Pluripotential stems? You know where his funding's coming from? Not the NIH, that's for sure."

"How much time have you been spending on me? I mean, you're not getting paid. I can't imagine I'm worth it just as a hobby."

"You're no hobby. I told you. You're a pain in my ass."

The woman was back at the door. "The boss usually comes back in around two. And we really do have appointments scheduled at-"

"We're done here." Medina waved the woman off. "You know something. I know you probably won't tell me. It's part of your M.O. You won't give anyone shit. The less they know, the less they'll blow, right? But eventually you're going to have to trust someone. You know why? You missed your parole. You probably think it doesn't matter. You're under the radar. You can just change your name again. Slip off to Oregon. Or Idaho. But they have you fingerprinted now. They have your DNA registered. They don't have your real name. If you actually have one. But it doesn't matter, does it? If they have your DNA, they have you."

She leaned in, stared me down. "So, if you think you're just going to run, you can't. Sooner or later someone's going to come find you. If it's not the cops, it's someone worse. And this shit you've gotten yourself into? It's a mile deep."

Medina waked to the door, her heels clicking loudly against the wood floor. "I'm leaving in an hour. We'll find Hunter. If we can tie him to Belladonna, that might help your case. If we can tie him to any of the girls, even better."

"What do you want me to do in the meantime?"

"I suggest you come clean. Nobody will believe you. At first. But the dates, the bodies, the locations will all check out. Heck, you don't actually have blood on your hands. They might even go easy on you. Pay your dues, you'd probably be out in a couple of years. But with a real name, a real life for once."

"I'd be an ex-con with no skills."

Medina stared me down. "As opposed to what?"

CHAPTER 44

Shimon was halfway up a stand ladder, noise-cancelling headphones over his ears, a cordless driver in one hand, a rotating camera in the other. Four or five fasteners stuck out of his mouth. It made me feel sick to my stomach.

It was the screws. I'd know them anywhere. Four and a half-inch lag bolts. Quarters. Hex heads with a box driver. Hot dipped galvanized. Three quarters of a millimeter of pure zinc surrounding a core of alloyed iron and low carbon steel.

They took me back to 2012. The first case I'd ever worked on. A missing thirteen-year-old, milk-carton smile, headgear, pigtails. It ended in a maintenance closet, the sour smell of machine oil and a whole box of lag bolts. Every psychopath knows where to find the worst possible torture implements. Home Depot. Lowes. Ace. Between the wood and the appliances. Brad nailers, u-staplers, and nail guns. I know the sound of each, but the sound of a drill, any drill, especially the high torque of a box wrench, coats my throat in a sour purge.

"Why didn't you tell me?" I asked.

Shimon wouldn't turn. He knew I was here. He'd seen me a mile away. He plugged another bolt in and my teeth stung.

"Shimon!"

"I had a friend back in the old country," Shimon said. "His name was Eli. We grew up on a kibbutz together. Kibbutz Afik. In the Golan Heights. We were like pilgrims in Indian Country. But we scraped something together. Chickens. Cows. Fruit trees. We ate together, studied together, worked the dairy together."

He pulled one of the earpieces off. He was swiveling the camera from side to side, lining up the trajectory. "But Eli was a year older so there was always this divide, you know, this knowledge that it was all just temporary. That eventually we wouldn't be friends anymore."

He came down the ladder slowly, his back still facing me. "Then it happened. He got conscripted, joined the IDF. It was 1982. Eight months later he was in Lebanon. They assassinated Gemayel a week after he got there and his company was assigned to a PLO refugee camp. Shatila. You might have heard of it. Their job was to blockade the entrances and provide cover. Sounded like a good job, a decent job. Keeping the bad guys out, yes? Until he heard the sounds. Like popping rocks in a can. He never went in, never fired a shot. But when he came back?"

He turned and looked at me. Through me. "Every time there was a sound, a dropped plate, a slamming door, he looked a lot like you do when a drill goes off. I don't want that for you, Portia. I'm trying to prevent-"

"So, what you're trying to say is I shouldn't be mad at you for lying to me all this time. I should thank you. For fixing me before I got too broken. What you're trying to tell me was that this all happened for a reason. That it was meant to be."

"None of this was meant to happen. I know it's hard to see it that way now. But life's messy. You plan for one thing to happen and, well, the point is, we didn't want you hurt. And you're not. Not yet."

"Boy, have I been ungrateful. Battery, assault, kidnap, rape. But at least I'm not dead, right?"

"You weren't raped."

"The hell you know."

"I know. I read the reports. You had some rope burn on your wrists, bruises on the abdomen, the oral trauma. Isn't that, what do they call it, the cost of doing business?"

"Fuck you, Shimon."

Frida was in the doorway, sloshing water from an oversized watering can. "Don't mind him, dear. He's from Israel. They mean well but they're not known for tact."

"How about you? How long have you known?"

"Long enough." She had the metal can braced across her chest like a weapon. "And tact or no tact, I think the old fool is right. Your hand twitches. Your eyes are squinty. You're looking at my watering can like you think I'm about to swing it at you. Break off the spout and drive it down your throat? You don't trust anyone, Portia. That's not a good thing. Once you stop trusting, you're already lost."

"Who should I trust? You? Him? You brought me in here on a lie. You two were lying to me before I even met you."

"They didn't lie to you. I did." A large man stood at the door, an oversized pair of sunglasses perched in the middle of a Prince Valiant haircut, like a bird in its nest. "And in my defense, Portia? I was protecting my daughter. Sad to say, I'd do it again. Even if she is a coke sniffing tramp."

He turned and disappeared into the house. I could see Steph standing behind him, wrapped in a blanket, a little girl waiting for her punishment. Like a long-restrained animal she came hurtling at me, clutching me desperately.

"I'm sorry," she cried. Her eyes were appropriately red, but the tears seemed forced.

I should've punched her. After everything, I had the right to do far worse. But my hands were loose, my temper well under control. I realized it never mattered. We were never friends. "You can dial it down, sister."

"You think this is a joke? Because I'm not joking. I never knew it would go this far."

"Well, you should've."

"No, not another word." I fully expected her to collapse on the ornate silk daybed, the back of her hand glued daintily to her forehead. "Not until I've explained everything." She pulled me into the kitchen. "Look, it's stupid, right? I know what you're thinking. Bunch of rich kids with nothing better to do. You don't know what it's like. You think it's just lying by the pool, finding ways to spend daddy's money."

"Sounds horrendous."

"You wouldn't know. You've been out there. You know what it feels like. To live." Her breathing was rapid, shallow. "I'm empty. I feel nothing. It's like I'm drowning every day. I can't walk by a kitchen knife without wondering how sharp the blade is. I can't look at a fan without wondering if I can swing a rope over it."

"Jesus." I spun my knife on the table, the handle facing her. "Go ahead."

"Portia-"

"Don't *Portia* me. You're sick. What about your parents? What about me?"

"I said I'm sorry. What do you want me to do?"

"Tell me where Hunter is."

"I don't know where he is. Seriously."

I was across the table and on her like an animal. The blade sat across her neck, the skin red and white under the serrations.

"Don't fuck with me, Steph. I know about Shawna. About Alexandra. About Belladonna. You don't want to tell me, then don't. We're going to find him. And when we find him-"

There was a look on her face, half fear, half delight. *Joy.* It was the same face I saw the first time I met her. In that little dungeon.

"You don't know shit, sister. You think you know, but you don't," Steph said. "But you'll find out. Soon."

I stood up, watched her cower. There was a break in the skin where I pressed too hard. A spreading stain across her hips. She dropped to her knees, smiling that terrible smile, holding her hands out like she was begging to be cuffed.

"You're sick."

"You already told me."

I turned and pushed my way past her. She had her hands around my knees. "Don't leave me alone," she begged.

"Sit down, Portia," Mr. Winter said. "We need to talk." He was behind his desk, signing a sheaf of papers with a gold Mont Blanc.

"There's nothing to talk about. I know how this works. You express your regret without actually apologizing. Throw a number at me. Pretend that I can just walk away."

He kept sifting through. The pen scratched the paper rapidly. "Why don't we do it your way then? How about you throw me the number?"

"Twenty-two."

"Twenty-two what?"

"That's the number. Twenty-two. That's the number of pigs off the streets. I know it doesn't sound like much to you, but it's something to me. They're not million-dollar contracts. But it's not about the money. It's about twenty-two animals that can't hurt anyone again. That's twenty-two animals that will never haunt a parent's nightmares. That's about one every four months. There's no law enforcement agency, no judiciary that can come close to it. I have thirteen more contracts out there. I have one I'm so close to, I can actually smell his stench. I'm so close, and the last thing I need is to waste my time on a teenage game. Are you even listening?"

"Yes." He put his pen down and looked up. "I hired you to find my daughter. She was kidnapped. You succeeded. Admirably, I must say. The rest is unfortunate."

"Unfortunate? She was kidnapped by a thug *she* hired. All you had to do was make a payment. Or sit and wait. She wasn't in any danger."

"I wasn't paying my idiot daughter a penny. I definitely wasn't paying her drug-dealing friends."

"You went with option C."

"Actually, option D. Option C was someone more experienced, more traditional. Someone like Medina and her crew. But Shimon said you couldn't be beat. He called you option X, if I remember rightly. He meant it as a compliment, of course. After seeing your work, I would agree. If I had to do it over, I'd promote you to option A. From a purely strategic standpoint, of course. But that's of no consequence now. The problems are not behind us. They're ahead of us. How we get you out."

He turned the sheaf of papers around and pushed them across the table.

"You think money's going to make me happy?"

Mr. Winter smiled. "Whoever said money doesn't buy happiness probably didn't have enough. Now you do."

I pushed the pile back. "You do realize I can't go anywhere. Not without leaving pieces of me behind. And I mean actual pieces."

"So? Leave the pieces behind. They're no good once you're gone. What you definitely can't do is stay here. I'm giving you a lifeboat. Don't expect a king-size bed to go with it. My attorneys assure me no one will be able to trace the money. It's in drop boxes anywhere you want it. You can access it wherever you go. I'd suggest leaving the country. Just in case. Ecuador. Thailand. Botswana. Plenty of nice places to live. You can retire at, what? Twenty-four? Twenty-five? It's not like this was going to last forever anyway. It's a dream."

I stood and settled the papers into a neat pile. "You know the difference between a dream and a nightmare, Mr. Winter? Perspective."

I threw the papers into the fireplace.

"You know that's not a real fireplace, Portia."

"It's not a real offer either."

"You want to know what's real?" He began to unbutton his shirt. I cringed. "Don't look at me like that, I'm not Weinstein-ing you. You're not my type, anyway." He pulled the collar down and exposed a pasty swath of skin. A pink scar ran across one nipple.

"So what, you got cut? I've got plenty."

The other flap of his shirt was off and I could see the pink lines connect from one side of the chest to the other. It wasn't a cut. It was an engraving. "It spells Dago, in case you were wondering. D-A-G-O. It's kind of hard to read now; that's what scars do after fifty years."

He moved over to the fireplace, ran his fingers over the ornate gold engraving. "I didn't grow up here, Portia. Not like this, for sure. I'm a mucker. Once a mucker, always a mucker. Onion muck. Back home in upstate New York. My father died when I was five. My brothers and I all worked the muck to help my mom out."

He turned and faced me his shirt still pulled open. "You're in the shit when it's July and it's so hot you have to rip your tongue off the roof of your mouth to put two words together. You're in the shit when it's October and it's already below freezing, and you still have six fields to go and a tractor to unstick. All you think of is, I don't know? Getting dry? Getting warm? Getting to bed? All you think is how the thirty bucks in your pocket is going to pay for the heat that comes out of the grate you sleep on."

He finally buttoned his shirt back up. Slowly.

"And then you get jumped because the quickest way home is through the Polish side of town. You get christened with a shaving blade. Do you know what Dago means? It's a corruption of the word Diego. That's what they called Spaniards, Portuguese, Italians. Because there were a lot of Diegos amongst us. We called the Poles *chucks*. You know? Because of how their names ended. Silly, isn't it?"

He popped up the globe and tapped the bottles on the cap. He ended at the Sazerac, pulled it out and handed it over.

"You don't need a glass, do you?" He took the Karuizawa and unscrewed the cap, and took a swig. "I'm not making excuses. I know you hold back puke every time you look at Steph and her friends, but before you look at these kids? Before you castigate them, brand them? Before you pretend you even know them, you might want to remember that we were pretty silly ourselves when we were young."

"I spent my childhood dodging punches and pervs. I didn't have time for silly."

"I won't pretend to know anything about your life, Portia. But you don't know much about Steph's either. I know that you won't understand the pressures, the conflicts, the terrifyingly privileged world out there."

"Terrifying?"

He chuckled and tilted the bottle at me. "There's the life I knew. And there's the life Steph knows. God knows, I'd pick mine. And despite everything, I know you'd pick yours. The point is, we both made our choices. We're not here because of Steph. We're here because of *us*. We'd be here eventually. One way or the other. Because we made our choices. That's life.

If I were you, I'd take the money. And get to keep making choices. What else do you want?"

As I stared at him and realized, for the first time, I wasn't sure anymore.

Shimon was sitting on the steps, sorting his tools into a tackle box. I sat next to him and wound an extension cord into a tight roll.

"What happened to Eli?"

"He died." Shimon snapped the chest closed. He looked at me. "He came home after that first tour. It was supposed to be a vacation, a happy time. His sister was getting married, the kibbutz was doing well, we were all doing well." He stopped.

"He didn't make it, did he?"

Shimon nodded slowly. "We found him hanging from a fan hook. They said he was weak, that he should have been put at a desk job, not thrown onto the frontlines. But Eli was not weak. He was good. And when good people have that stripped from them, they have nothing left. They're just a shell waiting to break up."

I handed over the cord and stood up. Shimon was right. The tight loop of wire looked just about the size of my neck.

"Portia, you've got that look in your eye too. Just go. Take the money. Go. Do something else. There won't be anything left of you."

"There's nothing left of me now."

CHAPTER 45

Dr. Zahn pulled into the garage and parked at the very last spot, near the exit ramp. He was driving a beater with a large dent in the fender. It could have been a lack of worldliness or just a healthy dose of respect for L.A. traffic. Either way, I was impressed. In a town where every other car was a Tesla, a ninety-six Oldsmobile Cutlass was a statement car.

I followed him up the stairway and into the marbled floor of the apartment building. The doorman was occupied with a busty young woman with silver-blonde hair and yoga pants so tight the black lycra was translucent. I slipped past, took the stairs two at a time, and exited on the sixth floor, following the sharkskin jacket down the corridor. I toed the door as it swung closed and followed him in, blade drawn.

This was a city that spawned not one, but two, night stalkers. Housebreakers in the city were a vicious bunch and most Angelenos are liable to have a can of mace or a stun gun near the key rack.

Zahn slipped off his coat without worry, hung it up on the rack, and checked his carefully moussed hair in the mirror. He was a good-looking man, even with his back to me, broad-shouldered, just enough gray in his beard to make him look distinguished but not quite old.

I made a mental target of the area between the shoulder blades. If I hit him hard enough I could have him arm-barred on the floor with minimal damage. But I didn't have to. Zahn already knew I was here.

"Put the knife away, young lady."

"Why don't you put your hands behind your back and I'll make this easy."

"No," he said. He clicked a button on his phone and faced it at me. It was a live picture of me following him into the bay doors. "I saw you in the lobby too. Edgar's a good man. If you just want your packages and mail delivered. Put a pretty face, or better yet Margaux Miller's booty in front of him, and he'd let the fifth fleet pass by before he notices. So, what would you like to drink?"

He walked over to the mini-bar, a single decanter and glass lounging against the ice-bucket. Everything in the apartment seemed lonely, like it had been broken off from a set. "Was I a hard follow?"

"No, that clunker is an easy tag in this neighborhood."

"Sorry to disappoint you. The Mercedes and most everything else went with the missus and her new boyfriend. But I'll trade you for your little red number. It's probably about the same level. Clunker-wise."

It was my turn to be taken aback. "You trailed me. I'm flattered."

"Don't be. I wanted to make sure." He tilted the decanter and squinted at it. "Apparently she took all the good liquor too. What'll it be? Mezcal or Mezcal on the rocks?"

"Make sure of what? You thought I was going to jump you? Now I'm really flattered."

"Isn't that what you're doing though? The knife's still in your sleeve."

He motioned me to a table in the corner and pushed a drink in front of me. "No, I'm not scared of being jumped. That was my first divorce. My second was a sucker punch. I was checking up on you. I had a feeling after that scene you made at the school so I made a couple of calls. I know who you are. Frankly I'm disappointed. I was expecting a little more Charles Bronson. A little less Joan Jett."

"I'm not a vigilante, if that's what you're going for."

"Let's see, you track violent criminals and kill them. That's pretty much the definition of a vigilante."

"I never killed anyone."

"No, that's right. You trap them, but you don't pull the trigger. What do you call that?"

"Justice."

"No courts, no defense, no chance? Some people would say that's the complete opposite of justice. It's a one-woman lynch mob."

"I was seven years old when my grandma died. My first foster parents were the Mays. Big stinky Charlie May and his little ratty wife, Meg. They had me take my clothes off in their living room. They filmed me. Called it a medical exam. Making sure I wasn't bringing fleas into the house is what they said. They sold the tapes for fifty a pop. Sold a hundred copies. This was before the internet got big. I'd have sold thousands now. Be a big star."

Zahn raised his hand, trying to stop me.

"You know what they said at social services when I told them? That I was lucky they hadn't touched me. Then when they did, I complained again. They said I was making things up. I ran away twice. Got beaten up twice. The second time they made a mistake and left a permanent mark below my neckline. You know how the Marines won't let you in if you have a tattoo below your sleeve? CPS doesn't like scars. Especially one that are visible with a t-shirt. You want to see it?"

"Okay, okay, I get it. You had a rough life. I'm sorry."

"I don't need your sympathy. I need an answer. I know what's going on. About Rosarito. Hunter. Everything. Frankly, I don't give a crap about how these little shits shake their parents down. But Shawna wasn't rich. Neither was Alex. They don't get to stick their toes into the sand while mommy and daddy wire their inheritance to the Caymans."

"You're right." Zahn piled them together like a deck of cards without looking at them. "Shawna isn't rich," he said. "She could've been, though."

There was a lightness to his tone I didn't expect. It was like a funeral director humming through an open casket service.

"I'm sure you know you've been fingered, haven't you?"

The way he put it made my skin crawl. Cold. Calculated. He'd been a step ahead of me since the school, and now he was the smart kid in class, prepped with all the answers. He patted the tip of his nose with an upraised middle finger.

"Word gets around," I said.

"In the appropriate circles."

"And which circle are you?"

"Jesus, you'll find me in every single one. Lust. Gluttony. Greed. Wrath." He stopped. "Avaritia. Greed. Don't listen to what they say. Greed." He swallowed his drink in one gulp. "It's not so good. Look, it's been a long day, so can I just dispense with protocol and wade right into the shit?"

"Go ahead."

"I'll need to pat you down first. Just to make sure you aren't wired." He showed me the back of his hands like a TSA officer and proceeded to pat me down the rib cage and up my calves and thighs.

I flinched, knowing what was coming.

"I'm sorry, especially considering, you know, your past. But I know a guy who did all his interviews naked in a hot tub so you're getting off easy." His hands climbed up the center of my thighs towards my panty line.

"Okay, that's enough. I'm not wired."

"I need to be sure."

My fingers balled up into fists. "Who am I wiring up for? The cops. The FBI?"

"True enough." He threw his hands up in mock surrender. "Okay, quid pro quo. You can search me if you want."

"Pass. Just talk."

"About five years ago I had a great job, a booming private practice. The occasional hospital stint, the occasional lecture. On the outside, you'd think things were great. But like most people, I wasn't happy. Isn't that the worst thing in the world? Happiness? I mean it's our national motto, isn't it? Life, liberty, and blah blah blah."

He folded his arms tightly.

"Well, I've come to find that happiness is the worst thing in the world. I mean, if you can just fall ass-backwards into it, if it's just dumb luck then, by all means. But it's the pursuit. It's that itch to give everything up just to find happiness because you think Joe Blow down the corner is happier. It's bullshit. No one's happy unless you're dumb, drunk, or drugged."

"I'm guessing you quit your practice and went into research."

"I have an undergrad at Stanford, a Master's degree from UCLA, and a PhD from USC. All in molecular biology. Dental school, surgical residencies just got sandwiched in there somehow. But lab work is my love. I know cells, I understand them. I've got a red thumb, if you will. I can grow shit out of a fragment of flesh or blood you wouldn't dream of. But when we discovered pluripotential stem cells, man, the lid was off and the soup was boiling. We just dumped the alphabets in and we were gone."

He put the decanter to his lips and drained half of it.

"All that was in my way was a cashflow problem. This was big money. Real money. But to make big money you have to put up big money. What I had from selling my office drained pretty quickly, and universities are particularly stingy when they don't have full control."

He rubbed his fingers together like he was counting bills. "The NIH, other major players don't want to invest in labs that aren't university-sanctioned either. Lone wolves tend to go belly up pretty rapidly."

He shook the decanter, looking at the sad pool of amber gathering in the crevices of the crystal.

"Anyway, where was I? Oh, yeah, no money. My wife was already seeing another man, my kids hated me, my mortgage was unpaid, but I just kept on chugging. I was hired by Neogen for some shitty lab-cultured meat deal. I assume you met with that schmuck Murphy already? Well that's when we got the call from Belladonna. Money finally wasn't an issue anymore, and at first everything seemed like it was on the up and up. I mean, it was a straight up investment. They never even asked for anything."

"So, you had no idea."

He cut me off with a swift slice of his palm. "Oh, come on, Miss Portia. Nobody invests that kind of dough without asking for something. It's like kissing someone's pinky ring and saying you don't know he was the capo. I just made it feel like we were disconnected. Like there was an information leak in the lab and there was nothing I could do to control it. Besides, we were do-gooders. We were growing people new skin, new cartilage, new bone. What could go wrong with that?"

"The possibilities are endless."

"Every new technology has its dark side. You can't stop progress on the off-hand that someone will find a way to use it."

"Hunter."

"What about him?"

"Did you deal directly with him?"

"Sure. He paid my checks. I guess you could say I was Botticelli, he was Lorenzo."

"Where is he?"

"Your guess is as good as mine. But the girls? That one I can actually answer." He turned his phone on and shuffled through the pictures. There was one of her, undeniably Shawna, sitting in a clinic room. "This is the one, right?"

"Yes."

"Shawna was a patient of mine. She had no money. No insurance. She'd just been in an automobile accident with her boyfriend. He'd been drinking. Quite heavily. Of course, he got away without a scratch."

I closed my eyes. "Quentin."

"She protected him, took the blame. Told the cops she was driving. And then the little shit turned around and dumped her."

"How badly hurt?"

"Broke a bone or two, nothing too terrible. But her ear was severed off. They tried suturing it back on, but it was too damaged. So, she was sent to me. I was already working with Hunter. We needed a test subject and she needed some work done. I had the stems and everything. All we needed was to buy the rights."

"But it wasn't money she wanted. It was Quentin."

"We evened the scales a bit."

"What about Alexandra Cooper?"

"You know how hard it is to break through that glass ceiling. Middle class in America? It just sucks. Might as well be poor nowadays. Alex was the girl in the middle. So, she did what she could. She knew the club kids, Shawna knew the street dealers. Made a pretty good team. Until Alex started using. You know they say a dealer should never use? No one told her that. God, she was probably snorting more than she was selling. Girls like that end up selling more than just drugs. I mean bodies. And not only in a prostitution sense. I mean, *bodies*."

Zahn placed a finger suggestively in the decanter and twirled it around. A drop of liquid hung onto his fingertip and he sucked it off.

"I suppose you want to meet them."

"Meet whom?"

"Shawna. Alexandra. They're here. I mean, not *here* here. But they come up for appointments on the regular." He shook the bottle, squeezing out the last drops. "In fact, I believe I'm seeing Shawna tomorrow. Six p.m."

He handed me a business card with an address on it. "Now I'm just putting you two in the same place at the same time. Nothing more. Don't expect me to introduce you. I'm her doctor. I'm still bound by the rules. I'm not breaking it because of your circumstances. If she refuses to talk, she refuses to talk. She has to think it's by chance, okay?"

He went to the door and stood by it, expectantly.

"There's no such thing as chance." I tucked the card into my pocket.

"Yeah. And you, of all people, should know that."

CHAPTER 46

The card was plain ivory cardstock, no embellishments nor embossing. In simple blue letters down the middle it said: BELLADONNA LAB-ORATORIES. The script was simple. It seemed like a card generated by a computer, one of those online deals; pick a color, background, and font and we'll send you the first five hundred free. It was a card for a corner cupcakery, the local electrician, not the nameplate of a high-tech startup.

Below the name was a phone number, an out of state code for an answering service that played early John Coltrane and Miles Davis, but didn't take messages. On the reverse was a handwritten note with an address way up in the Agoura Hills.

I was at the end of this road now, at a solid white gate in the middle of the woods. There was no signage nor security, just an articulated camera perched on the post. I stuck the business card out of the window and watched it zoom in, its black eye blinking as it recorded. The gate rolled open and I rambled up a grass-lined road that ended in a teardrop circle.

The building in front of me was a Dali painting come to life, a series of curved aluminum wings that folded over each other like the pages of a book aflutter. It was hard to tell where the entrance was without the series of granite paving stones.

A stream ran through the blocks, fifteen or twenty hungry Shubunkin gathering, nipping at the heels. The walkway ended at a sliding glass door.

The inside of the building was lab white, the reception desk covered in a single sheet of scalloped aluminum that matched the exterior.

"I'm looking for Doctor Zahn," I said.

"I know," the young man behind the desk said. He didn't look up. There was a waiting room with rows of chairs but no one waiting. I was obviously the only appointment.

"I'm early," I pushed. "I'm supposed to be here at six."

"I know." He was still at the computer, sliding his finger across a black tracing screen. "You like it?" he said finally.

"What?"

He waved his hand in an extended semi-circle, palm up, like a tour guide.

"Oh, yes. It's nice."

"Just nice?"

"It's Gehry gone wild."

"Gehry gone wild. I like that. Can I use it?"

"Sure." I looked around. There didn't seem to be anyone else in the building. "Listen, I left my car on the driveway. I won't be blocking any-"

"Do you want some water? Coffee?"

"No. Is Doctor Zahn coming?"

"Of course." He got up, ushered me into a meeting room that over-looked the parking lot. He was tall and skinny and stood at a list, like he was facing a headwind. I wondered if he'd been picked to match the architecture.

"I could move my car if you tell me where the access road-"

"You're our only customer today. Sure you wouldn't like some coffee?"

I relented. My stomach was roiling from the thought of seeing Shawna and I opted for safety. I nodded.

"Right away, then."

I dropped into a swivel chair and waited. It was exactly fifteen minutes past the hour when a silver Tesla convertible rolled past. Too big to be Zahn. Too male to be Shawna. It was a minute before the door swung open and the driver breezed in, two styrofoam mugs of steaming black coffee in his hands.

"I'm not late, am I? Because I could swear my car said eight o'clock, but man, you can't trust a Tesla. Can't trust anything that thinks it's smarter than you. You know why? Because it probably is."

I was staring at him, my mouth open and dry. I'd taken the cup without thinking, the heat barely bleeding through my numb fingers. Six months had changed little. His hair was cut tighter and the tan was darker. The suit was undeniably expensive, two-fifty, maybe three hundred count Australian wool.

"It's coffee. Black. That's what you asked for, right?"

My voice finally returned, but it was scratchy and husky. "Last time I took a drink from you, it ruined my life."

"God, don't be so melodramatic. It's just a game. And you know what they say; don't hate the player, hate the game."

"You are the game."

"Oh God no, all life's a game." He smiled, his teeth small and white. "I'm merely the jailor."

"I'm sure Nathan Hunter isn't merely anything."

"Flattery. From you? I guess I should have my guard up. But you probably have so many questions." He dropped into a chair and folded his hands on the table. "Go ahead, ask away."

"I don't have any questions."

"Really? Not one?" He twirled an index finger around like he was testing wind direction. "None of this begs questioning?"

"You extract tissue from some unsuspecting schmuck and, I don't know, you separate the cells by what? Apheresis? No, you seem like a centrifuge guy. Then you perform a forced re-programming. What do you use? Recombinant protein? Or Yamanaka transcription factors and-"

"God, you suck the fun out of everything. Look, you want to talk nerd, I'll call Zahn. He's the Woz. I'm the Jobs. I don't do science. I'm a businessman."

"And what business are you in exactly?"

"I thought you'd know by now. I'm in the business of justice. I do what you do, honey. Just way, *way* better."

"Nobody does what I do."

"On the contrary. You woke up in an empty apartment. Handsome, super-rich, wunderkind owner of said apartment is missing. And of all things, there's a finger in the refrigerator. There's no knife. How did you cut off the finger? Nobody cares. There's no blood spatter, no evidence of a clean-up. Nobody cares about that either. You didn't even take the damn car. You just killed a man in cold blood and went right back to sleep. In his bed. And yet the cops are stuck on the fact that, one, there's a finger wrapped in a zip-lock bag in the freezer. And, two, you were the last person to be seen with me." He wiggled his hands at me, ten intact, slender fingers.

"Nobody's going to believe you."

"Oh, they don't have to believe me. This a DNA world, kid. The flesh and gristle are just theatrics. Just to push the jury over the edge. You know how long a single strand of DNA is? Six feet. I can dig a pretty deep grave with six feet of DNA. If you're not sure, ask your buddy Quentin."

"I don't need to. Zahn told me. You used him."

"Him. Her. Don't look so horrified. Isn't that what we do? Use people? I needed a test case or two. A practice run. A beta test. You can't put product on the shelves that hasn't been focus-grouped, am I right? Alex was an addict. She was a smack whore. A smack-whore with connections. Shawna was a hood-rat with a crush. Quentin was a dealer. A low-end hustler. A ten-cent millionaire."

He placed the back of his hand on his forehead. "Then a tragic accident. And everything went to shit. Happens every day in the ghetto. So, we helped them out. Evened the scales of justice in one fell swoop. But don't thank me. Like I said, it was a test. A freebie. And Zahn was already seeing her, had her cells in the oven. It should have been a piece of cake. It was a disaster. But we made it work. And we learned from it. You should see what we can do now."

"Why me?"

"Fly, meet spider?"

"I don't believe it for a second."

"Okay, it's more than a random roll of the dice. You're good at what you do, how about that? You're good and I like a challenge. Plus, you can't go to the cops for obvious reasons. Neither can I. Kind of evens the playing field, doesn't it, Portia? You do like to play fair, don't you?"

"Do you?"

"No," he said. "Fair is for losers. I like to win. But there's no winning without a contest. So here it is." He tossed a file onto the table. A single photo was inside. It was a familiar face, brown skin, cropped hair, wide glossy eyes, dilated, hopped up on Scopolamine.

"This isn't Vegas. This this time it's for real." He leaned over. "I'm feeling generous here. I'm willing to start over. Rules are simple. I've got her locked up in a room. You need to save her. You win. I'll walk. I win. Well, you know. How about I give you till daybreak tomorrow? Then we cut her up and start dropping her all over the city."

"That's twelve hours to find a needle in a haystack."

"Oh God, no. It's not anything like that. You can bumble around a haystack for twenty hours and get poked if you're lucky. But there's no luck here. I know it's difficult. But I'm not asking this from some geek off the street. I'm asking you." He swiveled in his chair. "Play the game, Portia. Come on, it'll be fun. Like old times."

I was still staring at the photo. "This isn't a game."

"What?" He turned and looked at me.

"It isn't a game. It's not about winning and losing. It's about revenge."

"Revenge? That's so petty. That's so nineteen eighty-seven. My name is Inigo Montoya and you killed my father. Don't you see how tawdry and old-fashioned that sounds? People don't do revenge anymore. People don't care enough for revenge. It's too messy. No, what I want is for you to disappear. Pick up your ball and go home. You win, you stay. You lose, you go. You can have Omaha or Paducah. Just don't come back here."

"I'm not going anywhere."

His shoulders slumped like he was exhausted. "You think you have a choice?"

"I do. I'm not going anywhere."

He pulled a seven-millimeter Sig Sauer and slapped it onto the table.

"I've been so patient. I mean, Zahn keeps telling me I should just end it. We could get this over with right now, you know. The old-fashioned way."

A white rage came across me. The knife was out of my sock and swinging across the table before I could stop myself. The gun fired, missed. The handle of my knife quivered, the ivory glistening with blood. The blade had pierced between the radius and ulna, stapling his wrist to the wood. The pistol spun on the table in a lazy circle.

"Jesus, I didn't-"

Hunter grabbed the gun with his left hand and fired. The bullet went into the wall behind me, the plaster exploding. The door opened. The secretary stood there, his eyes wide. Hunter was screaming, firing in blind rage.

Two more bullet holes, one in the wall, the other in the ceiling. The boy dropped to the floor, his hands over his head. I grabbed his hand and twisted. Two more bullets, one grazing my ear, the sound loud enough to deafen me. I was over the table now, spinning on my hip, the heel of my boot catching him in the temple, his head jerking back, the gun releasing.

I stuck it in my pocket, still warm from the recoil, and ran for the door.

"I'm sorry," I said. "I really am. This wasn't the way I wanted it to happen."

Hunter stared at me, his eyes as red as the blood that pooled on the table.

"Run," he spat. "Do what you do best. Run."

CHAPTER 47

Ipulled up at the corner Save-a-Lot and killed the engine. There was no sense attracting attention here. The two blocks south of Easton was a popular pickup joint for hookers and tweakers and I wasn't looking for either tonight.

I settled in and watched the girls preening at the corner. They were young and their bodies were showroom ready, even if their hair had already begun to fall out and their teeth were mud-brown with rot. Their skin was colored with cheap tan, the clothes pop-button fastened for easy access, back alleys or rear seats where the lighting was dim and the elbow room minimal.

They weren't the kind who had convinced themselves that this was just transience, that the next trick would be the last before a career in porn or the escort industry would steal them away to the Hills.

These girls were the lifers, the cheap kind, the ones who charged straight twenties for anything you could think of, thirty if you wanted it twice. They're the ones who worked the graveyard shift every night until thirty-five or forty rolled around and the twenties became tens and the fives became ones. These were the kind of girls I could so easily have become had I been less skilled with a knife.

A small, pale-skinned girl with close set eyes and mostly white smile peered in. I rolled down the window. "I'm not buying, sister."

"Didn't say I was selling. Your boy said he'd be coming up around ten."

"Cool." As I rolled the window back up, her hand grabbed hold of the rim.

"Wait. That's half an hour. You want, I can entertain you for half an hour."

"Entertain?"

"Anything you like. So long as you pay up front."

I pulled the cutter and pointed it at her. "How much for me to cut you?"

The girl didn't flinch. "Fifty."

"Jesus," I said. I felt sick. In my back pocket was one of the fifties Jamal had given me. It was the last of my money. I peeled it open and handed it over. "Just go home. Take the night off."

The girl finally showed some concern. "What is this, some TV show? An undercover thing?"

"Go. Take the night off. Seriously."

The girl stepped back. She folded the bill carefully into her bra but she didn't go home. She was back at the corner with the other girls. Like I said. Lifers.

Around fifteen minutes past ten there was a rap on the window and Dog sat up and growled.

"It's okay, girl." I tossed back a snack. She guarded it with her paws, but she wouldn't eat. She was staring at the man at the window. I unlocked the door, Quentin slid in, and buckled the seatbelt. His hair was recently cut and combed, and his beard was neatly shorn.

"You're not going to hurt her, are you, Q?"

"No. Why you asking?"

"Because you're freaking me out. You smell more like Irish Spring than Irish Whiskey, you don't have any gold on, and what the hell are you wearing? Five oh fives? If you think this is some kind of hit, so help me-"

"I had a father."

"What?"

"What did you call it?" He looked at me, his eyes dark and soulless. "Strike one? Absentee father? Well, I had one. He was shot in a drug deal when I was fourteen. Died on the pavement like a dog. But he wasn't a dealer. He was a Ventura County deputy. He was shot five times on the one-oh-one by a crack dealer who thought five years in the pen was a worth killing a cop over. Two of the bullets were in his eyes. One in his mouth. That was after they killed him."

"Quentin, man-"

He waved me off. "My mom was an elementary school teacher. Between her paycheck and my dad's pension we did okay. No bars on the windows, an actual basketball hoop on the driveway, not a milk carton. It wasn't the Huxtables, but we did alright. She could have just given up. Retired. But she never stopped working. Not for a day. Because she never wanted me to think I could."

"I'm sorry, Q."

"I don't want you to be sorry. I just want you to know." He turned to the window. I could see his reflection, the tears brimming in his eyes. "I couldn't play ball either. That was never my get-out ticket. Long legs, long arms only get you so far without any real talent. I got good grades, loved organic chemistry. My aunt was a pharmacist back in Augusta and I thought maybe I could do something like that."

He drifted off.

"Shawna killed all of that. It was an accident. Yeah, I had a drink. But I wasn't drunk. I didn't ask her to take the blame."

He lapsed into silence, tapping at the window, tracing the smudges on the glass. "You know what hurts the most? My mom never even looked at me after that. Not once. It's like you see a cockroach in the kitchen sitting in your best china plates. You hate that it's there, but you can't kill it because maybe the whole set gets busted." Quentin reclined his seat and closed his eyes. "So, yeah, I'm not going to hurt her. I need her alive more than you do."

"Okay," I said. I dropped the clutch and put the van into gear. "Let's get this show on the road."

We slowed down at the corner of Hollywood and Wilcox. Vincent clambered over the gate, his feet squeezed sideways at the railings trying unsuccessfully to gain traction against the wet iron.

"Can't believe this freakshow's coming," Quentin muttered. "He's going to get us killed." Vincent made it to the top rail, swung a leg, the cuff of his pant catching on a spike as he vaulted the other leg over. He flipped over and hung there, dangling like a marionette. "If he doesn't kill himself first. Tell me again why we need him?"

"Four million people in this city. Twenty million if you include the greater L.A. area. That's a pretty big haystack and we don't have a clue where to start. You got a better idea?"

Vincent slid open the back door and hopped into the van. Dog nuzzled up against him. "Altman," he said, "Marlon Altman. Four-one-three-five South Flower Street. Six-five-seven-seven- nine-nine-three-one-one-five."

"What's he jabbering on about?"

"Mailing lists." I dropped a metal case onto his lap. "Plextor M5 Pro, solid state upgrade, 500 gigs-"

"I know what a goddamn hard drive is. Where did you get it?"

"Michael Duncan. The kid selling the Belladonna in Barstow. Vincent followed him home, stripped the hard drive. There were mailing lists on it. He memorized them."

Quentin's eyes widened. "That was six months ago."

"Branford. Robert Branford," Vincent continued. "Eleven oh five South Westlake in Westlake Village. Eight-one-eight-seven- six-five-"

"Yeah, I know." I looked at Vin, still rambling through addresses. "And one of the names on this list is Nathan Hunter," I said. "It has to be."

I pulled out onto the avenue. There was a large black sedan following us, an old Crown Vic, the police-interceptor type, grille and chrome spraypainted to blend with the matte finish. I sped up and took a sharp left across two lanes of traffic.

"Holy shit," Quentin said. He stuck his head out of the window, looking back.

"Still behind us? Black sedan. No front plates."

"No," he said. "Lost him."

"For now." I took another left, then hooked the next curve sharply, bumping the curb and narrowly missing the hydrant. Once we hit the freeway, there was no way they'd get to us.

"How many names on that list?" Quentin looked back at Vincent.

"I don't know. I lost count at forty-five."

"How much time do we have?"

I stepped on the gas. The old engine screamed. "Not nearly enough."

CHAPTER 48

I parked on Fourth Street, near the south entrance of the Los Angeles Public Library. The streetlights had turned on, buzzing with silvery halide intensity. A slow-moving car rolled up, paused, then moved on. The street was empty except for a drunk stumbling around with a paper-bagged can of malt.

"I think we're good," I said. I pulled the slide door and let Dog out. That girl had a nose for trouble. If there was something out there, she'd find it. And fast.

Quentin hopped out, pulling his jacket close. "Library closes at five thirty," he said.

"Good for you, Q. Didn't picture you as a reader."

"No, I'm not. I'm not a burglar either."

"Relax, we're not stealing anything. It's breaking and entering at worst."

"What's the difference?"

I shrugged. "About five years."

There was a light on around the side entrance and the door was open. A small man with a pencil mustache was waiting at the stairwell, his hat pulled low. He turned and walked in as we approached, his feet moving quickly, trying to outpace us.

"I never saw you, you never saw me," he said, walking faster. "Maintenance comes through this section around eleven so you'd better be out of here by then." He stopped at the computer lab. "And please, try not to break anything."

Vincent took out a screwdriver and began stripping the panels from the tower.

The man winced. "Or at least put it back when you're done."

By the time he disappeared, Vincent had switched out the drives. The printer whirred and sheets of single-lined paper spat onto the tray.

"How many?" Quentin asked.

"One hundred and sixty-two."

"Are you shitting me?" Q asked. "There's no way we'll even do twenty."

"The kid was selling street, Q. Oxy, PCP, crank. If we just keep the ones who bought Belladonna, we should be able to cut the list in half. Probably more."

I bit off the cap from a Sharpie and handed it over. "Want to make yourself useful?"

"What do you want me to do?" Vincent asked.

"Can you get me overhead views of the addresses?"

Vincent swiveled over to the next computer and began pulling up maps on the screen.

"Forty-eight," Quentin said, finally.

"Take away any that are over fifty miles out. And any orders that shipped over a year ago."

"Brings us down another six."

"It's probably somewhere without neighbors, right? Eliminates apartments or townhouses."

"And he'd have a secure area. A holding cell for the girls. A basement. Maybe a shed." Vincent pulled up maps of the remaining addresses and pulled the cursor around the houses. The printer started whirring again, spitting out black and white pages.

"Can you Google-check these names, see if there's something on them?"

"This guy's in prison." Quentin crumpled a sheet and tossed it over his shoulder. "And this one's dead. Nothing on the rest. No Facebook, no Twitter, no footprints." He looked up. "Twenty-eight. There's no way we're making that tonight. It'd be like throwing darts at a board and hoping the first few stick."

"You're right," I said. "Medina was right."

"What?"

I could have kicked myself but she was right. I was in a hole and I wasn't thinking straight. "The addresses are buyers. Not sellers."

"And how does that help us?"

"We're tracking delivery addresses, Q. We don't need to know where the Belladonna went. We need to know where it came from. We need to track the money in the other direction."

"Won't work. It's all crypto. There's no money trail with cryptocurrency."

"How about phone numbers, email addresses?"

"They'll be burn numbers. And spoofed addresses."

"Well, do you have a better idea?"

The printer began whirring. Vincent grabbed the sheet and crumpled it. "Drops," he said.

"What the hell are you talking about?" Q asked.

"You can track address logs through Dropbox if they're on the same account." He ran through the code on his computer. "After that just bomb the IPs to the source and hope their ISP doesn't use dynamic rotation."

"English please," I said.

Vincent handed over the paper. It was an address in the Rialto section of San Bernadino.

"That's it? You sure?"

Four more sheets spat out onto the tray. "Five," Vincent said.

"Twenty percent chance we get it on the first try." Quentin said. He crumpled up the papers and tossed them into the trash basket.

"That's close enough," I said.

Dog smelled them before we even saw them. Two men, dark suits and heavy soled boots, poking and prodding at the windows and doors. One of them popped the front lock and settled into the front seat, his hands on the steering wheel. He ran his fingers over the dash, then under the instrument panel.

"What do you want to do?" Quentin asked. "Looks like they're packing."

"I'm packing too." I pulled the pistol out from my waistband.

"Where the hell did you get that?"

"Never mind. We'll wait them out."

"Like hell we're waiting." Quentin grabbed the gun and crossed the road, arm outstretched, gun held sideways. "Get the hell away from my car, man."

I closed my eyes. "Vincent?"

"What?" he asked.

"Tell me when he gets shot so I can call 911."

"Actually, he's not doing so bad."

I looked up. Vincent was right. A little theatrical but, effective. The two men stepped away and disappeared down the street. Quentin was in the front seat, running his hands over the dash and under the steering column.

"What if they were planting a-"

"A what?" I asked. "An incendiary? You know how long it takes to wire in a bomb to the ignition?"

"Maybe they were trying to jack the car," Quentin said.

"And they chose this one?"

"Last option is the worst," Vincent said.

"What's that?" I asked.

"There's a tracker."

"And that's worse than a bomb?"

"Yes," Vincent said, shuddering.

I closed my eyes, turned the ignition, and listened to the engine rumble.

"Well, we're not dead yet," Quentin said.

I popped the van into gear. "Don't get comfortable."

It was 11.29 p.m. when we arrived in Rialto. The house on Lincoln sat at the end of the street, a two-story Victorian that hadn't seen a coat of paint in fifty years or more. The weeds were calf-high and the mesh fence was clogged with creeping vines and trash. Dented plastic toys dotted the yard. An entire truck engine sat partially protected by a ripped blue tarp.

"This isn't it?" I said.

"How do you know?"

"Place is a walking violation. Last thing you want to do is have a nosy inspector knocking around on your foundation when you got something to hide. This looks low-level, two meth-heads and a bucket of phosphor."

"So, we move on?"

"Yes." I paused. "No. Give me five minutes." I got out and looked around. The street was empty. No one had followed us out from the city.

"Keep the lights killed." I pointed through the trees behind the house. "Park on the next street over." I crossed the road and hopped the fence. The yard smelled of dog excrement. Fresh. I was glad I had left Dog in the car with Vincent.

Quentin was behind me, huffing. "What about me?"

"What about you?" I rummaged through the junk pile and found a rusty crowbar and a bent screwdriver. "Here." I handed him a bracket from the junk pile, a five-pound rock of aluminum. "Give me five minutes; no, seven. If I'm not out, then break a window. Front window. Preferably the one by the door. Then find Vincent. If I'm not there in ten minutes, get lost."

"I'm not just going to leave you-"

"This isn't the Marines, Q. If I get caught, busted by the cops, anything, you're out of here, get it? Now go."

I was covered in dirt and grass from inching over the lawns and under the shrubs to get to the crawlspace that accessed the basement windows. The window was covered by a metal grate, but it was attached to the rotting frame, not the concrete. A last wrench of the bar popped the struts off, and I cracked the glass and slid in. There was a smell worse than dog-shit here. I shuddered. It smelled like shit. But human.

The flashlight cut across an inky black basement. I could hear the steps above me, boots; the heavy kind with the hard rubber sole and metal ribs. Not the kind you wear indoors. Definitely a drug house. I hoped it was something tame. Heroin or crack. MDMA, if I was lucky. I was never that lucky.

I pushed through the piles of junk in the room. There were moldy carboard boxes piled to the roof. I sliced three open. Grocery store plastic filled with stuffed animals and children's clothes. A pink bear stared at me plaintively, its black button eye hanging by a single thread.

I edged from room to room. There were four in total, divided by two by sixes and single panels of drywall, unpainted, unadorned. The central room leading to the stairs was filled with more boxes stacked like walls, rooms within a room.

The opposite side was covered by a moldy bath curtain, faded flowers on opaque plastic. I was at the bottom of the steps. A light turned on behind the basement door, broken by a pair of feet. I heard the handle turn, the heavy snap of a shotgun safety. If that door opened I was in the light and in the line of fire. I jumped.

As I pulled the curtain shut, the light from upstairs flooded the basement. It took a few moments for my eyes to adjust before I saw it. In the corner was a child-sized creature shackled to the floor.

CHAPTER 49

The voice behind the curtain was deep and gravelly, a construction worker or lumberjack, someone accustomed to working with ear-plugs in. The plastic snapped back like a Band-aid ripping off. My pupils constricted again, trying to adjust back to the light. A man stood across from me, a wad of patterned drape in one fist, a Beretta in the other.

"Hey, Guerrero," I said, "didn't expect to see you here."

The gun didn't waver. It was still pointed directly at my chest. "I would say the same, but I've learned not to expect anything from you."

"Are you going to shoot or not?"

"Depends. How about the knife in your pocket first? And the one in your shoe."

I passed over both blades. I felt as good as naked now.

"Okay, let's go."

"What about-" I turned around. The room was now brightly lit. A mannequin sat in the chair behind me. A single line of duct tape sealed its lips together. The hollowed eyes were wide open, staring off into space.

"Don't ask," Guerrero said. "I don't want to know either." He motioned with the gun. "Just come with me."

As I stumbled up the stairs, I checked my watch. Eight minutes and counting. I prayed that Vincent and Quentin had been smart enough to leave.

Guerrero was on the phone as we drove back into the city. The call kept dropping, and he redialed three times before his conversation ended. Finally, he turned.

"Medina's on her way over, but she's delayed. I guess it's just us now."

"Great," I said. "What are we doing exactly?"

"I don't know what you're doing. I'm just here to protect you."

I couldn't help but feel a small pinch of relief. "Protect me from whom?"

"Yourself."

"I'm fine by myself."

"Look, I wasn't supposed to stop you. Get involved. But clambering into someone's basement like that? You were liable to get shot. How about you let us handle this from now on."

"How about no." I pulled at the door handle. It wouldn't budge.

"How about yes," he said.

The offices of Medina and associates sat on the eleventh floor of the 301 on the outskirts of Century City. The space consisted of three adjoining rooms lined with computers and television screens. The paint still smelled fresh. Guerrero sat me on a couch in front of a bank of monitors.

"Don't say anything. Just watch." He picked up a remote from the desk and turned four screens on, the pictures dark and blurry, the angles bouncing madly. "The bodycam footage is live. Chest mounted. We see what they see. Minus a foot correction. Top left is from a house in Calabasas. Top right, a shed in Fontana. Got a warehouse in Murrieta. A beach house in Capistrano."

"Where did you get this?" I stopped, feeling stupid. I remembered the two men poking around my van. This was *my* list.

"We had our own running list." He dropped sheets of paper onto the table. They spread like snowflakes. "Tustin. Cerritos. Carson. El Monte. Nothing. Then we found yours."

"Stole it," I said.

Guerrero tossed a crumpled ball toward me. "It was in a trash basket. In a public library. That you had broken into. Now you have a front row seat. In the safety of my office. And I don't have to explain to Medina why your brains were splattered all over Encino on my watch."

Guerrero left the room. I heard it lock and bolt. Fifteen minutes passed. The first monitor flickered and went dark. The second and third followed over the next five. Twenty minutes later there was just one.

The camera approached a door, glistening green in the lumi-light. A metal-cutter latched its beaks on the padlock and ratcheted up. The bolt snapped and camera light shone around the inside of the room. A six by ten cell. A set of manacles were bolted to the floor, a metal bucket; a rudimentary toilet.

The door unlocked and Medina entered, phone in hand. "Time to go."

"He's not done."

"It's over, Portia. There's no one there. You lost. Hunter's just going to keep playing you like a mouse, batting you around here and there. One day he's going to tire of you and he's going to pull those claws out. They'll lock you up for years."

"Not unless Shawna or Alex turns up alive."

Medina dropped a pile of photos onto the table. "That was at the Palacio Azteca in Tijuana two days ago. They're alive. But you'll never find them. New passports. New identities. They could be anywhere by now. Brazil. Suriname. Ecuador. From there they could hop a flight anywhere in the world. And I knew you were going to ask, so I did some digging. The registered guest on the room? Hotel records has him as Michael Duncan. AKA Mickey Deez."

Medina tossed another photograph on the desk. "Found him in an empty mansion in the Hills this evening with a bullet through his head."

"I didn't kill him."

"Oh God, Portia, does it really matter? There's no way you're getting out of this mess. Even if you do find Hunter."

"I would have found him. If Guerrero hadn't butted in."

Medina sighed, exasperated. "You don't have a clue where he is. You have an empty crackhouse in San Bernadino. You have an empty hotel room in Tijuana. You have four people missing or dead. And you're the only one with links to all of this. At this point you really shouldn't be worried about finding Nathan Hunter. You should be worried about them not finding you."

She dropped a bag onto the table. "Game's over, Portia. Guerrero did you a favor and packed a bag for you." She looked at her watch. "You have five minutes."

CHAPTER 50

A white passenger van with the blue insignia of the ICE deportation unit rolled into our lane as we ramped up toward departures. There were over a thousand repatriations from LAX alone, mostly non-violent offenders, traffic stops, minor drug convictions, and major overstays on their visas. Many of them were sent out in exodus on specially chartered flights insiders called ICE air. On occasion, individuals were transported on regular commercial flights, watched over, cuffed and shackled, constantly supervised by an agent till debarkation.

I felt like one of these faceless persons now, unwelcome and unwanted in a country I had lived in since birth. The passport in my hand now identified me as Ana Maria Souza, citizen of the Federal Republic of Brazil. The re-lamination process made my skin darker and my hair bigger, both of which I would grow into south of the border. I waited for a sense of relief to wash over, but it felt steadily colder, like a shower running too long.

"Don't look so glum," Medina said from the front seat. "Money, freedom, sunshine. People would kill for that."

I stared at her.

"Sorry, wrong choice of words." She turned back and looked at the traffic piling up on the ramp. "There's nothing left for you here anyway. You should be happy. At least the girls are safe."

I looked out of the window. An airplane was roaring up into the night, red lights blinking, then disappearing into the clouds.

"There's still something that doesn't make sense. All that money that Steph transferred? Repeat payments of half a million? If it wasn't ransom, then what was it for? That kind of money's not just for hotel rooms."

Medina peeled through her folder. "Three and a half million dollars in total." She passed the sheets over. "The money was a donation. It's on Mr. Winter's tax return. Everything checks out."

"You're going to tell me how a construction company, an operating business, gets a tax-deductible donation?"

"The donation was not for Azteca," she said. "The money went to rebuild a church that burned down in Zona Rio."

"Steph donated money to a church? In Mexico?"

"What?"

"Steph's an atheist."

"Doesn't mean that she can't donate money to a church."

"Do you really think an atheist is going to donate three and a half million dollars to a church? In a different country? Don't you think that's a little suspicious?"

Medina turned. "I'm a little tired."

"What's the name of the church?"

"Does it matter?" Medina glanced at Guerrero.

"Yes."

Medina sighed and looked through the sheet again. "It's San Huberto. Does that satisfy you?"

I stayed silent. But my mind was racing. Saint Hubert. Patron saint of the hunt. I had to find a way to get out.

I stared out the window. There was a long line of cars pulled up to the curb unloading baggage of every size. I marveled at the organized chaos. There was no place in the world with so many unoccupied cars with engines running.

The passing lane was open as Guerrero wedged in. He popped the back doors. I waited for Medina to open her door before I made my move. As she stepped out I slid over to the driver's side, popped the lever, and jumped out. Medina was shouting, but she was on the wrong side of the fire-drill and she had the curb and a line of bags to hurdle.

I jumped into the first car up, a white Camry, easily the least conspicuous car in the lineup. The owner was a middle-aged man slinging two full size suitcases and a double set of golf bags. He didn't stand a chance.

Neither did Guerrero. He raced along for a while but I swerved across two lanes into the traffic. In the rearview I could see Guerrero standing in the middle of the road doubled over, panting, his palms on his knees. I hit the accelerator and screamed down the ramp, my door only shutting as I took a forty-mile an hour hairpin drift onto Sepulveda.

CHAPTER 51

I clambered over the barbed wire fence and dropped onto a soft carpet of grass, recently turfed and well hydrated. Zoysia, I thought. At least he was listening.

The side door to the church was open, the nave empty, save for the pew-bolts that still penetrated through the concrete floor. The altar was stripped bare, the white marble of the canopy covered with a thin layer of dust. In the open tabernacle was an icon, engraved wood and rich gold leaf in traditional Orthodox style. The features were unmistakable.

"It's beautiful, isn't it?"

I turned and looked at the man in the sacristy. His bull-like shoulders brushed both frames of the door.

"Judas the Apostle, circa nine hundred and sixty, one of the few images that survived the Byzantine iconoclasm."

"Judas Thaddeus. Patron saint of the impossible. Not Judas Iscariot, the betrayer."

"I didn't betray you. I was never on your side."

"Siyad means Hunter in Arabic." I pulled out the phone and slid it over the altar. "You've been the Hunter since I got here."

Jamal smiled. "You're smart. Like a whip. No, not like a whip. Whips are fast. But you're here. Finally."

"I had to drive from LAX to Imperial. Then I had to ditch the car because it was probably already reported stolen. I had to walk across the border and hitch. And you have to be careful. I was in Zona Norte. Most guys there see a single girl and think they're a hooker."

Jamal laughed as he looked me up and down. "You'd probably make more money that whatever it is you do." He turned to the back wall and scanned his palm. I followed him down the stairs to the laboratory. The promenade was dark, the machines silent, just the steady breathing of forced air from the overhead ventilation units. We walked over to the end, to the glossy black door beyond the packing tables.

"I never got to show you our hot room, *bint*."

"Let's get it over with."

"Get it over with? No, *bint*, I've spent a lot of time on this. It's been, how would you say, a passion." He swiped his finger over the screen. "At the risk of spoiling the surprise, it's not Shawna. Or Alexandra."

"I know."

"But if it makes you feel better, it's the girl I wanted all along." The door opened with a swoosh. It was about the size of a surgical operating room, the walls and floor lined with non-skid. In the middle was a Stryker table, pieces of a naked female body lying perfectly still on the spotless white sheets.

"What do you think?"

I couldn't speak. I was prepared for this. I thought I was prepared for this. I wasn't. No one could be prepared.

"Is it bad? I know it's just bits and pieces, but do you not recognize her? Because I swear we did the best we could."

I recognized her, of course. It was me.

"I own you, *bint*. Genetically. Molecularly. Every cell, every shard of bone. All the meat and gristle. Packed away in little zip-lock bags. I knew you'd come. Eventually. I mean, where will you go? Anytime I want, I can drop a little tissue, some cells, put you in the middle of every crime scene in the country. God, I can send your liver to Oregon. Your kidneys to Alabama. I can have every police department in the country cross match your DNA with every cold case they have. I can make your life a living hell."

He poked at the body on the table. "What are you going to do? Oh, I know, you could take your cells and burn them, destroy them. But that's just the main course. You can burn down the lab. I'll build another one. The recipe? The ingredients? I have them. I can do it again whenever I want. You want to live, you live by my rules. Your only other choice is to get rid of me."

He spread his hands out wide.

"And you won't. You know why? Because I haven't done anything wrong. I've just done what you've been doing for the past ten years. We're a lot more alike than you think. You're not a fly, *bint*; you're a spider. We're both spiders. And spiders don't tolerate each other. One either submits or it dies."

"I'm the fly." Quentin was standing at the end of the promenade, his face a dark scowl.

"Quentin, you finally made it. Now it's a party. Did you tell him, *bint*? That it was never about Shawna? That this was always about you? Oh, God, you didn't. Of course, you didn't. You used him like you use everyone else. At least I pay him. You know what the real irony is, though? I spent all this time, all this money building you so I could set you free. I could have just killed you in the first place and got it for free. But then you'd be dead and that would be a waste. I hope this won't be a waste. Anyway, I'm talking too much."

He turned to Quentin and cocked his finger.

Quentin pulled out a gun and aimed it at me.

"Thanks a lot, Q," I said.

"Don't thank him," Jamal said. "He just does what he's told. That's what flies do. Now, *bint*. Tell me what you want to be. A spider. Or a fly? What-"

Quentin had turned slowly until the gun pointed at Jamal.

"God," Jamal said. "He's on your side now? You turned him?" He laughed. "Seriously? This is your partner? He can't even hold a gun right. He watches a couple of gangster movies, but that's it. He's a street softy. A pussy."

"Shut up."

"Please, Quentin, you can't even hold that thing right."

"Don't, Jamal. I swear. I'll shoot."

"Yes, Quentin, I'm sure you will." Jamal walked up to him, his frame taking up the entire door. He pushed himself up, the muzzle of the revolver sinking into his thick chest. "Go on Quentin. San Quentin. Big man on the streets. Go on, shoot me."

Quentin's hands trembled. He backed up a step. Jamal grabbed his wrist and twisted it, the barrel pointing up, his trigger finger locked. Jamal plucked the gun out and pointed it square at his forehead. He pulled the trigger. It clicked. Once twice.

"Quentin, you stupid bastard! You didn't even load it? See, *bint?* This is the problem with flies. You can't trust them to do anything right." He stormed back across the promenade, slammed the muzzle against my temple. "This why sometimes you need to do it yourself. You need to…"

He stopped and looked at the gun. The grip glistened in the light. "What the hell is this?" The gun dropped, clattered against the floor. His palm was wet like oil.

"You should know," Quentin said. "You made it." He peeled the brown vinyl glove off his hand and dropped it over the side of the promenade into the pit.

Jamal dropped to his knees heavily.

I squatted next to him. "It's a darn shame your hands are so thick. Or maybe your Belladonna is just not that good. Anyway since we have some time, let's chat. Because once I'm dead and you're in jail, we won't get the chance."

"You're not dead yet."

"No, I'm not. But Portia is. I could drop her into a canyon, give it a couple of months in the woods, let the coyotes and the bugs have at it. Or I could just leave her around here." I patted him down, found a Beretta tucked into his waistband. I went over to the table, and fired a couple of shots into the dissecting table. "What are the chances the bullets found in her abdomen will match your casings and bore? Probably match the bullets that killed Duncan. And if that's not enough, someone's going to squeal. I mean, Zahn's a real liability. He'll squeal easy. Heck, Steph will too. Just apply a little pressure. She's crazy enough to do it. But again, we don't need witness testimony, do we? Like you said. All we ever needed were a few cells."

I stopped and wiped the sweat off my brow. Digging a grave, even a shallow one, is a real workout. Especially when you're digging your own. The pieces of flesh were scattered in the hole. I packed the mud back into place and rolled the sod back into position.

"What do you think?" Quentin asked.

"I think they're not going to ask too many questions."

Quentin pulled out a cell phone. "Federales should be here soon. You probably want to disappear."

"I'm pretty good at that." I turned. It was a long walk back to the border.

"Hey, Portia?"

"Yeah?"

"Where you going?"

For the first time in a long time, I knew exactly where I was going.

"I've got a dog to pick up," I said.